Sign up for our newsletter to hear
about new and upcoming releases.

www.ylva-publishing.com

THE
CLUB

A.L. BROOKS

ACKNOWLEDGEMENTS

Firstly, I want to thank those wonderful women at Ylva for seeing something in my writing they wanted to publish—you made a girl's dreams come true!

I particularly want to thank Astrid Ohletz for offering me this chance, Gill McKnight for her amazing project management, Gill and Jove Belle for editing the book to within an inch of its life, and Andrea Bramhall for her fantastic support and encouragement from start to finish.

Next, my beta readers—you know who you are—who gave me valuable feedback and also immense encouragement on this, my first novel.

Thirdly, all my wonderful friends and colleagues for being so excited about this on my behalf and never letting me forget that this is a pretty amazing thing to be doing. Though, let's be honest, it's not likely I'd forget in a hurry anyway.

And lastly—you, whoever you are, holding this in your hands right now. Thanks for reading, I sincerely hope you enjoy...

DEDICATION

For Y&T—you know why

PROLOGUE

Brixton, 1993

Mandy grinned as Laura pushed open the cubicle door and pulled her inside. The main door to the toilets swung shut behind them, muffling the thump of the music coming from upstairs in the main room. The rave was in full swing, the dance floor jumping with the movements of hundreds of people all sweating out a good time.

Laura slammed the cubicle door shut behind them, and Mandy pressed up close against her in the confined space. She reached for Laura as she pushed the bolt across. Laura turned, and instantly her tongue was in Mandy's mouth, hands pushing inside her tee shirt. She cupped the bare breasts, squeezed, and then groaned as Mandy's nipples hardened under her palms. Mandy pushed up into her, breathing raggedly through her mouth. The air around them stank; the toilets here were not ideal, but sometimes there was no other option. When the need took her, as it had fifteen minutes ago when she and Laura had met in the middle of the dance floor, she made do with what was available.

Mandy had noticed Laura some time before they'd started dancing. Her bleached-blonde hair, cropped nice and short, smoking hot body, and those vivid green eyes that sparkled under the club lights... She was breathtaking. Mandy hadn't been able to look away. The heat between them had been instant and intense, and when Laura had bent to Mandy's ear and offered her a quick fuck with no questions asked, Mandy hadn't hesitated.

Just as Laura's fingers started to pop the buttons on Mandy's faded Levi's, the outer door opened again. Two women entered, chatting to one another. Laura didn't pause, and Mandy ignored them in favour of concentrating on Laura's fingers as they worked their way into her underwear. Laura ran her hand through the wetness of Mandy's pussy and rammed two fingers straight into her cunt. Letting out a loud groan of satisfaction, Mandy threw her head back. It thumped against the cubicle wall, and she giggled at the sound.

"Yeah, you like that?" asked Laura, her eyes darkening to a deep jade colour.

Mandy panted. "Fuck, *yes.*"

"Oh shit, are you fucking kidding me?" a woman said, followed by her hitting the partition, making the wall of the cubicle shake. "Hey, fucking carpet munchers, take it someplace else!"

Laura's fingers stopped mid-thrust, and she and Mandy looked at each other, grinning. Then Laura moved again, and Mandy groaned again.

The woman hit the door, twice.

"I'm fucking serious, lezzas! Get the fuck outta there. Some of us need to piss!" The woman was angry.

Mandy twitched slightly. This might get nasty. Laura stopped moving and met her gaze. Her eyes held the same hint of the doubt Mandy was feeling.

"Jesus, are you serious? Are they fucking in there?" The second woman sounded younger and considerably more amused than the first.

"Yes," snarled the first woman and followed up with a kick to the door.

"Shit," murmured Mandy, and Laura nodded slightly. She pulled her fingers out of Mandy, and Mandy did up her fly.

"Sorry," whispered Laura, shaking her head.

"It's okay; no point putting ourselves at risk. Sometimes you get away with it, sometimes not." Mandy shrugged and planted a kiss on Laura's lips before she shifted to give Laura room to slide the bolt back.

They shimmied around the door in the enclosed space and met the glare of the angry young woman. She was tall, too thin, and wore her blonde hair pulled back in a tight ponytail. Her neck was covered in tattoos, and her face twisted in hate.

"About fucking time. Disgusting cunts."

"Oi, no need for that!" snarled Laura. "We're going, all right?"

"Fuck off, lezza bitch."

"Hey, get over it!" snapped Mandy as she pushed past the woman with Laura right behind her.

"Don't know why you lot don't just stay in your own clubs. Stop bringing your fucking queer shit to our places."

Mandy turned back to the woman. Laura carried on walking, calling over her shoulder, "Leave it; she's not worth it."

Mandy looked the woman up and down. "Yeah, you're right," she said with a sneer. As she turned to leave, the woman slapped her. Mandy saw it coming, but not quick enough to avoid it. When it connected with her face, it didn't have enough power to send her to the floor, but it still rocked her back on her heels. Her lip stung as if cut, and a moment later, her mouth filled with the coppery tang of blood.

"Jesus!" The younger woman pulled at her friend's arm.

Laura grabbed Mandy and yanked her towards the door.

"Come on, enough. Let's get out of here," she said firmly.

Mandy went with her, stumbling as she tried to get her brain to engage with the rest of her body. The bitch fucking *slapped* her! What the fuck?

She wiped the blood from her mouth with the back of her hand. The cut stung like fuck. People stared as Laura led her to the cloakroom upstairs. Mandy ignored them.

"Where's your ticket?" Laura asked her. Mandy rummaged in her pockets, found the green stub, and handed it to the girl working the counter. The girl stared at Mandy's mouth for a moment, and Laura gave her a dirty look. She hurried to retrieve Mandy's bag and jacket.

Out in the cool evening air, they walked down Brixton Road towards the Tube station. After a few moments, they came to a bench. Laura tugged Mandy over to it, pushed her down, and stood in front of her.

"You got any tissue to clean that up?" She pointed at Mandy's lip.

Still in a slight daze, Mandy nodded, undid her bag, and found a packet of travel tissues. She pulled one out and dabbed gently at her lip. After cleaning around the cut, she pressed the tissue against it to staunch the flow. It wasn't bleeding heavily, but it was annoyingly persistent.

Laura ran her hands through her short hair and puffed out a big sigh as she locked her hands together behind her neck.

"Sorry," she said, looking down at Mandy.

Mandy waved one hand in the air between them. "Shit, not your fault. You don't need to apologise. It's a risk we take in places like that."

"I know, but... Well, it just fucking annoys me, you know?"

"I know."

And she did know. Mandy didn't like to take women home to her place—her flat was private, and she didn't want strangers in it. But equally, she'd had one too many morning-after conversations when she'd gone back to other women's homes. She wanted her sex life uncomplicated, no strings. The only way she'd found that worked was random encounters such as the one she'd been in the middle of with Laura, quick and hard in some secluded part of a club. Unfortunately, most times that meant mixed clubs, as there just weren't enough lesbian ones available, even in a city as big as London.

Mixed meant risk. The risk of being found, of being verbally abused, of being thrown out, or—as she'd discovered tonight—worse.

"Look, are you okay to get home?" Laura dropped her arms to her sides and shuffled on the spot, clearly keen to get going. Mandy couldn't blame her.

"Yeah, I'm fine. You take off."

"Look after yourself," said Laura.

"You too. See you around."

Laura turned and marched off, tucking her head down into the collar of her jacket.

Mandy shivered and pulled her own jacket tighter around her body against the wind that knifed up the road. She didn't blame Laura for disappearing, but it did rankle a bit. Left on her own in the middle of Brixton with a bleeding face wasn't exactly her idea of a great night out. But then, what did she expect? She and Laura had only shared first names and about five minutes of interrupted intimacy. She wasn't pretending it was something it wasn't.

She pulled the tissue away from her lip and then patted the cut tenderly with a fingertip. The blood seemed to have stopped, thankfully. She dipped into her handbag again and found the little tube of lip salve she always carried around with her. Using her fingertip, she gently covered the cut with the soothing balm and then stuffed it, along with the tissues, back in her bag.

She stood up, took a deep breath, and started for home. So much for an easy, fun Saturday night out. She was fed up with this—too many nights ended in disappointment these days. She was thirty-two, way too old to be slapped down by some stupid bitch in a toilet.

She needed a change of scenery.

CHAPTER 1

Manchester, present day

Kath held the steaming hot mug carefully in one hand as she flicked off the main kitchen light. By the soft light of the under-cupboard spotlights, she made her way out of the room and down the hall.

"Mum, I've got your cocoa," she called and nudged open the door to her mother's bedroom. She stepped into the warm room. The bedside lamp was on, casting its muted light in a small pool that left most of the room in darkness. At first it looked as though her mum was sleeping upright, but she was merely gazing off into space, eyes unfocused. Kath put the mug on the bedside table. Her mum slowly turned towards her.

"Is that you, Kath?" Her voice was tremulous as she clearly struggled to focus in on Kath's face in front of her.

"Yes, Mum, it's me. Got your cocoa," she repeated; sometimes it took two or three goes for things to register.

Her mum managed a weak smile. "Oh, you are a love," she whispered and tried, unsuccessfully, to push herself a little more upright.

"Here, let me." Kath kept her voice light and cheery. She slipped her arms around her mum and gently pulled her up. Before resting her back against the headboard, she made sure the pillow ran dead centre down her spine.

"Thank you, love," her mum whispered again.

Kath swallowed hard. Sometimes it really was just too much. The pain of seeing her mum like this and the energy Kath expended on caring for her… All of it threatened to overwhelm her. But what was she to do? Care for her mum fell to her as her brother refused to help.

"We should put her in a home," he'd said. "It's too much for you to take on, and frankly, I don't have the time to just drop everything when you can't cope. I have a wife and kids. It's not fair to them. It was your decision to take her in, your decision to leave the professionals out of this." His words, delivered in his usual clipped tones, rattled around her brain, their sharp edges catching her like needles. There was a lot right in what he had said. But the idea of her mum going into care was far too upsetting for Kath.

Her mum sighed and reached for the cocoa. Kath intercepted her.

"I've got it, Mum," she said brightly. She held the mug close to her mum's lips, letting her come forward slightly to sip, trusting she still had enough awareness not to gulp the hot drink too quickly.

Later, after her mum had gone to sleep, Kath tucked her in, switched on the night light, and left the room. She leaned against the wall outside for a moment and breathed deeply. Today had been a long one. She rubbed at the back of her neck, trying to ease out some of the tension that seemed permanently knotted there these days. She rolled her shoulders, pushed herself away from the wall, and walked down the hallway to the kitchen. As she passed the table, she picked up her fags.

She stepped out of the back door into the cool May air and plopped herself down on one of the plastic patio chairs. She lit her cigarette, inhaled, and let the smoke trickle gently out of her nostrils as she gazed up at the night sky. It had been a beautiful spring day that had left a pink tinge on the horizon with the streaks of cloud stretched like layers of a creamy cake across the sky. It was almost perfect, and sitting out here, experiencing it alone, made her heart clench just a little.

Maybe she should call Julie, talk a bit more about their plans for tomorrow. At the thought of Julie, she smiled. Julie, with the long black hair that draped so seductively over Kath's face as she straddled her, riding out her orgasm as she thrust down hard on Kath's fingers. Julie, who didn't really understand Kath's home arrangements and didn't understand why Kath couldn't come running every time she called.

She stubbed out her fag in the overflowing ashtray and walked back inside for a cold beer. She popped the cap and strolled into the living room. Her phone was on the sofa, right where she'd left it earlier. Glancing at the screen, she noticed one missed call and a voicemail. She checked the missed call—Julie. As she listened to the message, the sound of Julie's voice made her smile. Then, as she took in the words, her smile faded. Key phrases zapped into her ears and ricocheted around her mind.

I need to end this.
Too difficult to find time to be together.
Found someone more reliable, more committed.
Sorry to do this.
Really thought we could have had something, but I can't share you.

Kath hit the "end" key and dropped the phone. She was numb. Sure, Julie had been struggling with Kath's need to put her mum first, but she hadn't realised it had got this bad. Briefly, she considered calling Julie back, but then she replayed the words from the voicemail in her head. It was a lost cause.

They had only been dating about three months, but she, too, had thought they could have had something very good together. But caring for Mum as she did challenged Julie's ideas of how a relationship should normally progress. Last minute cancellations. Too many nights settled in to watch a DVD rather than out on the town as promised. Quick sex sneaked into the few free hours she had.

She should have acted sooner. Instead, compressed under the weight of all she was juggling, she had hoped it would miraculously resolve itself.

Well, in a way, part of it had.

Kath exhaled, slumped back against the sofa, and took a long pull on her beer. Her brother's words mixed with Julie's and echoed through her mind. She had some difficult choices to make.

"So," Jacky handed Kath her pint of lager, "how's the new carer working out for your mum?"

They were in the Soldier's Arms, their favourite haunt. Jacky was Kath's closest friend; the one person she didn't have a problem confiding in. Strange, as Jacky wasn't the touchy-feely type at all. She was often thought of as all surface and no depth. But Kath knew differently. Jacky's stocky, butch exterior, almost a mirror of Kath's own, contained a warm heart and a lot of love for the people closest to her.

They'd not seen each other since Jacky and Tania got married back in April. Yet another reason why she'd re-evaluated her life, worked out her money and her priorities, and got in touch with a private home-care agency.

Leaning back against the bar, Kath took a big gulp of her beer and smacked her lips in pleasure as the cool liquid slipped down her throat. "Great, actually," she said. "They're not cheap, but something had to give. So it's worth it."

"How many nights are they in?" Jacky's gravelly voice rumbled across the space between them.

"I've got them four evenings a week, Tuesday to Friday, seven until eleven. Just couldn't afford the weekend option, as everyone wants that. But this way, I at least get some time out. I can go to the cinema or hit the bars or clubs if I want to."

Jacky nodded. "It's good that you've done it. We missed you for sure, and Tania was getting so worried about what it was doing to you, cooped up at home all day and night."

"Well, it did get a little claustrophobic, I must admit."

"See, so it worked out okay in the end. I know Julie leaving was shit, but she kind of did you a favour; didn't she?" Jacky wasn't one to mince words.

Kath nodded ruefully. "Yeah, she did. Bit of a hard lesson to learn, but hey, I'm there now, and things can only get better, right?"

"Definitely. So, any hot chicks on your radar?"

Kath snorted. "Well, that's the fucking irony of it. Ever since I've had all this extra time to play, I haven't found anyone who interests me enough. Mind you, I'm still getting used to all this…freedom… so I'm not even sure I want anything serious anyway."

"You should get yourself down to the Ace, find a little one-night-stand action." Jacky grinned.

Kath thumped Jacky in the arm, laughed, and mimicked a vomiting action with her finger near her mouth. The Ace was a cheap club tucked into the bowels of Stretford, somewhere she and Jacky had frequented years ago, before they knew any better.

"Ugh, no thanks. The trash that goes in there, I wouldn't touch with a barge pole. And anyway, you're a happily married woman. What would you know about the pulling possibilities at the Ace these days?"

Jacky smirked. "Nothing at all. I'm just guessing it hasn't changed."

Kath smiled. "No, not one bit, so I've heard." She mock-shuddered. "I have no intention of setting foot in there again. Still, a one-night stand would be quite nice, actually. It's just knowing where to go to meet someone who'd be interested."

"Ever done the chat room thing? You could always use it just to find out where all the women go these days. Or have cybersex."

Kath grimaced. "No thanks. I want a real woman, hands-on, thank you very much. But yeah, maybe going online just to find out where everyone goes would be a good way to start."

Kath sat back in her chair and raised her arms above her head to stretch. She moaned loudly, the pull on the muscles of her back feeling *so* good. She'd been at her desk since eight thirty in the front-room-turned-office where she carried out her tax consulting work. It was now—she glanced at the clock in the top right of her screen—two in the afternoon. Although she'd looked after her mum's needs during that time, she had neglected her own. Her water glass was empty, and she couldn't remember when she'd last filled it. Had she eaten? Her stomach growled. Okay, that would be a no, then.

She pushed back the chair and stumbled to her feet, her legs wobbling from their lack of use. She did some more stretches and then headed out of the room to check on her mum. Kath paused at the doorway of her mum's room, not wanting to march in if she was sleeping. Her mum was sitting up in her armchair, staring at the small flat-screen TV. Rather than stepping in and talking to her, Kath hesitated. She just didn't have it in her right now, and from the looks of it, her mum was off in another world anyway.

Kath sighed, stepped quietly from the room, and headed to the kitchen. Sun streamed into the large room from the patio door at the back, and she took a few minutes to have a quick smoke outside before she made herself lunch. The garden looked as though it needed some work again. Maybe Saturday she'd help her mum out to one of the patio chairs while she worked out there. Maybe.

She pulled together a glass of orange juice with a thick doorstop of a roast chicken sandwich and headed back to her office where she tucked in. When her mum had first started…drifting…and it became clear she needed around-the-clock care, it had been a no-brainer for Kath to move back in to the family home. Her mum had been rattling around alone in the four-bed detached in Sale ever since Kath's father had died the year before. After tidying up all the remnants of her dad's will and estate, Kath had rented out her flat in Stockport and moved into the big front bedroom. She and her brother had reconfigured the house so that her mum could stay on the ground floor—there was a small walk-in shower room and toilet downstairs already, so they'd only needed to rearrange furniture.

With a small sofa and a TV, the old dining room became the new living room, somewhere Kath—and now the carers—could sit in the evenings and still be able to hear her mum in the next room. Her dad's study-cum-library was just big enough for a single bed and an armchair, so it was transformed into a bedroom for her mum. The front room had been turned into Kath's office. It was cold in winter and too distant from the rest of the house to serve as a bedroom. Kath had worried about keeping her mum within earshot.

As workplaces went, it wasn't that bad. And again, she was thankful that she was able to work from home, for the most part. She went into the city one afternoon a week to meet with Jude, her manager. Jude had been instrumental in transitioning Kath's role from office based to home based. Each Wednesday, she spent the afternoon catching up on clients and forthcoming work with Jude at the office, while Mrs Davey, a neighbour from across the road, sat in with Kath's mum. She always brought over a small cake and sat in the living room chatting around whatever TV programmes they watched until Kath got back at five. She seemed to genuinely enjoy her Wednesday afternoon visits. And the twenty quid Kath slipped her on the way out didn't hurt, of course.

Her phone rang just as she finished her sandwich. She swallowed the last mouthful quickly and answered it on the fourth ring.

"Hi Kath, it's Jude."

"Hey, how are you?"

"I'm good. Listen, just a quick call—any chance you could come in earlier tomorrow? I know it's difficult with your mum and all, but I've got a family thing I need to get to and have to leave earlier than normal. Sorry, I would have asked sooner, but I completely forgot it was this week."

Kath's mind quickly spun with the arrangements she'd have to make. Mrs Davey probably wouldn't mind, especially if Kath threw lunch into the mix. She'd have to scoot over the road straight after this call, though, to catch Mrs Davey before she went off to bingo. Tuesdays was always bingo.

"I'll need to check with the neighbour, but I'm sure that will be okay. What time do you want me in?"

"Say noon, so a couple of hours earlier than normal? I need to get out of here at three to catch a train to London at three thirty."

"Off to do anything nice? Oh wait, you said a family thing—I'm guessing not so nice then?" Kath made sure to put a laugh into her voice.

Jude snorted. "Yeah, you guessed that right. Father's birthday. I have to meet them at some fancy restaurant in Covent Garden and then stay overnight before catching a red-eye train back here Thursday."

"Okay, let me go and talk to the neighbour right now. I'll send you a quick email once I know it's going to be all right. If not, I could always see about coming in on Thursday instead?"

"Sounds good, let me know either way. Thanks."

Her visit to Mrs Davey was short and sweet—yes, there was no problem with her coming in a little earlier to sit with Mum, and her eyes definitely brightened up at the thought of lunch. Kath made a mental note to pop out later to Tesco and get something nice for the pair of them to eat.

When she got back to her desk, suddenly she wasn't in the mood to work. She'd done pretty well this morning, so an hour off now wouldn't kill her. She sent the quick email to Jude, then, smiling to herself, she opened up her personal laptop and resumed her search of sites that could help her in her...research. So far, she'd signed up for a couple of chat rooms that looked promising, and through them she'd made contact with two women who sounded as if they knew of a place.

One of her contacts was online and in a chat room already. Another homeworker maybe? Or someone sitting at her desk in an office, bored out of her mind and sneaking a little lesbian chat to pass the day?

Kath sent a message and got an instant reply. The afternoon was definitely looking up.

Kath pulled on her black leather trousers and zipped up. God, it had been so long, she'd forgotten just how good they felt against her skin. Black shirt next, over the black bra she liked to wear for nights out. She smiled to herself as she did up the buttons on the shirt. She was excited, and it had been a long time since she'd been excited about a night out.

She'd lost a bit of confidence since Julie left, making her self-conscious and nervous on the couple of occasions she'd gone to bars in the Gay Village in the last month. She'd left early both times, unable to see the evening through to the conclusion she'd wanted.

Time was she could walk into any bar or club and get off with someone, even for just a snog and grope. But now, all these months of looking after her mum had taken their toll. Julie leaving had been the final straw, somehow knocking her confidence back decades to when she was a gangly eighteen-year-old, fresh out of the closet and not a clue what to do about it.

She splashed a bit of CK One on her wrists, slipped on her watch, and ran her fingers through her dark, shoulder-length hair. Okay, ready as she'd ever be. She switched off her bedroom light, ran lightly down the stairs, and grabbed her long leather coat from the hallway cupboard. It was August, but she went nowhere without that coat. She stuck her head around the living room door to say a quick goodbye to Milo, the carer who was in tonight, and then headed out the door to the taxi waiting outside.

Her insides did a little flip. The promise of the night stretched before her.

Twenty-five minutes later, she climbed out of the cab just up the road from the club. The black door was hidden in the shadows, but she found it easy enough, having done a drive-by in daylight the week before.

Through her chat room research, she'd ended up on a site where fellow lesbians looking for that no-strings action could swap stories. There, she'd learned about this club, and Kath's pulse had quickened at some of the stories. Hot femmes after a quick, hard fuck from a dominant butch. Straight, bi, gay, it didn't matter—it was all about the essentials, the basics, the needs. Behind that black door lay three rooms offering her all sorts of possibilities to quench her thirst for physical contact with another woman, without the long-term complications getting in the way. She was genuinely excited about how this could fit into her world, her life.

She paid the cabbie and watched him drive off before she lit a fag. As she strode up to the door with her head held high, she smoked it quickly, sucking down the smoke in long pulls. She smiled to herself. She was ready for this.

She was admitted to the club at the first buzz on the bell and handed over her money.

"Welcome," an older, rather striking woman greeted her. "I'm Mandy, the owner."

"Hi," Kath replied as she accepted the change. God, the woman had the most amazing blue eyes. Kath tried not to stare, but they were incredible.

"We have a locker for your coat, if you like?"

Kath nodded and gratefully slipped out of the leather jacket. It was warm in the hallway. She followed Mandy's directions to the small room further down the hall and stowed her coat. When she turned back, Mandy blinked rapidly and glanced away. Wondering what that was about, she cleared her throat slightly before speaking.

"So, through that door, then?" She pointed to the only other door in the hallway.

"Yes, sorry. That's right. Do you need me to give you a rundown on the facilities first?"

Kath shook her head. "I'm okay, thanks." She knew all she needed to know from her research; all she wanted now was to get in there. She straightened her shirt a little, hitched up the leather trousers, and then took a deep breath before heading along the shadowy corridor.

Mandy fanned her face after the butch walked away from her. Jesus, talk about pheromones. She heard a giggle and looked over her shoulder. Dee, her assistant, smirked at her. Mandy gave her the finger.

The club had been open for about nine months now, and Mandy had seen plenty of women of all shapes, sizes, colour, and looks come through that door. She was proud to give them this space to enjoy—a place to let themselves go, let themselves find something, whatever that might be. She hadn't ever factored in her own needs, even though the idea of the club was based almost entirely on her memories of those needs. But occasionally, like tonight, a woman would walk through that door who made Mandy's pulse race and her clit throb. And that woman, although nothing amazing to look at, had the kind of...charisma that worked for Mandy in all the right ways.

Maybe it was the leather trousers—she'd always had a thing for leather. Especially when they fit someone as well as that. She tore her gaze away from the woman's broad ass as the doorbell rang behind her.

Back to work, you silly bitch, she chuckled to herself.

Kath entered the Green Room—a space where it was just bodies, no toys or BDSM equipment allowed here. There were other rooms for that, rooms that Kath fully intended to explore at some point. Her body immediately responded to the darkened atmosphere, the dim lighting, the muted music, the carnal sounds, and the sex she could almost taste on the air. She bought herself a beer and sat at the bar. Her old self was quietly returning, and the buzz of the evening permeated her, setting her nerves alight. She settled in her seat. She wanted to watch first, check out what everyone else got up to before she made her move. She had no doubt she would fuck someone tonight—this was definitely not just a reconnaissance mission. It had been too long, and she needed it. Badly. Three months wasn't that long to go without sex, but somehow the way Julie had left and the toll of caring for her mum made it seem much longer. And her need that much greater.

She sipped her beer while her gaze roamed her surroundings, taking in all the action. It was gone eleven by now, and the room was fairly busy; she counted ten couples already hard at work and another half a dozen or so unoccupied women placed strategically against the walls. Her blood warmed as she watched the couples who were active. There were hands, tongues, and fingers all being used to good effect, and she was getting wet at the ecstasy playing out on the faces around her. Oh God, to feel that again… She focused her attention on one couple in particular—a curvy blonde being caressed and kissed very slowly by a soft butch. The woman wore a black muscle vest and black jeans. Her dark hair was cut short in a feminine spiky look that highlighted her beautiful face. Though the two women were presumably strangers, they were totally into each other. What they were doing to each other made her realise that, for some, this place wasn't just about quick, hard fucks.

Tonight, however, quick and hard was what Kath wanted.

After watching them for a few more minutes, she finished her beer. With her arousal building rapidly, she was ready—there was no point waiting any longer. Her need consumed her, raging through her veins, making her skin tingle and her cunt throb. Her fingers ached to plunge deep inside someone's hot wetness, and she searched the room for that someone to feed her fire.

She passed over the first three women she checked out. None of them gave her a spark that flashed a "go." But she stopped dead on the next woman. Oh, hell *yes*. Blonde, curly hair tumbled over her bare shoulders where her clingy black top had slipped down to pull tight across very full breasts. A black skirt, possibly leather, with a long split up the side, showed off bare thigh. She appeared a little younger than Kath's thirty-six years and oozed sex appeal, and Kath practically drooled as she made her way over. Her target caught her movement and met Kath's gaze, and Kath's stomach lurched. The woman's eyes said yes in no uncertain terms, especially when she ran her gaze deliberately down the length of Kath's body and back up again.

The woman splayed her hands back against the wall just as Kath reached her, and that gesture of submissiveness sent Kath's pulse racing. She didn't bother with pleasantries; she didn't care what the woman's name was. She just had to have her. Their lips met, and Kath pushed her tongue deep inside the woman's mouth. Bracing her hands on the wall to either side of the woman's head, she let their bodies barely graze each other, hinting at what was to come. She felt, rather than heard, the woman groan, and kissed her even deeper. And still the woman kept her hands splayed back against the wall. Kath was the one running this show.

After a few moments, Kath pulled back. The kiss sent hot blood coursing through her veins. It was all she could do to keep some kind of restraint on herself and not just rip every bit of clothing off the woman. With her teeth.

Instead, she took a deep breath and stared into the woman's eyes as she slowly, and very deliberately, ran her hand down the woman's body. Down her neck, over her bare collarbone, over the lush swell of her breast, registering the hardness of the nipple as she did so. Then past her hip and down to the split in the skirt. She skimmed her fingers over the—*yes*—bare skin and the soft, pliant warmth of her flesh. Gripping her thigh hard, Kath's desire flared brighter again. Jesus, this was sexy. She had no idea who this woman was, could possibly pass her in the street the next day and not recognise her. But here Kath was, about to run her hand up inside that skirt and find out what delights awaited her. The thrill of it left her breathless. She had finally found the solution to the imbalance that had plagued her life since her mum's condition had taken over.

Kath moaned loudly when she discovered the woman was, as she had hoped, not wearing any underwear at all. As she let her fingers move without hesitation into the—significant—wetness that awaited her, she stared into the woman's eyes. The woman gasped and thrust against Kath's hand.

"Oh no," whispered Kath, pulling her hand back. "No, no, no, that's not how it goes. You have to wait until I let you, understand?"

Kath dropped into dominant mode as easily as she had slipped on her coat earlier. She mentally grinned. *Oh yes.*

The woman, panting in front of her, nodded. Her eyes were bright, desire written all over her face, and heat surged through Kath's veins again. Oh, this fuck was going to be perfect. What a way to get back in the game.

"Stay still," said Kath, the strength of the command in her voice thrilling herself as much as it did the woman in front of her. "Don't move. Take everything I give you and… Don't. Fucking. Move."

Even during her best nights with Julie, she had never seen such utter surrender, such willingness to give everything—and take everything—written all over someone's face.

She pushed her hand back between the woman's legs and nodded slightly in satisfaction as the woman contained her reaction, keeping her legs wide open but not moving her hips. The control that must have taken… Her muscles quivered beneath Kath's hand. She ran two fingers through wet outer lips, down to the entrance of the woman's cunt where she hesitated, her fingers poised but not moving. She kept her gaze locked on the woman's eyes, kept her fingers still, and leaned down to kiss her, letting their lips just brush, nothing more. She pulled back and then kissed her again, just as lightly, this time keeping their lips in the merest of contact rather than moving away.

The woman moaned, and Kath smiled. The woman still hadn't moved, even though Kath's actions were clearly torturing her in the most exquisite way. She moved her fingers slightly, maybe a centimetre or so, letting them slip just inside, and then stopped. The woman whimpered and panted against Kath's lips.

"Do you want me to fuck you?" Kath said against the woman's mouth.

"Oh, Jesus, *yes.*"

"How much do you want it?" Kath moved her fingers in a bit further.

The woman didn't move a muscle, even though she groaned, loudly, and her breathing increased against Kath's mouth.

"God, like nothing I've ever wanted before," replied the woman, voice thick with desire, eyes hooded. For all Kath knew, she'd said the very same words to someone else only half an hour previously. But it didn't matter. That was the beauty of this club; they could all play the game because they could all win at it.

Kath's clit pounded against the seam of her tight leather trousers. Her boy shorts were soaked as her cunt released gushes of juice at the woman's words, her gasps, and the look in her blazing eyes. This was what she had missed these past couple of years. Kath was back, with a vengeance, and oh, God, it felt *so* good.

She pushed inside then, unable to delay. In future nights, she might play this out longer, but the consuming need was too great not to act, not to follow her true desires. Two fingers, straight in, all the way up to the furthest knuckles. The woman cried out against Kath's mouth, and Kath devoured her, tongue pushing deep, lips crushing lips as her fingers pumped in and out.

Bracing herself against the wall with her right hand, she pressed her body closer and used her thigh to force her fingers even deeper inside this beautifully wet cunt. The woman ground down on her, and it was Kath's turn to groan. She pulled back a little so she could look into those eyes as she fucked her relentlessly. Her own clit and cunt were throbbing from the sensations coursing through them.

And then she saw it in the woman's eyes, saw the orgasm growing, and she flicked her thumb over the woman's clit to bring it ever closer. The effect was instantaneous; the eyes widened then closed, the hips thrust upwards, and the woman gushed all over Kath's hand, arching her back to push her body tight up against Kath's as she rode it out.

Kath maintained their body contact even as the woman relaxed back against the wall, kissing her neck, her collarbone, her lips.

"Oh my God," whispered the woman as Kath nibbled along her chin. "That was...incredible."

Kath nodded, breathing heavily. Torn between giving the woman time to get her breath back and the desperate ache between her own legs that needed immediate attention, she withdrew her fingers.

"What do you need?" The woman brushed her lips across Kath's. "I can see it all over your face—what do you need?"

Kath brought her hand up and wiggled her fingers.

"Lick these clean and then lick me," she said, her voice so hoarse with desire she barely recognised it.

The woman groaned and lunged forward to take Kath's fingers into her mouth. She sucked and licked with relish. And then, with a strength that both surprised and delighted Kath, she grabbed Kath's shoulders and pulled her around to lean against the wall. With an oh-so-sexy smile, the woman dropped to her knees in front of Kath and reached for the zip on Kath's trousers. Kath's clit pulsed in response, and she helped with opening her trousers. She pushed her boy shorts down enough for the blonde to get her head—and more importantly, her tongue—into position. At the first touch of that warm tongue bathing her clit, Kath groaned from deep within herself and pushed her hips forward. Oh God, yes, she needed this...

She happened to glance across to the central bar and caught the approving nod of another leather-clad butch who, it seemed, had been watching their show. Kath grinned, and the butch laughed, and then all of Kath's attention was drawn to the tongue and lips working between her legs. She closed her eyes and let herself be taken to a level of pleasure she hadn't known in a very long time.

The blonde was *very* good at what she was doing—good, firm strokes that took Kath to the edge, then soft, gentle sucks that kept her hovering in limbo, just below orgasm. Then, with another few hard strokes with the flat of her tongue directly on her clit, the blonde brought Kath to a spectacular orgasm that ripped through every fibre in her body.

She clutched at the woman's head as she gasped for breath. Before she could ask, the blonde rammed a finger inside her, giving Kath what she needed to finish off her pleasure. Kath ground her teeth and thrust against the finger, letting it perpetuate the aftershocks of her orgasm through her entire body.

After a few moments, the blonde withdrew and stood. She pulled Kath's underwear and trousers up as she did so. Kath drew her close and kissed her, tasting herself on the woman's lips.

They pulled back, and their gazes met.

"Amazing," said the blonde, smiling. "Thank you."

"No, trust me, I'm the one who's thankful," said Kath, surprised at the emotion that bubbled up and threatened to spill over into tears. "Thank you for being so perfect."

The blonde dipped her head in a display of coyness that really touched Kath. Then she raised her head for one more kiss before making her exit.

Kath slumped against the wall, breathing slow and deep. Her emotions were still very close to the surface. The encounter had restored her in so many ways, not just physically. Somehow, in all her planning, she hadn't anticipated that and was at a loss as to what to do with herself and the rest of evening. She didn't want to go home yet, but she was *almost* sated from just that one experience.

First things first—another beer.

She sat at the bar for her first few gulps, gazing into space, still enjoying how it felt to command a woman that way again. The ease with which she slipped into the dominant role thrilled her. Her confidence was back in bucketfuls, and it felt wonderful.

"She's something else, that one, isn't she?" a woman said. The butch who'd caught her eye earlier on eased her way onto the stool next to Kath's. "Had her last week. Best fuck I've had in a *long* time," continued the butch. "Seen her sometimes in the Blue Room. She loves getting it from behind. A few of us have had her that way. Rumour is she's straight. Well, married to a bloke at least. Comes in here for a couple of weeks at a time, then no one sees her again for a few weeks. But fuck, she's worth it."

Kath didn't know how to respond, so she just nodded and grinned inanely. It should have occurred to her that anyone she met here had probably been before, but somehow knowing the blonde visited so often threatened to take some of the magic away. How stupid was that? It's not like she came here looking for the love of her life, so why should she care how many times the blonde had been here and who she'd been fucked by?

"First time here?" asked the butch.

Kath nodded, not trusting her voice just yet.

"Well, you certainly hit the jackpot, then, didn't you? Fuck!" The butch laughed and took a long swig of her own beer. "You should bring your cock next time and get in the Blue Room—you get some seriously good action in there, believe me."

"Yeah," said Kath finally. "I may just do that. Excuse me, I think I'm just going to go and check it out now." She didn't want to talk any more—she didn't want anything else the butch said to diminish her high.

Kath strode into the Blue Room without looking back at the action in Green—she definitely didn't want to see the blonde involved with anyone else tonight. The Blue Room was accessed from a door in the corner of Green. The door to the Red Room, the BDSM space, was in the opposite corner. The atmosphere changed the minute the door closed behind her. The Blue Room was…grittier…harder.

There was an edge, something she couldn't define, but it set all of her senses sparking again. She inhaled deeply as she looked around. She'd had a fair amount of sex in her life, a lot of it purely physical with no emotion involved at all, but the rawness in this room took her breath away. She walked to the centre bar and took a stool on the end to make sure she had a clear view of events. She drank it all in, and her body responded with an immediacy she wouldn't have thought possible so soon.

Immediately to her left, a naked woman was bent backwards over a stool. Standing between her legs, fucking her slowly with a substantial dildo was a tall, striking woman dressed entirely in leather. A femme dressed in a short skirt paired with a tight top that let her substantial cleavage spill over its very low-cut neckline stood opposite the butch. She had her hands full of the naked woman's breasts, kneading and pulling at them while she watched. Clearly all three of them were getting what they wanted from the evening. Kath glanced around. She wasn't the only one watching; they had quite an audience.

God, she loved this place.

She let her gaze roam across more of the room. In one corner, a woman with long auburn hair hitched up her skirt and straddled another woman—a solid black butch with multiple piercings—who was seated in a chair. Slowly, she inched herself onto the dildo her partner wore, her head thrown back in ecstasy as she did so. The butch pushed up her tight tee shirt and buried her head between the femme's breasts as she rode her. Kath watched until the red-haired woman came, and her own cunt contracted in response.

Kath kicked herself for not bringing her own harness and favourite toy. When she'd planned the night, all she'd thought about was skin and wetness and heat. But now, watching all of this, she was totally turned on at the thought of strapping on again. She drank more of her beer, shifting her gaze to two women directly in front of her.

One was braced against the wall, legs spread wide. Her skirt was pushed up to her waist and underwear down around the ankles. Her partner rammed into her from behind, hard and fast, gripping on to handfuls of the skirt to give herself leverage.

Kath almost groaned aloud. That was her favourite position for giving. Julie had loved it, absolutely *loved* it. Kath had taken her that way in nearly every room in Julie's house—against the bedroom door, across the kitchen table, over the sink in the bathroom. The idea of doing that again, in this room filled with lust and sex and desire, made Kath nearly tremble with need.

As she finished her beer, she sat and watched the room. She wondered about paying a visit to the Red Room—she'd dabbled in a little BDSM over the years—but that wasn't what she was looking for right now. Unfortunately, without her harness and dildo, she couldn't have what she really wanted.

She sighed, resigning herself to going back into the Green Room to find another woman to explore with her fingers and tongue. Not that it would be a hardship, but next time she came here—and there would *definitely* be a next time—she would come better prepared.

As she made to leave, she caught sight of a redhead leaning against the wall nearby. The woman smiled, cockily, and raised a hand to beckon Kath over. Kath ran her gaze down the redhead's curvaceous body. She wore black jeans tucked into knee-length leather boots and a tight-fitting, long-sleeved top that hugged her ample breasts and the top of her wide hips. She wasn't skinny by a long shot, but she wore her curves as though she was born to seduce anyone who took her fancy. Kath raised her gaze. This time, the woman's face featured a quirked eyebrow and a hint of impatience.

The redhead crooked her finger again, and Kath found her legs responding before her brain could question it.

She reached her in a few paces and discovered herself inexplicably tongue-tied when she got there. The woman, older than Kath by some years, oozed a surety and sensuality that completely unsettled Kath, yet her body ached to connect with her.

"Hello," said the woman, her voice like velvet, sending shivers down Kath's spine. "My name is Vivian, and I want you to fuck me."

Kath blinked, shocked at the directness from such a femme. She'd thought Julie could act the seductress when she wanted to, but Vivian could have given her lessons. To PhD level.

"I-I'm sorry," stammered Kath, embarrassed by her inability to form a sentence. "I don't actually have my strap-on with me."

Vivian reached out a finger and laid it over Kath's lips.

"Not to worry, honey. I brought my own."

Kath's eyes widened, and Vivian chuckled throatily.

"Don't look so shocked." She leaned forward until her lips were a breath away from Kath's. "I know what I want, and I make sure I get it. You just get to enjoy the ride. Okay?"

Kath nodded, the power of speech having totally left her. All she could focus on was the lushness of Vivian's lips and the warmth of her breath fanning over her mouth, sending bolts of heat straight to Kath's clit. She moaned and attempted to lean in closer for a kiss of those plump lips, but Vivian pulled back sharply.

"Sorry, honey, I don't do kissing. Just fucking. Now, you reach down and find what you need in the bag at my feet while I get comfortable."

And with that, Vivian turned to face the wall and began undoing her jeans. Kath blinked a couple of times, then mentally shook herself into the here and now. While she normally wanted—needed—to dominate a situation like this, Vivian's cool commands had had a profound effect on her. She obeyed without question, dipping down to find a large black leather handbag next to Vivian's legs. Inside the bag, she found a soft harness and a six-inch ribbed dildo. It wasn't as large as she would have expected. Somehow Vivian's confidence had led Kath to believe she'd want to be fucked by something big. As she fiddled with the bag, she glanced up, and her breath caught in her throat. Vivian had dropped her jeans to the top of her boots and pulled her tight top up over her ass to reveal two pale, very round, very squeezable buttocks. The strong scent of Vivian's arousal, along with the way her pussy glistened in the low light, made Kath clench down deep in her own cunt.

Kath stood and glanced at the harness in her hands and then down at her own clothing. Moving as quickly as she could, she undid the buckles on the harness, unzipped her trousers, and pulled them down just enough to slip the harness straps between her legs. Once it was in place and set, she pulled the trousers up over her ass; she felt a little too vulnerable with her hind end hanging in the wind. Then, finally, she stepped behind Vivian, who was looking over her own shoulder with an amused smile on her face.

"Comfortable?" she asked with a smirk.

Kath nodded, willing herself not to blush. For fuck's sake, she'd done this a hundred times or more. Why did Vivian make her feel like such an amateur? And yet somehow this didn't knock Kath's confidence. If anything, it was inspiring her to rise to the challenge, to show Vivian that she knew *exactly* what she was doing.

"Good," purred Vivian, her voice strong above the background music. "Then coat that little baby in my juice and fuck me."

The blood in Kath's veins came to a momentary stop as a tsunami of desire swept through her body. Never had a woman's words had such a physical effect on her. She nearly whimpered with it. Vivian caught her eye, one eyebrow raised.

"Problem?" she asked, glancing down once at the dildo between Kath's legs and then back up again to meet Kath's eyes.

"God, no," groaned Kath and ran her hand through the sexy, hot juice leaking out of Vivian's cunt. She eased the dildo through that wetness, using the motion, plus her own very wet hand, to give it a good covering. To Kath's delight, Vivian trembled slightly as she did so. Vivian's composure wasn't total after all. Confidence surged through Kath, and she teased Vivian once more. She ran both hands through and over her wet cunt lips to brush ever-so-casually over her clit. Vivian groaned aloud.

With that groan, she decided to test Vivian's mettle and make her wait just a little longer. Show her who was really in charge now.

Leaving the dildo between Vivian's legs, pressed up into her lips lengthways, so that it didn't penetrate, she put her hands on Vivian's waist and inched her fingers under the tight top.

"Fuck, what are you waiting for?" Vivian growled.

"Shush," whispered Kath close to her ear. "This is my show now, babe."

Vivian growled again and turned to meet Kath's eyes. She paused for a moment and then swallowed. Kath had won this round. Vivian smiled, slow and sexy and turned back to the wall.

"Give me your best, then, honey," she said over her shoulder, her voice that soft velvet again, and Kath chuckled.

"Oh, I will." She pushed her hands up inside Vivian's top to grasp her abundant breasts, revelling in how they overspilled her hands. Vivian pushed into her, forcing her nipples into Kath's palms. Kath arched her fingers to pull at each hard centre and twisted them roughly. Vivian let out a guttural moan and pushed her chest harder against Kath's hands. As she did so, the arch of her back made her pussy ride along the dildo and pushed her ass back into Kath's groin. Thrusting gently, Kath helped the motion along, letting the dildo slide through Vivian's lips to tease her even more. Vivian's moaning grew louder as she murmured "fuck" and "yes" over and over.

Kath smiled to herself; it was time to put Vivian out of her misery. She grasped the dildo and placed the tip of it against the entrance to Vivian's cunt and then gripped Vivian's shoulder with her other hand.

"Ready?" she asked, pressing her mouth close to Vivian's ear.

"Yes. *Jesus*," hissed Vivian.

Kath pushed and watched as the dildo slid into Vivian. There was a little resistance, and then Vivian opened herself and the toy sank into her. Kath groaned as the full length disappeared. With one hand clutching Vivian's shoulder and the other on her hip, she braced herself against Vivian's luscious body. And then she started thrusting, pulling about halfway out before driving deep inside again. With each thrust, Vivian's head arched back. She pressed so strongly against the wall, the veins stood out along the back of her hands. Vivian gasped, her ecstasy obvious, and Kath responded to each sound, thrust, and arch. Her clit pressed nicely up against the base of the dildo, and she had every chance of coming in this position. But first, Vivian. After a few more deep thrusts, Kath moved her hand from Vivian's hip around to find her clit.

"God, yes!" cried Vivian, and Kath didn't hesitate, starting slow circles over Vivian's engorged clit. She increased the pressure and speed with the increase in volume of Vivian's cries, all the while watching the dildo move in and out. As she brought Vivian to the brink, as she controlled the pace of it, Kath set aside one small part of her brain to register just how important this night had been for her. Vivian came, thrusting back against Kath, fingers clenching into fists against the wall, and Kath sucked in a deep breath.

A cry formed somewhere deep inside that threatened to become a sob in the next moment. The joy, the pure ecstasy running through her body was almost a physical thing in itself. In the instant after that realisation, her own orgasm crashed through her, weakening her knees. Vivian groaned in tandem with her. Kath stilled her thrusts, leaving the dildo buried deep inside Vivian, and she wrapped her body over Vivian's to pull her close. Vivian tipped her head back and let Kath nuzzle her neck.

"Thank you," Kath whispered. Her emotions were of no relevance to Vivian, but the heartfelt words escaped her without warning.

Vivian turned her head slightly and stared at Kath for a few moments, her eyes not revealing any of her thoughts. Then she smiled. "Trust me, the pleasure was *all* mine." She winked, and Kath grinned.

"Oh, I don't know about that," replied Kath, also winking. She pulled out slowly, bringing one last hiss of pleasure from Vivian as the dildo left her body. As she removed the harness, Vivian rearranged her clothing. Then Kath passed over the kit to Vivian, who stooped to pick up the bag. With a final smile, Vivian walked away without so much as a backwards glance, but Kath didn't mind. She felt drained and elated all at the same time. She zipped up her trousers and stumbled over to the central bar. Her legs refused to cooperate fully with her brain's commands, much to her own amusement. She slouched on one of the stools, gaze unfocused, and closed her eyes as she replayed the last twenty minutes or so in her mind. Somehow, even though Kath hadn't started as the dominant one, this encounter had been even more fulfilling than the one with the blonde earlier. She'd had to work at this one, prove herself just a little bit, and the satisfaction was all the greater because of it.

Without a doubt, her weekends for the foreseeable future had a new, exciting look to them.

When she felt her legs could actually support her, she stood and stretched. She left the Blue Room, walked back into Green, and stopped for a moment to soak up a bit more of the atmosphere. She didn't focus on anything in particular beyond just being there.

Then she took a deep breath and made to leave and head home, only to have a cute little thing who'd just walked in catch her eye.

The short, tartan skirt showed off a fine set of legs, and the sheer top that covered her upper body left little to the imagination. The woman's eyes flashed a very definite "go." She couldn't, could she? Not three in one night? And then her clit butted into her thoughts. *Sure we can*, it purred. *What are you waiting for?*

Chuckling to herself, Kath took a step forward.

Mandy watched as the butch she'd lusted after earlier departed Green and headed for the locker room. She emerged wrapped in her long leather coat again, and Mandy couldn't help but ogle as the woman walked towards her. She was taller than Mandy, probably about five nine, and carried her big build with a swagger that made Mandy grin. As she passed, she met Mandy's gaze and smiled. Mandy returned the smile with a blush and pulled back into her office to hide it, embarrassed beyond measure at showing herself up in front of a customer. The woman left, and Mandy let out a breath. She could almost hear Rebecca's voice next to her. *Oh, so that's really your type, is it? Big and butch?*

There would be humour in the tone, a hint of teasing, but it would be done with love. Mandy's smile faded as the pain hit her, stuttering her heart. Just over a year since Rebecca had gone. A year of battling her emotions while pushing on with opening this club. The joy of that tempered by the emptiness left without Rebecca to share it.

"You okay, Mandy?" Dee's voice was laced with concern. She had worked for Mandy as the assistant manager since the day they opened, and they'd become quite good friends.

Mandy blinked back tears and inhaled deeply.

"Fine," she replied, her voice quavering more than she liked. "I'm fine."

CHAPTER 2

Melbourne, 1997

The music was thumping through the floor of Toolbox, the small, dark club Mandy had discovered during her first week in Melbourne. Saturday night was in full swing with wall-to-wall dykes bumping and grinding to the beat, and the air was hot and sweaty. Just the way Mandy liked it. She urged Suzy to follow her to the back of the club, but Suzy was dragging her heels a bit, which Mandy *didn't* like.

She'd thought she'd read Suzy's responses to her overtures on the dance floor correctly, but now she wasn't so sure. She pulled her into the toilet cubicle anyway and locked the door shut behind them. She gently pressed Suzy against the door, and leaned into her firm body. If Suzy was having a few doubts, Mandy was happy to assuage them. She dipped her head and trailed open-mouthed kisses down the length of Suzy's neck. Suzy trembled beneath her, and Mandy smiled into the soft skin beneath her lips. Moving upwards, she found her earlobe and nibbled lightly before biting down a little harder. The small groan that Suzy emitted sent a nice little pulse of desire to Mandy's clit.

"Okay, baby?" Mandy whispered against Suzy's ear and was rewarded with another groan. Suzy latched onto Mandy's hips and pulled her closer. *Oh yes, job done.* Mandy pulled Suzy's tee shirt from out of her cargo pants and ran her hands straight up her body and over her breasts. It had been obvious on the dance floor that Suzy wasn't wearing a bra. Her breasts were small, not even a handful, really, but Mandy didn't care because Suzy's nipples responded just the way she liked, hardening rapidly and pushing into her palms. Every touch she bestowed on them had Suzy grinding just that little bit harder against Mandy's thigh.

The night had started out so slowly. Her friend Stacey hadn't shown up, which had put a damper on the start of the evening. Mandy was perfectly happy to spend a night alone in a club, and had frequently done so, but she'd been looking forward to hooking up with Stacey. They hadn't seen each other in a couple of weeks and had a lot of catching up to do. No doubt a woman was the reason for Stacey's absence; it usually was.

So, Stacey had ditched her tonight, and Mandy had two choices— go home or make the most of it. She chose the latter, and Suzy's soft breasts in her hands vindicated that choice. She needed this—it had been a long week at work. She'd been in Melbourne for six months now and had landed a job in a friend's club. Despite her protestations that she knew nothing about running a bar, he'd waved her off.

"Look, love, I'll give you a month to try it—if you don't like it, no hard feelings, and if you're shit, you're out, simple as that."

She'd started the following week and never looked back. She was a natural—having spent so many nights in clubs herself, she'd become adept at reading the crowd, picking up on the atmosphere, and understanding what the punters wanted. Mandy had found her new niche and was working flat out to build her reputation within it.

For now, as Suzy responded eagerly to the touch of her hands, all thoughts of her long, tiring week were fading into the recesses of her brain. Time to up the ante. Mandy reached down to the zip of Suzy's pants and started slowly undoing it. Suzy's hand shot down and stopped her in her tracks.

"No, wait," panted Suzy against Mandy's mouth.

"Something wrong?" asked Mandy in her most seductive tone.

There was a slight hesitation, and then Suzy pulled her mouth away and looked at Mandy.

"I'm just not… That's not what I do, not with someone I've only just met." Suzy's soft Aussie twang trembled with a clear mix of desire and nerves. "I don't mind a bit of a pash and a grope, but… well, I'd rather get to know you a bit more before…you know."

Oh shit. There was a determination behind Suzy's words that told Mandy all she needed to know. She had definitely read this one wrong.

"Oh, right." There really wasn't a lot else she could say to that. Suzy's entire demeanour made it clear there was no point in going down the teasing, coaxing route, as she'd sometimes done in the past. And Mandy wasn't the sort of woman who needed—or wanted—to force an issue.

She stepped back and pulled her tee shirt down. Her skin was already cooling where Suzy's hands had been only moments before.

"Well, I guess I'll say goodnight, then," she said as she reached for the lock.

"Hey, wait." Suzy's voice registered surprise. "Don't you want to swap numbers, maybe arrange a time to see each other?"

Mandy breathed out an elongated sigh.

She turned back to meet Suzy's gaze. "Sorry, love," she said quietly. "Not my style. Have a nice night."

She unlocked the cubicle and left before Suzy could get a word out.

On her way back through the club, she immersed herself in the music once more. She was filled with a strange mix of denied arousal and exhaustion and didn't have the energy to make another conquest. She danced her way towards the front of the room, angling herself away from the angry looks Suzy and her group of friends were shooting her way. Lovely. Maybe it was time to call it a night—she really didn't need the hassle. *Get over it, girls*, she mentally threw their way. *Nobody died.*

She made her way to the exit. The night was balmy—February in Melbourne carried the warmth of late summer long into the evening, and she loved it. She strolled away from the railway arches that housed the club and wandered up Flinders Street towards the station. She had just enough time to get the tram home rather than a cab.

She shared the tram ride with a group of very drunk, very young girls who gave the conductor quite a hard time all the way back to St. Kilda. He took it well and caught Mandy's eye as she hopped off at the Esplanade, raising his eyebrows in a resigned manner that suggested this was nothing short of a usual Saturday night for him. She pitied him.

She walked the short couple of blocks to her apartment and rode the lift up to the fifteenth floor. Once inside she opened up the balcony doors and stepped out to gaze at the surf that crashed gently on the beach across the Esplanade. She couldn't really see the waves in the dark, but she could hear them, even above the traffic that rose up to her in fits and starts along the road below. That was enough. She stepped back into the apartment and pulled an ice-cold Carlton from the fridge. As she took a couple of quick gulps, she noticed the light flashing on her answer machine. Her mum's broken, aching voice came over the machine to deliver a message that crashed into her brain.

"Mandy, sweetheart, it's your mum. I think you'd better come home, darling, if you can." A pause, followed by a sob. "It…it's your dad. H-he hasn't got long. Please, come home?"

CHAPTER 3

Manchester, present day

The door was nondescript, inconspicuous. Black, which made Max smile weakly. What other colour would it be? She stood across the street, hidden in the shadow of the railway bridge above, and wondered, again, if she could do this. In three attempts, this was the furthest she had got. The two previous journeys had ended at Stoke, as the fear of taking such a step far outweighed the hunger, the need, inside her. But now, two weeks later, she'd stayed on the train to its final destination, Manchester, and having gone that far, it seemed her legs had decided she might as well reach her final destination without any more delay.

She'd arrived at the hotel, in the city centre near Piccadilly Gardens, at about five o'clock that afternoon. The room was small but nicely furnished, and the bathroom was gorgeous. She'd eaten early from room service and had one glass of wine to settle her rampaging nerves. Then she'd had a long soak in the bath and washed her hair, taking her time, again hoping the warm water would calm her. She wanted to do this. She did. At the same time, she was terrified about what it meant for her life and her relationship. She refused to listen to the answer.

At nine thirty, she'd summoned a cab. The ten minutes in the car sent her stomach churning and her mind whirling. Twice she'd nearly asked the driver to take her back to the hotel, and twice she'd resisted.

So here she stood, body trembling from nerves or from the cool September evening air; she couldn't tell which. She hated the lies she'd told these last two months about imaginary meetings in Manchester that didn't finish until after seven. Somewhat to her dismay, the lies had come easily.

She'd blamed her job—working in PR for a drug company meant she constantly had to…massage…the truth. Telling little white lies was second nature to her. But Sue didn't need to know the truth. Sue, whom she loved dearly and had loved for nearly eight years. Sue, who was twelve years older than her, who was deep in the throes of menopause, and who had lost all interest in sex, even in intimacy. Sue, who hadn't kissed her properly in a year.

They'd talked about it, and there had been genuine regret in Sue's voice. Max had accepted it and told her it was okay, told her it didn't matter. Their love was too strong to let this one small thing get in the way. Their love was built on a more intellectual basis, always had been. That had been fine when they first got together; in fact, it had been exactly what Max had needed. Sue was a wonderfully undemanding escape from the unhealthy craziness that Max had dealt with in her previous relationship.

Only now, however, Max needed something else. At first, she'd just blamed it on Sue's menopause because that seemed the easiest excuse. But the more she struggled with what she was feeling, the more she analysed it. The more she delved inside herself, the more she realised it was not about Sue at all. Something had cut loose inside Max over the last two or three years.

She didn't know how it had started, particularly, although her brief…interaction…with Lucy had definitely been part of the trigger. Lucy had worked as a temp in Max's office a few years ago. And she had sent Max's head—and other parts of her anatomy—spinning. Lucy was hot. Absolutely smoking hot. It had shocked Max—she'd never even so much as looked at another woman since meeting Sue. Yet something about Lucy sent Max's pulse racing, and gradually some very inappropriate thoughts crept into her head.

Nothing had ever happened between them, although Lucy made it clear she was amenable one night during after-work drinks. Pressing herself up against Max in a quiet corner of the bar, she'd dared Max to kiss her. Max, of course, had run. At the time, she took it as clear proof that she was totally committed to Sue despite the raw, passionate feelings Lucy stirred in her. But over time, those feelings hadn't gone away. If anything, they'd increased.

And that had coincided with Sue's diminishing lack of interest in all things sexual, leaving Max frustrated and angry at herself for being so. Surely what she and Sue had should be enough? Shouldn't it? Why did something as silly as the need for sex have to get in the way? She continued to ignore the little voice deep inside her that said it wasn't just the sex…

So she masturbated—frequently—to take care of that silly urge, but it was never enough, never fully satisfying. Max craved the sensations of another woman's hands and tongue and skin. Sometimes she absolutely ached from it, and it drove her to tears. After years of careful, gentle passivity from Sue, she wanted passion—something harder, something…more. Something that Sue couldn't give her.

Underneath all her introspection about the physical, Max had gradually let that little voice inside her get louder. The differences between her and Sue were getting wider and scarier and more difficult to manage. And the differences weren't just about the physical. Their earlier connection, the reason they had fit so well in the beginning, was lost to her. She looked at Sue sometimes and wondered, *if I met you now, would I even give you a second glance?* Thoughts like this terrified her.

They'd bought a flat together, talked about getting married. How could it all unravel like this? Blaming it on a lack of sex was a huge cop-out, but it was all Max could handle right now. She wasn't ready to face what she knew, deep down inside, was really wrong. So she had focused on the lack of sex and wondered if there was something she could do about that. Maybe, if she could get this out of her system, she and Sue would be okay.

She'd discovered the club purely by chance. After a late night at work, heading home on the Tube through the West End, she'd picked up a magazine left on a seat. The front featured two women in a semi-naked embrace. It was a gay magazine, one she'd never even heard of, such was her distance from the scene since finding committed bliss with Sue. She flicked through it as her train trundled on and came across an article. She'd read every word and found herself surprisingly turned on by the descriptions of the clubs. Clubs that offered a new variation on the darkroom scene—for women, by women.

Over the next few days, she hadn't been able to stop thinking about the article. One club in particular, located in Manchester, was seared into her brain. She'd deliberately not registered the names of the two clubs in London—she'd never take the risk of running into someone she or Sue knew. The one in Manchester sounded like it was a cut above what she expected—classier, if that were possible. It even had a code of conduct to ensure that everyone had a fun yet safe time. After tormented thoughts that kept her awake over many nights, she finally took a minute to look it up on Google Maps. It was centrally located, easy to get to from a train into Piccadilly station, if one was travelling up from London.

Another few weeks of thinking about it. Another few weeks of doubts and questions with very few answers. Another few weeks of getting herself off in the shower in the morning. Another few weeks of justifying the plan to go—she wouldn't really be cheating on Sue if it was anonymous… If it was just a quick fuck… If it was just to scratch an itch…

It would be fulfilling a need, similar to the way eating a meal fulfilled hunger. It would be getting this damn sex thing out of the way, once and for all, so that she could focus on what was important between her and Sue.

Too bad she couldn't quite remember what that was.

A cab pulled up a little way up the road from the door, and a woman got out. She was quite tall, wearing leather trousers and a long leather coat, and she carried a small pack slung over her shoulder. Her dark, shoulder-length hair lifted slightly in the breeze as she strode confidently towards the black door. She looked perfectly normal. Ordinary, even.

Max chuckled to herself—what had she expected? Two heads? The woman waited for the cab to drive off before knocking. A small shutter opened at eye level, and then the door opened, and she disappeared inside.

Easy as that.

Max took a deep breath, trying to calm the butterflies that were now in rampant flight in her belly.

A part of her wanted to laugh—never in her lifetime did she think she'd be standing here, planning to step inside a building in search of a woman to fuck her. Any which way she wanted. For as long as she wanted. She never needed to know the woman's name or, if it was as dark inside as the article claimed, what she looked like.

Another part of her wanted to cry. She really shouldn't be here, standing in this quiet, dark street, contemplating fucking someone who wasn't her partner.

Suddenly, it was as if a dark wall dropped down in her mind, cutting off her feelings with a sharpness that made her feel almost amputated from her emotional self. Without really being aware she was doing it, she crossed the road and knocked on the door. Her breath caught in her throat as the shutter opened from the inside. A woman's face appeared in the small window. Her sharp blue eyes looked at Max intently.

"Do you know where you are?" she was asked quietly.

"Yes," Max replied and smiled with more confidence than she felt. "But it is my first time," she admitted as a slight blush stole across her cheeks.

The woman smiled in return, and then came the sound of the lock being turned.

She stepped into a hallway that was painted deep red with dim lighting to guide her steps.

"Welcome," said the woman. She had handsome features to go with her intense eyes. "I'm Mandy, the manager. I don't like to waste a lot of time here on the doorstep, but as you're new, would you like a rough idea of what's on offer?"

In the semi-darkness, Max's blush deepened. She nodded, shoving her hands into her pockets to hide their shaking.

"It's twenty pounds membership for the evening, which includes the use of the showers, but you'll pay for whatever drinks you want. There are three rooms, each with their own bar. Each room serves a different purpose. The Green Room is, shall we say, vanilla—no toys, no bondage."

Max nodded, involuntarily licking her lips, which suddenly seemed very dry.

"The Blue Room is the toy room. Just to be clear on what can be expected, dildos are definitely allowed."

Max again fought a blush as thoughts of toys filled her head.

"And the Red Room is the BDSM room. Pretty much anything and everything is allowed in there. We have various pieces of equipment that allow a certain level of play without being too dark."

Max made a mental note to avoid Red—BDSM was definitely not something she'd experienced, and she didn't intend to stumble into something she couldn't handle.

The corners of Mandy's mouth lifted slightly. "The basic rule for all rooms," she continued, "is that if you want to participate in any way, you find a space along a wall. That signals your availability. Obviously, it's up to you whether you want to be approached or do the approaching. If you just want to watch, take one of the bar stools, and no one will touch you. Anything happens that you think is against the spirit of the room you are in or the place where you are sitting, you just get hold of one of the bar women. Okay?"

Max nodded again and reached into her bag for her wallet. She pulled out the twenty pounds, heart pounding in her chest. A mildly nauseating mix of fear and excitement pitted deep in her stomach.

"I can give you a locker for your jacket and bag if you want?"

"That would be good, thanks." She pulled cash from her wallet, stuffed it into the pocket of her jeans, and returned the wallet back into her bag. She followed Mandy to a side room, deposited her stuff in the locker, and pocketed the key.

"Green is the first room you'll come to, through that door there." Mandy motioned towards the end of the hall. "The others are through that room. You can't miss them." She paused and smiled. "Hope you find what you're looking for."

Even though her mouth had gone dry and her lips felt like they would never part, Max returned the smile and made herself walk purposefully to the end of the corridor. Her fingers trembled as she reached for the door handle.

She pushed open the door and stepped into an equally dim room, this one painted a forest green. Music played just loud enough to cover quiet sounds, but she would still be able to hear her temporary lover. A cry of "Oh *yes*!" came just as she stepped into the room. She didn't dare look round for the source. Not yet.

She took a deep breath. The room opened up to a large space with a tall bar table and stools in the centre. A handful of couples were pressed up against the wall. She turned to the bar, feeling the need for something to relax her a bit before she allowed herself to participate in any way, even just by looking.

"What can I get you?" The dim lights of the bar cast a gentle glow up into a friendly face framed by blonde hair chopped into a funky cut. She had the sort of face that instantly put one at ease with its softness.

"Whisky and ginger. A double."

"Coming up."

As the drink was poured, Max resisted the urge to wipe her damp palms on her jeans. She stepped up onto a stool and perched on it, safe in the no-touch zone. She was grateful that the club had such a simple method of communicating her intentions to others. She took a good pull on her drink as soon as it was handed to her, and the warmth of the whisky eased its way down her throat to her belly. After a couple of sips, she felt brave enough to look back to the room.

Near her, a dark-haired woman was on her knees in front of a blonde, her head bobbing up and down between the other one's legs. With her head thrown back against the wall, the blonde's gasps were audible above the music if Max listened hard enough.

Desire thrummed between Max's legs, and she couldn't help smiling to herself. At least one part of her had no confusion about why she was here. When she finished her whisky, she ordered another and continued to watch as a few more women arrived. Some walked straight through to the Blue Room—clearly identifiable by the small blue light above the door—and two others stayed in Green. Both immediately leaned up against the wall. The dark-haired woman who had minutes ago been tonguing the blonde got up and without so much as a backward glance, walked across to a new arrival wearing a short tartan skirt. The dark-haired woman shoved the skirt up, yanked the underwear down, and dropped to her knees. As she pressed her face into the newcomer's pussy, Max's mouth went dry again.

Was that what Max wanted? Quick, no foreplay, instant gratification? She wasn't sure. That would be almost too clinical, too much like masturbating, really. All of her torment about the physical aspects of her relationship with Sue had been about the lack of connection, so surely that should be what she was looking for here, not just a quick-fire orgasm that she could have given herself back in her hotel room.

She let her gaze slide round the room and spotted a couple in the corner near the door to Blue. This couple was kissing deeply, hands roaming over each other's bodies underneath their tee shirts. Without thinking about what she was doing, she strolled into the centre of the room, took a seat on a stool at the high table there, and sipped her drink while she watched them. Heat rose in her face again as she blatantly stared. She had to admit, being a voyeur was turning her on. A lot. The one with her back to Max was taller, and she was the first one to undo her partner's jeans. They both groaned as she did so, and Max's cunt throbbed in response. Oh God, to have someone want her that much, to have the *thought* of someone's fingers inside her make her so wet.

Tonight, she needed to deal with her physical self, the one that was aching to be wanted. And then, tomorrow, she'd let that wall come down and deal with the aftermath.

The tall one slid her hand inside the jeans and then, clearly, straight inside the other woman, who arched and moaned and called out, "Fuck me… oh *God*, fuck me…"

Max finished her drink and dragged her gaze away from them, acutely aware of the throbbing ache between her own legs. She needed to find someone to take care of that, and soon. The thought of it made her nearly moan out loud with want. Fuck yes, she *needed* it. A woman walked past, taller than Max, with short, dark hair and a spicy scent that spun Max's heightened senses into overdrive.

She walked slowly past the table. Her body was lean with strong shoulders beneath a muscle vest and long legs encased in tight denim. God, *yes*.

Almost on autopilot, her mind shut down and her body fully awake and alive, Max stood, walked across the room to the opposite wall, and turned to face the woman as she strolled around, gaze sweeping the room. When she landed on Max, she stopped roaming. Max sucked in a breath and waited. Her nipples hardened with the anticipation and pushed against the confines of her bra. The woman slowly stepped towards her, and Max's heart threatened to stop.

You are actually going to do this.

The whispered thought rattled repeatedly through her brain. The woman came closer, her blue-eyed gaze locking on Max's. She hesitated a moment, then lifted a hand to Max's face and ran her fingertips from Max's eyebrow to her neck. Max's entire being focused in on the gentle touch of those fingertips on her hot skin. She was vaguely aware the woman's fingers were trembling. Nerves? Or desire?

"I want to take my time, okay?" the woman said; her quiet voice held a slight tremor in it. All Max could do was nod; the power of speech had abandoned her. "I...I need to feel." She dipped her head and brought her lips to Max's neck. "I need to...taste." Her voice sounded strained as if she had her own battle raging. Max had no idea what that was and, to be honest, didn't care. Max moaned, unable to help herself, and her whole body pushed up towards the stranger.

"Oh *yes*." Max, finally remembered she had arms and hands of her own and brought them up to grip the woman's hips. She cupped her ass and pulled her in tight against her.

The woman moaned, and the tension in her body relaxed at Max's touch. Her whole stance softened as Max held her. Perhaps she wasn't as confident as she had at first appeared. And then Max's thoughts fluttered away as the woman's lips trailed a path across her chin to find her mouth.

Max didn't hesitate. Her lips opened, and for the first time in over eight years, she felt a new tongue push into her mouth, a tongue that sent shockwaves of heat and want pounding through her veins. At the back of Max's brain, a sliver of guilt writhed but was tamped down by the overwhelming physicality of the moment. They devoured each other's mouths, long, deep kisses that elicited moans and whimpers from Max that she'd forgotten how to make. It was hard, messy, and passionate, yet tender all at the same time.

"What's your name?" whispered the woman in Max's ear. Her tongue lingered to lick and probe and send shivers down Max's spine. "Just your first name…"

Max trembled. "Max. Yours?"

"Lou."

Lou's hands pushed up underneath her tee shirt then, and her warm fingertips stroked their way upwards. In a moment of clarity, she suddenly realised she was oblivious to everyone and everything else in the room. It was just her and Lou and their mutual need, which pulsed between them like a living thing. Lou's fingers reached Max's bra, and Lou reached round to unclip it. She freed Max's full breasts and cupped them in the next instant. Lou moaned and teased her nipples with her nails. Max whimpered with pleasure, pushing upwards, desperate for more contact, more pressure. Jesus, she had been so long without this. She feared she would come too quickly and then almost laughed. So what if she did? That was the beauty of this place—she could take what she needed and not worry about how she did it. As Lou feathered her fingertips around her nipples, Max moaned, murmuring words like "harder" and "more," unable to form full sentences, yet trying to communicate her need for Lou to apply more force. Lou responded. She pinched both nipples between her fingers, rolling them, kneading them, making Max gasp with desire.

"You feel amazing, Max," murmured Lou, close to her ear again, and then she was gone. She pushed Max's tee shirt up, baring her breasts, and sucked hard on one nipple, then the other. Max groaned with every pull of Lou's lips, her teeth, her tongue.

Without warning, Lou moved, kneeling, her hands undoing Max's jeans. She pulled them down to her ankles, spread Max's legs, and when she pressed her tongue to Max's clit, Max thought her knees would give. Max opened her knees wider and pushed her hips up, wantonly giving Lou more room. Lou licked the length of her, dipping her tongue just inside and then out and over her clit, her strokes hard. As she lapped up Max's juices, Lou dug her fingers into her thighs, pulling Max even closer to her face. Max was panting, her heart thumping in her chest, her pussy throbbing.

"Oh God," she breathed, her head buzzing with the pressure Lou was building in her body. "Fuck me...*please.*"

Lou pushed one, then two fingers inside Max, her tongue still slicking over her clit while she fucked Max with her fingers, thrusting slow and deep. She felt, rather than heard, Lou murmur her name against her pussy as she fucked her harder still. Max's orgasm came over her in huge, warm waves that curled up through her body from her toes and fingertips. Jesus, it had been so long since Sue had brought her to this point—and it hadn't ever felt like this, so all-consuming, so...everything. She breathed out a loud, guttural moan when it hit her, hips pumping against Lou's face, pushing herself down harder onto Lou's fingers, her hands in Lou's hair, keeping her tight against her while her clit throbbed out the last exquisite sensations.

Max slumped against the wall, head thrown back, breathing ragged. Oh God, that had been good. Jesus... After a few moments, she tipped her head forward to look at Lou, still on her knees in front of her, her forehead resting on Max's abdomen, her breath warm on Max's pussy. She reached down and tugged Lou up; the glassy look in Lou's eyes could mean only one thing. She did up her jeans, then reversed their positions. Lou's breathing hitched as her back hit the wall.

"Inside. Please," Lou said, trembling as she gazed into Max's eyes, and Max nodded. She undid Lou's jeans and slid her hand down. Her fingers slipped through soaking wet curls, and Lou let out a long moan. Heady with the power that washed over her, Max groaned. Lou arched as Max slipped her fingers over and through wet folds to glide into Lou. She was so wet...so open... Max pushed three fingers inside, filling her.

Lou shuddered, and grabbed onto Max. Pulling Max tight against her, she kissed her deeply. Max matched the thrust of her fingers with her tongue—long, slow strokes, deeper inside Lou each time. She angled her hand so that the heel of her palm pressed against Lou's clit and moaned at how fucking good it felt. She set a strong, steady rhythm, nothing too fast just yet, keeping Lou just away from the edge and loving the sound of Lou whispering her name as she fucked her.

"Faster, please," begged Lou, and Max responded, driving deeper and faster and harder until her wrist screamed its pain. When Lou came, bucking and writhing against Max's hand, Max groaned aloud with pleasure. Lou gasped in her ear as she drowned her hand with her juices. Max dropped to her knees, yanked down Lou's jeans, and began licking. Not to arouse, but simply to taste, to drink. Oh God, she tasted so good, and it had been *so* long. Lou gasped again, her hands frantic in Max's hair.

"Oh, that's so good, don't stop." Lou's voice was quiet and strained. She was close to a second orgasm, and Max changed the tempo of her tongue, changed her purpose. As she licked and sucked, she eased over lips, dipped inside, and then drew back over Lou's swollen clit. Lou whimpered, a sound that had the capacity to drive Max to a second orgasm of her own without any further manual manipulation.

She let the flat of her tongue lap over Lou's clit, faster and harder until Lou thrust her hips upwards. A harsh sound escaped her, and her grip on Max's head tightened to the point of pain. Max stayed where she was until Lou slouched back against the wall, then Max slowly stood, keeping her body pressed against Lou's as she moved. She pulled Lou close, kissed her, and her own flavour mingled with the taste of Lou on her mouth.

"Is 'thank you' inappropriate?" whispered Max once she could find her voice. She involuntarily gripped Lou's waist tighter, not wanting to let this incredible woman go just yet.

Lou smiled, shyly, which Max found utterly endearing. "Not at all. That was pretty amazing." She smiled again, zipped up her jeans, and planted a quick kiss on Max's swollen lips. "Thanks," she said, averting her eyes as she stepped back. Max reluctantly released her hold. The tension from earlier regained its hold on Lou's body, and Lou turned and walked towards the exit.

Although a little stunned at the speed of Lou's departure, Max took a deep breath and smiled ruefully to herself. This was what this club was about; no point hankering after an extended intimacy, a post-coital cuddle. What she'd just got was exactly what she had needed, and clearly it was mutual. Of course Lou was going to move on quickly afterwards, and Max should do the same or risk those emotions getting the better of her again.

She rearranged her clothes before heading off to find the bathroom. There were two cubicles, each like a small self-contained en suite, with toilet, basin, and shower. Towels were stacked on shelves, and liquid soap, tissues, and moisturiser were in baskets on the floor. She stepped into the first cubicle and locked the door behind her. She leaned against the door, closed her eyes, and breathed deeply. She could still smell Lou and brought a hand up to wipe at the slick juices coating her lips and chin. She licked her fingers, moaning at the taste. Too long…

As she washed her hands and face, she had no idea who this woman was looking back at her in the mirror. How had she just done that? How had she let go so quickly with a complete stranger? But oh God, it had been the most incredible experience.

She dried her hands on a small towel and then, with detachment, pulled down her jeans and cleaned between her legs with a moist tissue.

Did she feel any guilt at what she'd just done with Lou? She closed her eyes and searched deep inside. No, it wasn't there. She could easily conjure up Sue's face in her mind's eye and felt a rush of tenderness as she did so. But love? Deep, fulfilling love that was required to keep two people together? That she wasn't so sure about.

She opened her eyes and looked at herself in the mirror again. Where did this version of Max come from? Surely she should feel some shame, but she just couldn't find that in her. Tonight, she had experienced a release of pressure, a purely functional yet utterly pleasurable sharing of sexual expression that meant nothing. And yet everything.

But what about tomorrow? Could she just walk into their house tomorrow morning and lie through her teeth about her night away in this city? She gripped the sink with both hands as a stunning thought pitched into her head. She couldn't imagine, right here and now, having a problem doing that.

She looked away from the mirror, unable to face herself any longer, and took a few deep breaths. What now? Go back to her hotel or stay for a little longer?

She finished cleaning up, and as she towelled off, her body was still humming from that second orgasm she'd given Lou. She ached for more. Well, the genie was well and truly out of the bottle now. She stood quietly for a moment, shutting down her emotions yet again. A flush ran over her skin as she delved deep inside her fantasies and knew, without a doubt, what would round off the evening for her. She was walking a very fine line here—that little voice was persistent, if nothing else. If she let herself think about anything for too long, she just might unravel completely. So she closed it all off, kept her focus purely on her body, on her desire.

Would she find someone willing to indulge her? Toys had occasionally played a part in her sex life with Sue, back in the early days, but she hadn't been fucked with a dildo in years. The idea of it now made her breath quicken and her cunt pulse. Taking a deep breath, she ruffled up her hair, straightened her clothes, and walked purposefully out of the bathroom. She headed across Green to the door with the small blue light above it.

The Blue Room was just as dim, but seemed to have the same basic layout as Green. There was a bar in one corner, and she stopped there first to get a bottle of water. She followed her same pattern, perching on one of the central stools to observe before committing herself to something. There were fewer couples in here—two engaged in fucking, one talking and kissing occasionally, and two unattached women at opposite ends of the room. She watched one of couples for a while, getting even more turned on by the steady rhythm they set, the noises they made, knowing just how good it would feel to be on the receiving end. She became aware of being watched herself and turned slightly to her left. Leaning against the wall was the dark-haired woman from the cab outside, watching Max watch the couple. The woman moved her hand to her crotch and ran her thumb up the length of the zip in her leather trousers. Max's breathing quickened.

Almost without conscious thought, as it had been when first approaching the club outside, she slid slowly off the stool. Keeping her gaze on the woman, she walked towards her. When she reached her, she nervously wet her lips, not sure how this scenario would play out. The atmosphere was different in here—harder, more urgent.

Without preamble, the woman ran her open hands over Max's tee shirt to her breasts and squeezed sharply. Max gasped as wetness flooded between her legs.

"Undo your jeans," said the woman, her gaze never leaving Max's.

Max moaned softly and reached down to do as she was commanded. Oh yeah, the atmosphere in here was *very* different. And she loved it.

When she'd undone her jeans, the woman reached out to Max's hips, and flipped her round to face the wall. She pushed her up against it and brought her hands around to squeeze Max's breasts again. Max thrust backwards, pushing her ass into the woman's groin to find the hardness of the dildo inside her leather trousers. She moaned again, pushing harder. God, she was so ready for this.

"Easy," whispered the woman, her breath hot against Max's ear. "Soon, I promise. First I want to play a little." The woman grabbed both of Max's wrists and pushed her arms above her head slightly.

"Brace against the wall," she said, and Max did as she was commanded, splaying her hands out to give herself a steady balance.

"Good girl."

Those two words sent a shudder down Max's body. Another fantasy, of being dominated by someone a little butch, looked like it was about to come true.

The woman moved her hands over Max's body, underneath her tee shirt, and undid her bra. As the cups fell forward slightly, she grabbed handfuls of breast and pulled at Max's nipples until they were hard. She thrust her hips, grinding against Max and making her whimper. "Please...*please*."

"Not yet," said the woman, her voice firm, not tinted with anything resembling desire or passion. Just control. "I set the pace, remember?"

Max nodded, unable to speak.

The woman pinched one of Max's nipples sharply. Max gasped at the hint of pain that rapidly translated to pleasure pulsing in her clit.

"Who sets the pace?" The woman's voice was a little firmer, and she squeezed the nipple between her fingers even harder.

"You...you do." *Oh Jesus.*

"Good girl," said the woman again, and then she yanked down Max's jeans and underwear to her ankles. Max pushed off her short boots, and the woman helped her step out of the clothing. She pushed Max's legs apart, eliciting a deep groan from Max. She felt deliciously exposed. The sound of the zip of the woman's leather trousers being undone, followed by the condom wrapper being torn open, made her weak with anticipation. After a slight pause—presumably while it was rolled into place—a hot hand slipped between her legs, raking through her curls, her lips, getting covered with her juice.

"Fuck, you are *so* wet," groaned the woman, the timbre of her voice the first hint that she was enjoying this as much as Max.

And then it was Max's turn to groan again, loudly, as she felt the silicon against the back of her thigh. The woman grabbed hold of it, guided it to where Max desperately wanted it, and braced herself behind Max, one hand on her hip, one on her shoulder. Then, exquisitely, she pushed inside Max, taking her time, seeming to revel in the loud groans that escaped Max's lips with each inch further she went. The dildo was big, thicker than she was used to, but she was so turned on. Max wanted it faster...harder, but it was pointless. Her partner would go at whatever pace she chose, and Max had no say in the matter. When the woman thrust deep, fully inside Max, she thought she might actually die from the intense pleasure. She cried out, pressing her hands even harder against the wall to push herself back against the woman.

Max gave in. She opened her legs wider, begged for more as wave after wave of extraordinary feeling coursed through her. The woman slammed into her, thighs pressed against the back of Max's. It drove her utterly insane with pleasure. The sounds her partner was making—deep groans—heightened her own pleasure. She didn't care that she was panting and moaning loudly. She didn't care that she was being fucked hard by a complete stranger in a room full of strangers. This was years in the making, and she wanted it all.

On the brink and ready to spill over, she asked, "Can I rub my clit?"

The woman replied with a sharp "Yes."

Max moved her right hand from the wall and pressed her middle finger against her unbelievably swollen clit. It was almost too sensitive, and she pulled back slightly. It took a minute to find the right spot, the right angle, but when she did… Oh God… So good.

Her partner slammed into her, her groans intensifying as her thrusts became erratic. She was close. Max continued working her clit; she wasn't far off herself. With a couple more deep thrusts, her partner came. Her cries were loud in the air around them, and that was all Max needed to tip her over the edge.

Her climax was hard and sharp and blinding. A scream wrenched from her throat as her body melted into a quivering mess. Her knees gave out, and the woman chuckled and caught her. She held her up as Max laughed and caught her breath, revelling in her afterglow.

Once she could breathe normally and hold her own weight, she eased herself off the dildo and stood up fully. Leaning forwards against the wall, she gave her leg muscles a few more moments to wake up. The woman zipped up behind her and then passed Max's jeans and underwear to her.

"Thanks," Max said, turning to face her after she slipped into her clothes.

The woman smiled and leaned in for a kiss. She tasted of beer and cigarettes, and Max could not have cared less.

"See you," said the woman with a wink, and she walked off towards the bathrooms.

Max leaned back against the wall, her breathing still unsteady. She couldn't decide what she'd liked most about that experience—the actual fuck or the hint of dominance that had tinged the proceedings. She'd fantasised about it often enough and read some very erotic short stories that had got her soaking wet. Experiencing even just a hint of it, though, had sent her mind reeling.

She pushed her feet back into her boots. A rather intimidating butch who'd just strolled into the room was eying her up, so Max moved away from the wall. She definitely was not looking for a third round. Staying where she was sent a very wrong message. She walked across the room, avoiding the butch's gaze, and entered the bathrooms.

As she shut the cubicle door behind her, muting the sounds of the music and enthusiastic fucking, a wave of tiredness washed through her. She slumped down on the closed lid of the toilet and shut her eyes as she leaned back against the cistern.

She gave in to her tiredness, and that hold on her emotions, which she had largely held at bay all evening, began to loosen. Unbidden, Sue's face popped back into her mind's eye, and the emotions that image engendered brought a sudden sob to the back of Max's throat. She gripped the sides of the toilet lid with her hands.

No, not now. I can't deal with it now. Later.

Swallowing back the sob, Max released her deathlike grip and pushed herself up to standing.

She cleaned up again, just enough to be comfortable getting back to her hotel. She needed to leave. Now. She claimed her stuff from the locker and shrugged into her jacket.

"Everything okay?" asked Mandy, perhaps concerned about her newbie.

"Absolutely," Max said, but her voice held a tremor, and she couldn't meet Mandy's warm eyes.

Oh dear, thought Mandy, watching the woman walk out the door. *That was a strange one.* When she'd first arrived, there had been a fear in her eyes that Mandy hadn't been able to decipher. Whatever it was, Mandy wasn't sure coming here was the right thing for her, and from the look in her eyes as she left, her evening hadn't been quite what she'd expected.

She turned away from the front door and caught Dee's gaze as she reached the office door.

Dee tilted her head slightly to one side, watching Mandy. "You okay?" she asked.

Mandy sighed and smiled wanly. "Yeah. Just… Sometimes this place just doesn't work for everyone. I know it's not the club, per se, but still."

Dee nodded but kept silent, and Mandy appreciated that. She knew a lot of women were excited about the thought, the fantasy, of no-strings sex, thinking nothing could be simpler. They craved the freedom and the opportunity to forget everything else in their lives, even for just an hour. For a lot of the women, that was fundamentally true. It was one of the main reasons Mandy had designed the club in the first place. But for others, the emotions involved in such an intimate act interfered.

She suspected the latter was true of the hazel-eyed, curly-haired cutie who'd just walked out of here with a haunted expression on her face.

Mandy stepped up to the desk where Dee was lounging, playing Candy Crush on her phone.

"Bored?" Mandy smirked, thankful for something mundane to focus on.

Dee chuckled. "Just killing ten minutes until Cassie takes her break. Don't distract me, I just got to level eighty-three."

Mandy laughed, but her mind immediately drifted back to the sad woman. Even when the bell rang at the front door and she went to see who the next customer was, the woman who had just departed was at the forefront of her mind. She took the new customer's money, went through her usual spiel, and tried very hard not to worry about what this new woman was looking for in her visit. Not all of them left here looking lost and forlorn. Not all of them came here for the wrong reasons. At the end of the day, she wasn't actually responsible for any of that. She provided an opportunity to explore. What they did with that and how they reacted was entirely out of her control.

Max walked out into the cool night and took a few deep breaths of the relatively clean air. The atmosphere in the club had been a little claustrophobic at the end. She pulled her wallet from her bag to check that there was enough cash for the cab back to the hotel. She walked up to the main road, stood on the corner, and looked in both directions for a cab. Traffic was busy, but after a couple of minutes, she was in luck and flagged one down.

During the ride, she watched a city she didn't know drift by through the window. The cabbie tried to start up a conversation, but after several one-word answers, he gave up. Before she knew it, they pulled up outside her hotel, and she handed over the cash.

When she got to her room, she poured herself a neat whisky and took a couple of sips while she let the shower warm up. She stripped off, her mind still in the cotton-filled daze it had been in since she'd left the club. As she stood under the hot water, washing away all traces of her hedonistic evening, she let a few memories wander into her mind. She considered them with a detachment she hadn't felt at the time. It was as if she were watching someone else do the things she'd done. Someone else going down on Lou so eagerly, someone else bent over getting fucked from behind by that strong butch.

She stepped out of the shower, towelled herself dry, and sipped more of the whisky that was warming its way down her insides.

Her mobile rang, and she jumped. She glanced at the clock on the TV and took a deep, shuddering breath. Eleven thirty. At this time of night, it could only be Sue calling her. Probably wondering where she was, because—stupidly, she now realised—Max hadn't called her at all this evening.

Oh God, how was she supposed to talk to her as if nothing much had happened, when exactly the opposite had occurred? She'd had her mouth and her fingers on another woman's pussy. She'd had another woman fuck her from behind with a good, hard silicon cock.

And then, as if a dam had been broken with the insistent shrilling of her ringtone from deep inside her handbag, the sob that she had bitten back earlier broke free, followed by many, many more. The phone stopped ringing, and in the silence left behind, Max wept like she'd never wept before. All the fears and doubts and guilt and confusion over who she was, who Sue was, and who they were together overwhelmed her. Wrapped in a towel, she dropped to her knees in the middle of her hotel room floor.

Oh, fuck, what was she supposed to do now?

CHAPTER 4

Manchester, 1997

Mandy watched the removal men carry the last boxes into the house, squeezing her mum's shoulder gently.

"You okay, Mum?"

Her mum turned in her direction; her eyes shimmered with tears.

"That's it now, isn't it?" Her mother's voice quavered. The tears would surely start to fall soon.

She nodded and squeezed again. "Why don't you go and put the kettle on, and I'll see them out, okay?"

Her mum gave her a grateful look and headed down the hallway towards the kitchen.

Mandy turned to the removers and shook their hands.

"Thanks, guys. You did a good job. Appreciate it."

"You're welcome," said the more senior of them. "If I could just get a signature?"

Once she'd finished with the paperwork, she waved them off and then shut the door. She found her mum in the kitchen, two mugs of tea on the counter. She was gazing out of the window at the small garden of her new home. Five months since Mandy's dad had died, and her mum still looked as stricken as if it were yesterday. Mandy hoped the relocation, near to some of her closest friends, would help her move on with her grieving. Then it would be time for Mandy herself to move on. She'd given up her life in Australia to support her mum, but now she was getting antsy to proceed with her plans to get reestablished here at home.

Her mum turned as Mandy stepped further into the kitchen.

"Oh, sorry, darling, I didn't see you there." Her voice was quiet and thin, and it tugged at Mandy's heart strings.

"Why don't we sit down, and then we can plan the rest of the day?"

They drank their tea, and gradually Mandy got her to talk about today and tomorrow and the days after that. They came up with a plan for unpacking the house in the order that she would need things, and she could tell her mum felt better for it.

"If I haven't said it before," her mum said as they set their empty mugs down on the kitchen drainer, "I am so grateful to you for coming back here to help me. I know that must have been hard for you, to walk away from your life there so suddenly."

Mandy shrugged. "I didn't have to think about it, really. You needed me, and I wasn't not going to be here for you, was I?" It *had* been hard, but her mum didn't need to hear that. She'd stayed with her mum at the family home in the Cotswolds for these past few months, getting her through the worst of her grief and helping her sell up the old house and find this one.

Her mother pulled her in for a quick hug, something they rarely shared, and it touched Mandy.

"Well, thank you. I couldn't have done this without you." She paused and pulled back slightly to look at her daughter. She had crystal-blue eyes and pinned her with a piercing gaze. "Now, as much as I am grateful, I'm also a little worried."

"Worried?"

"Well, you've been here, with me, for five months now. You don't have a job or a partner, and you never really mention any friends. I certainly don't expect you to stay here forever looking after me, so what are you going to do? I worry that you think you need to stay, but that isn't a life you should lead. You could always go back to

Australia, you know. I have my friends close by to keep an eye on me."

Mandy smiled, touched by her mother's concern. She'd never really expressed it before, always shaking her head at Mandy's fierce independence, but never commenting one way or another on what Mandy did with her life.

"Don't worry, Mum. I do have a plan. I was getting ready to talk to you about it tomorrow, actually."

Her mum smiled and gestured to the chairs around the small table in the centre of the room.

"Well," continued Mandy once they'd sat down. "The guy I worked for in Australia, he knows some people here who run bigger clubs than his. He thinks he might be able to set me up a job, and he's arranged for me to meet a guy next Friday. He runs a club in the centre of the city."

"So, you'll stay in the UK now?"

Mandy nodded. "Yeah, I think so. I know you've got your friends to look out for you, but you are my only family. Suddenly being on the other side of the world seems too far away."

Her mum smiled. "Well, I can't say I'm upset about that. I like having you nearer." She hesitated a moment before clearing her throat. "And this job that your friend has organised, what will it be?"

"Managing the bar, just like I was doing in Melbourne. Only it's a bigger club, with more staff working for me, so I'll get much more experience."

Her mum looked away and back again. "And is this what you want to keep doing? Managing bars?"

Mandy picked up on the slight disparagement in her mother's tone and sighed.

"I know you don't think it's much of a job, Mum. But I really enjoy it. And I'm good at it. I do have a dream to open my own club one day, and I can't do that without a bit more experience of working in them. It's a step towards something bigger for me. I...I hope to use the money Dad left me to help set up my own place one day."

Her mum nodded, and smiled more brightly than Mandy had seen her do in months. "I think he would have liked that—having a daughter who ran her own business. He would be proud of you."

Tears formed behind her eyelids, and Mandy blinked them back. "Thanks, Mum. That means a lot."

God, she hated the pricks that came to this club on a Saturday night. Fridays weren't so bad, but somehow on Saturdays, every tosser in the north-west who had a bit of money walked through those doors and into her bar, and Mandy detested every single one of them. But like the good professional she was, she plastered that fake smile on her face and made sure the champagne fridge was stocked for when they wanted to flash their cash.

It had been a year now. Although she would have preferred to work in London, no jobs had been forthcoming there. She had, however, been pleasantly surprised by Manchester. There was a good vibe to the city and a great little Gay Village with plenty to keep her amused for a while. She hadn't done too well on the sex front since she'd been here, but she didn't have the energy for it. Dealing with death and grief had left her little enthusiasm for anything else.

In the last three months, she'd had two...interludes. Hidden in the shadows of a gay club that didn't get that many gay women visiting, neither of the experiences had been at all satisfactory. She hadn't been able to come—something held her back from really letting go. So now she'd pretty much given up on all that for a while. Instead, she was focused on doing this job as best she could, getting a reputation established here and building her experience for the future.

What she really wanted next was to get into one of Robbie Chapman's clubs—biggest club owner in the north-west, and rumoured to be looking to set up another huge club in the city centre, for which he would need experienced staff. Working in one of his places, and being good at it, would set her up nicely for the future. But she wasn't stupid. She hadn't been in this game, or this city, nearly long enough to set her own place up just yet. No, a few more years of learning from the best, and then she'd be ready to make her move.

Raised voices came from the end of the bar, and she glanced up. One of the tossers was leaning across the bar with his finger in Chris's face. She was one of her youngest—and best—barwomen. Mandy reached for the small radio attached to her waist and thumbed the mike.

"Pete, meet me at the main bar, please."

Pete gave an affirmative response as she moved down to the trouble spot.

Putting a hand gently on Chris's shoulder, she stepped past her to face the angry man across the bar.

"Good evening, sir, what seems to be the trouble?"

His eyes, glazed from a clear case of overconsumption of alcohol, moved from staring at Chris to staring at Mandy. He took the time to leeringly look her up and down, and she resisted the urge to shudder. God, what a fucking snake.

"The trouble," he started, his voice slurred, "is that your bitch here won't serve me anymore."

"I'll ask you to refrain from abusing my staff, sir," said Mandy in her firm but hey-let's-all-just-take-it-easy voice that she reserved for occasions such as this. She held up a hand to him when he made to speak again and turned to Chris.

"Why did you refuse to serve the gentleman?" She hoped Chris could read enough in Mandy's eyes and face to know that this wasn't a telling-off. Chris had quite rightly refused to serve him.

"I'm afraid the gentleman used some abusive language when placing his order, and I wasn't comfortable with that."

"Stupid fucking cunt bitch!" His voice was almost a scream. Clearly, this was a man used to getting his own way, and he definitely didn't like being told no.

Before Mandy needed to respond, Pete was there.

"Thank you, sir," said Pete loudly. "That's enough of that." And before the drunk knew what had happened, he was frogmarched away from the bar and out of the club.

Mandy and Chris looked at each other and chuckled.

"Saturday fucking night," said Mandy quietly, and Chris grinned. Mandy patted her on the shoulder and walked back to retake her station at the rear of the bar.

She took a deep breath and watched the room again. Oh yes, another three months, and she was definitely out of here.

CHAPTER 5

Manchester, present day

"Come on, baby, come for me now," whispered Jacky hoarsely as she drove her fingers deeper into her wife's gorgeously hot cunt.

Tania groaned, and her walls closed in with the throb of her orgasm. She cried out, arching upwards and thrusting her hips towards Jacky, giving her a prime view of her fingers buried in Tania's cunt. As long as she lived, Jacky would never tire of that view. She'd known from the first time she'd fucked Tania that she'd never want another woman in her bed. Tania had taken everything Jacky gave her and still begged for more, and Jacky, butch as she was, wept silent tears as she plunged ever deeper, ever harder.

They'd married after only a year together. Jacky had bent down on one knee, mindless of the few other people sharing the beach in Norfolk that cold March day. Tania had cried and shouted, "Yes!" Then they'd kissed and laughed, and Toby, Jacky's four-year-old beagle, had hopped around between them in excited confusion.

After much discussion, they had mutually decided they couldn't handle the fuss of a big wedding and had quietly organised the briefest of ceremonies at the local registry office. They'd made it official only a month later in front of their two closest friends. Kath had stood as witness for Jacky, and Tania's oldest friend from school, Marie, had signed the register for Tania. This earned the wrath of their families for having been excluded from the celebration. Jacky didn't blame them for wanting to be a part of the celebration, but they couldn't wait. Jacky and Tania simply belonged together. They were a perfect fit except for one minor thing.

Despite the incredible sex they had on a very regular basis, there was one thing Jacky couldn't give Tania. Although Tania usually hid it well, she clearly struggled with it. Despite how happy Jacky was to lick Tania's pussy all day, she could never bring herself to let Tania reciprocate. Only one woman had ever had her mouth on Jacky's pussy, and after the excruciating embarrassment and shame of that event, no other woman had ever been allowed near there again. And no matter how much she loved and trusted Tania, she just couldn't do it.

Every now and again, Tania would broach the subject by suggesting counselling, books, or whatever it would take. Unable to explain, Jacky walked away from the conversation, and Tania would feel guilty for pushing. For a few days, things would be awkward between them, but eventually it smoothed out. They repeated this cycle every few weeks.

To say it was causing a rift in their relationship was overstating it. But it was always present. The elephant in the room.

Tania flopped down on the bed after riding out the aftershocks of her orgasm, panting heavily. Jacky lay down beside her, draped an arm over her rounded belly, and pulled her in for a tender kiss. Tania's body was luscious and beautifully curvy, and the soft glow of the bedside lamp accentuated all those curves. Tania complained about being at least ten pounds overweight; Jacky said she was perfect just the way she was.

"Okay, babe?"

Tania nodded and smiled and kissed her again. All was good, this week.

Jacky walked into the pub, clapping her hands together to take the chill out of them. October was kicking in with a definite bite.

The Soldier's Arms was quiet tonight, and she nodded a hello to Tim, the barman, as she walked further into the main room. This place had been her favourite haunt for many years. It was a good old-fashioned pub that had a few tasteful modernisations in place that didn't detract from the original character. The old wooden floor, polished smooth from years of workmen's boots clumping over it each day, was paired with modern comfy chairs and tables. Plus, it was close to her work and was convenient as a meeting point for her regular—or, lately, not so regular—catch-ups with Kath.

Kath was already there, leaning against the far end of the curved bar, wearing her trademark long leather coat, and nursing a pint of lager. Jacky strolled over and slugged Kath in the arm.

"Hey, what's that for?" asked Kath with a smile. She had dark circles under her eyes.

"That's for not calling me in forever," replied Jacky, slugging her again, but gentler this time. She ordered herself a pint of Guinness and then demanded, "Where the fuck have you been?"

"Yeah, I know, sorry about that. It's been a bit of a crazy time." Kath's face clouded over, and Jacky cringed at her insensitivity.

"Shit, your mum again?"

Kath nodded and took a big gulp of her beer.

"Sorry, I suppose I should have realised that."

"Hey, don't worry. You weren't to know. How's the lovely Tania?"

Jacky couldn't help it—her eyes glazed over as she thought about her beautiful wife, and Kath chuckled.

"Oh my, what a softie," she said, laughing as Jacky made to slug her again.

"I can't lie; I'm beyond happy." Jacky's big butch exterior turned to mush at the mention of her wife.

"So, where is she tonight?"

"Home, planning on a long call with her sister to catch up. So, want to order some food and grab a table?"

"Oh yes, I'm in need of a big burger. With all the trimmings."

"Mate, you are speaking my language."

An hour later, stuffed to the gills with a second pint in hand, Jacky sat back in her chair and groaned.

"Overdone it, my friend?" Kath winced as she eased back in her own chair.

"You and me both, by the looks of it," replied Jacky, grinning.

"Whatever."

"So, given that things have been tricky with your mum again, I guess there's still no love life of yours to speak of? No juicy goss you can share with me?"

Kath smiled mysteriously and shifted in her chair a little.

Jacky sat up straighter.

"What?" she asked. "Come on, spill the beans, you bitch!"

Kath laughed but blushed a little too, her gaze darting away from Jacky's and back again.

"Come on, bud. What's going on?" Jacky pushed. "Anyone I know?"

"Ah, it's… Well, it's not quite what you might imagine." Kath took another big gulp of beer and then let out a sigh. She leaned forward onto her forearms. "Okay, I'm going to tell you, but I'd really appreciate it if you didn't get too judgmental on me. Please, just accept that what I've found really works for me and I'm in a good place with it, okay?"

"Fuck. Okay. But now I really am wondering what is going on."

"Well," began Kath, "I've been visiting a club. A private club that caters to very, shall we say, special desires."

"A club? What, like a nightclub?"

Kath grinned. "Well, it is a club, and it's open at night, but it certainly isn't the kind of nightclub you're thinking about."

"Oh, come on, stop stringing me along." Jacky was losing patience.

Kath chuckled. "Okay, okay, I'll tell you." She took a deep breath and puffed it out. Then, lowering her voice, she said, "It's a lesbian sex club."

Jacky was thankful she wasn't holding her drink at that moment, as it would surely have ended up all over the floor.

"Say that again?" she said.

"Remember, you agreed not to judge." Kath's voice had an edge to it, and Jacky held her hands up in a placating gesture.

"Sorry," she said softly. "Please, tell me what you mean."

"Well, like I said, it's a sex club. I found out about it online— remember you suggested chat rooms?"

Jacky nodded. Kath had been pretty down after Julie left her and desperate to get out of the house for some uncomplicated fun. Jacky had thought that would mean she'd find herself a new dance club or bar to hit, not a sex club.

"Well, I got chatting to this other woman who, like me, just wanted the odd uncomplicated…moment here and there, with no strings attached. She'd found this club; doesn't really have a name. It's just kind of known about. It's amazing. It's like if someone asked you to design the perfect place to go and meet other women who just wanted sex for the evening, you'd come up with something pretty close to this."

Kath's face glowed as she talked about it, and Jacky couldn't remember the last time she'd seen her so lit up about anything.

"So, how does it work? I mean, you just stroll in, pick a chick you like, and get on with it, or what?" Jacky's curiosity was rampant.

Kath grinned again. "Well," she said. "How much do you want to know?"

On the train, Jacky couldn't stop thinking about the club. By the time she got home, a crazy plan had formed in her mind. The tricky thing would be selling it to Tania. On the short walk up the main road from the station, she ran through the words she wanted to use, rehearsing them until they sounded just right in her own mind.

The light from the living room spilled out between the cracks of the blinds. That meant Tania was still up and likely laid out on the sofa. Their house was small and modern, not quite what either of them had ever pictured for themselves. But it was all they could afford in their up-and-coming suburb. She didn't care, though. It was theirs, hers and Tania's, and that alone made it perfect to Jacky's way of thinking.

Jacky opened the front door to be greeted by Toby, who whined and jumped up at her until she ruffled his head and ears just the way he liked it.

"How's my boy, then?" she said, bending down to be eye level with him and using her special Toby voice. "Did you miss me? Yes, you did, didn't you?" She chuckled at herself. She was such a bloody softie for that dog.

In the living room, Tania semi-reclined on the sofa, dressed only in her red satin robe with the TV on in the background. She always loved the way Tania looked in that robe and took a moment to drink in the sight as she shrugged out of her jacket and threw her wallet and keys on the side table. Toby, content that his mistress was now home, followed her into the room and flopped down in his basket by the radiator.

"Hey, babe," said Tania as Jacky walked into the room. Tania turned her head to look at her wife over the top of the sofa, smiling sleepily as she did so.

"Hey, beautiful." Jacky walked around the sofa, knelt on the floor in front of Tania, and ran her fingers through Tania's lustrous auburn hair. She leaned into her for a series of quick sexy kisses.

"Hmm, feels good," Tania whispered as Jacky let her fingertips gently graze her scalp.

Just like that, it was there. That spark, that jolt of lust that made Jacky's breath hitch with a desperate need to have her hands on Tania's skin.

It seemed the reaction was mutual, as Tania planted a lengthy, smouldering kiss on her lips. Then, as they kissed, Tania reached between them to undo her robe. Once her heavy breasts had tumbled out of the fabric, she reached for Jacky's hand and placed it firmly over her left breast. Jacky rolled the nipple between her fingertips, bringing it to instant hardness and making Tania whimper softly.

Jacky lifted her head from the kiss. "I need to fuck you," she said, her voice gravelly with desire. "Now."

Tania groaned and fell back against the couch, parting the robe and her legs. Jacky stroked her way through the wetness already seeping out of Tania's cunt.

"I love you." Tania moaned as Jacky pushed two fingers inside her, going deep. Jacky bent down and kissed her. She thrust her tongue into Tania's mouth, forcing it open wide while her fingers pumped hard in her cunt. Tania came quickly, and Jacky smiled as her wife lay back on the sofa, basking in her post-orgasmic glow. Jacky leaned forward, still on her knees, and propped her head on her hands with her elbows supporting her on the edge of the couch. She gazed down at Tania.

Tania chuckled. "What brought that on?" she said teasingly. "I mean, don't get me wrong; I love you coming home horny, but did you spot some gorgeous chick out tonight who got your juices flowing or something?"

Jacky blushed, and Tania sat up suddenly, her expression turning serious.

"Whoa," Tania said. "That was meant to be a joke. What have you been up to tonight?"

"Nothing. You know I am yours and yours only. 'Til death us do part." The last thing Jacky wanted was Tania thinking she wasn't completely committed to her.

"I should think so too—I am not sharing you with anyone."

Jacky deflated slightly at Tania's statement. Tania frowned and reached up to cup Jacky's chin. She stared intently at Jacky, who squirmed under her scrutiny. "What's going on, Jack? You're acting a bit weird, and I've got to tell you, it's worrying me."

Jacky huffed out a big breath. Tania's words about not sharing had kind of taken the wind out of the sails of her crazy plan.

"You'll think I'm stupid," she said.

Confusion played out on Tania's face.

"You know I was out with Kath tonight, right?"

Tania nodded.

"Well, we got talking about how Kath doesn't have time for a love life now that her mum's taken a bad turn again."

"Oh, shame," said Tania.

"Yeah. Well, anyway, it turns out Kath has found quite a… different way to deal with her situation."

Tania raised her eyebrows.

"She's visiting a lesbian sex club," said Jacky in a rush.

"She's *what*?" Tania's expression switched from quizzical to incredulous in an instant.

"It's not seedy or dodgy or anything like that. It's run by this really cool dyke who makes everyone abide by a code of conduct, and it's, like, this really safe place to go and meet other women who want the same thing."

"Which is what, exactly?" Tania crossed her arms over her chest, sounding distinctly unimpressed by what Jacky was telling her.

"Hey, don't get on your high horse! This is Kath we're talking about. You know how decent she is. She's hardly likely to hit some sleazy joint for a shag with a prostitute, is she?" Jacky's voice was sharp in defence of her friend.

"Hey, it all sounds a bit odd to me." Tania held her hands up. "Sorry, sweetheart, I don't mean anything against Kath personally."

"Well, anyway," continued Jacky, slightly mollified and determined in a fatalistic kind of way to finish telling Tania about the club and her crazy plan. "The thing is, it sounds like she's had some really good experiences there. All of the women know exactly what they are there for. They all play it safe, and yet they can all go and indulge in whatever kind of sexual experience they want with no questions asked." She paused, choosing her words carefully. "So, the thing is, I kind of got this idea in my head after she told me, and I wanted to run it by you and see how you felt about it."

Tania took a deep breath and gave her a dubious look. "Go ahead."

Jacky ploughed on. "I want to use the club as a way to get you what I can't give you." The words sounded so loud in the room. Tania's eyebrows rose slowly upwards.

"You mean...?" Tania's voice was strained and hoarse, and Jacky winced in fear.

"I love you," whispered Jacky. "And I want you to be able to have something you really desire." Jacky trembled as unwanted memories pushed to the forefront of her mind. She quickly rammed them back where they'd come from, swallowing hard before continuing, "I thought we could go to the club and find you a woman who would let—"

Tania placed a hand across Jacky's mouth, stopping her from finishing the sentence. Tears fell from Tania's eyes, and Jacky's heart clenched. She never meant to hurt Tania or upset her.

"I'm sorry." She hung her head, unable to look at Tania.

Tania suddenly grabbed Jacky and pulled her tight against her chest.

"I can't...I can't believe you would do that for me," she said roughly. "I mean, I'm disgusted and overwhelmed by how much you love me, all at the same time." She pulled away from Jacky to smile weakly and wipe away her tears. "That really is one fucked-up idea, but I know it came from the best place." She touched Jacky's chest, just over her heart. "I know you truly meant that to be all about pleasing me."

Jacky nodded and pulled Tania back to her, so relieved that she hadn't blown it completely. They held each other close.

"I will never, ever put pressure on you about this again. I swear," announced Tania.

Jacky looked up at her, questioning.

"If you think me wanting to go down on you and you not wanting it or being able to do it has put some kind of block in our relationship, I don't ever want to bring it up again. It is just one thing, one silly thing that I can totally live without, and I would rather do that than have you doubt us in any way, okay?"

Jacky smiled. "But that's the thing. I've never doubted us, not ever. It's not about that."

Tania looked puzzled.

Jacky blew out a breath in frustration. Her eyes fell on a framed photo on the bookshelf. They'd spent the day at Alton Towers, and Tania went on every ride. Jacky grinned and turned back to Tania.

"Look, to me, offering that to you was just like saying I wanted to take you to a fun fair so you could ride rollercoasters all day. You know I fucking hate them, but I would quite happily watch you having fun on them as long as you wanted, because we'd still be sharing something that you loved."

"Wait a minute," exclaimed Tania, looking shocked and sitting bolt upright on the sofa. "You're comparing me eating out some strange woman's pussy to a day riding *rollercoasters*? Are you fucking *crazy*?"

Jacky laughed, then stopped when she saw Tania's face. "Babe," she said, reaching slowly for Tania's hand. "From what Kath said, there doesn't have to be any emotion attached to it. It's purely about meeting a need with none of the complications that go with trying to pick up a woman at a club and take her home. Yes, it might seem cold, but Kath says somehow, if you're both in it for the right reasons, it's really enjoyable and…freeing. I honestly thought it would be something exciting we could share." She took a deep breath. "I would find it totally arousing to watch you do that to someone, knowing you were imagining it was me, knowing how much enjoyment you were getting out of it, but knowing as well that the only one you want in your bed every night is me."

Tania sat back, her mouth open in shock. "You wouldn't get jealous or find it odd or…painful to see me doing that?"

Jacky couldn't tell from her tone what answer Tania wanted to hear, so she decided honesty was the best policy. "No, I truly wouldn't. For all the reasons I just gave. It wouldn't be watching you have an affair. It would be watching you eat something you love to taste. Like that double chocolate fudge cake we get from the pizza place sometimes."

Tania stared at her, then burst out laughing. "Oh my God," she said. "I just cannot believe we are having this conversation. Please don't tell me you mentioned this to Kath?"

"No, of course not! This is between you and me."

There was silence for a while. Tania sat back into the sofa and pulled her robe tight around her. Jacky gazed at her for a moment and then got up to make some tea, leaving Tania alone with her thoughts. Toby jumped up and followed Jacky to the kitchen, clearly expecting a late-night treat.

Tania vaguely listened to the muted sounds of Jacky filling the kettle, pulling mugs from the cupboard, and jokingly admonishing Toby for some minor doggy indiscretion. Their entire conversation had completely unsettled Tania. She pushed her hands through her hair and tried to make sense of the disjointed thoughts spinning around her head.

The issue over Jacky refusing to let Tania go down on her had not been a big deal in the early days of their relationship—there were so many other distractions and joys to explore that Tania hadn't really noticed it. But over time, she had come to realise that it was a serious psychological issue for Jacky, and although she'd tried to be understanding and patient, somehow she just couldn't shake it off.

It wasn't Jacky's refusal of the act itself. It was the frustration that there was something so important behind this, and Jacky felt as though she couldn't share it with her. For the other ninety-nine per cent of their life, they were completely together. She'd just always thought if she ever found her soul-mate, she'd get one hundred per cent of that person, and it pained her that Jacky couldn't take that one last step to full completeness with Tania.

Given everything else Jacky would do to her, the responses she could draw from Tania's body, Tania had no reason to keep dwelling on it. It was just that she missed the taste of pussy and would love to know how Jacky felt under her tongue. Never mind that it had always been one of her most favourite things to do in the history of the world.

When Jacky had first mentioned the club, Tania had feared she wanted something Tania wasn't giving her, and that had started a small, fiery ball of jealousy, hurt, and anger in the pit of her stomach.

Her head was still spinning. Jacky would do something like this to please her. Jacky admitted she'd find it a turn on. Tania closed her eyes and breathed out slowly. The most unsettling thing, of course, was the one thing she was trying extremely hard not to think about.

She hated to admit it, but deep down inside, she wanted to say yes.

Jacky slipped out of the bed at five thirty the next morning, careful, as always, not to disturb her wife. Tania had another two hours before she needed to start her day. In her sweatpants and tee shirt, she padded downstairs, slipped on her boots and jacket, and grabbed Toby's lead off the peg in the hall. He came barrelling down the hallway, and she clipped him into the leash before opening the front door. She always took him for his first short walk of the day—not too far, just enough for him to sniff his way around a few streets and relieve himself before they headed home. Tania would take him out again when she got up.

Once back in the house, Jacky topped up his water, gave him a handful of the crunchy snacks he loved, and headed back upstairs to shower and dress. Her mind felt woolly, as if she'd drunk much more than she actually had the evening before.

Last night, after she'd returned to the living room with their tea, they'd not mentioned her mad plan again. Instead, they'd watched some crime drama and then snuggled into bed with only a quiet "goodnight". There was a tension between them, and she was at a loss as to how to resolve it.

As she drove herself to work, she ran through it all again. She'd never meant to upset Tania, but it had seemed like such a good idea on the way home. Plus, she'd meant every word—the idea of watching Tania eat some woman out *was* hugely arousing.

Maybe that's what had put Tania off. Maybe Tania didn't like the idea of Jacky getting turned on by it. Whatever it was, she couldn't leave things where they were. Tonight, after dinner, she'd take a deep breath and bring the subject up again.

Tania had done nothing all day except pretend to work on the same spreadsheet. She had barely spoken a word to any of her colleagues, and her thoughts constantly returned to Jacky's mad idea. Lunch had passed in a blur—she couldn't even remember what she'd eaten now. So far this afternoon, she'd stumbled her way through a meeting with the new business analyst, Stephanie. The woman was rather gorgeous, and she gave off confusing signals to Tania's gaydar. They were supposed to work together on a new project along with the quiet woman from IT, Lou.

Then, out of the blue, between bullet points in the all-staff briefing, her mind had opened up and acknowledged what she'd been trying to fight.

She wanted to do it.

She wanted to sink her face into a woman's wet cunt and lick her senseless. She wanted to taste, feel, suck, and fuck with her tongue. It had been nearly three years, and God, yes, she wanted it.

Yes, she wished with all her heart—and other, lower parts of her body—that it could be Jacky's pussy, but Jacky wasn't ready. So, Jacky offered her the next best thing—a means to satisfying the desire in a way that allowed them to share the experience nonetheless.

Would it be strange to do that to another woman while Jacky watched? How exactly would it play out? Would Tania just pick someone while Jacky stood nearby and watched? God, no, doing it that way sounded awful. No, if it was going to happen, then it had to be shared as much as possible. It had to involve more than just Tania going down on someone. She needed there to be some sort of foreplay, some sort of…connection. Most importantly, she needed to be able to imagine it was Jacky beneath her tongue and Jacky's sounds of arousal reaching her ears.

"Okay," said Tania as they finished eating their pasta later that night. "How would it work, exactly?"

Staring at Tania across their small dining table, Jacky carefully swallowed her last mouthful of food, wiped her mouth on her napkin, and sat back in her chair. "How would what work exactly?" she asked, knowing precisely what Tania meant but needing to hear it nonetheless.

"The club," said Tania, staring deep into Jacky's eyes. "How would we…choose her?"

Jacky exhaled slowly and gripped the edges of the table tightly. "You mean, you might want to try it?" She couldn't believe Tania had brought it up first and in this way.

Tania nodded and smiled shyly. "I can't believe I'm saying it out loud, but yes, I want to try it."

Jacky grinned. "Fuck, I really didn't think you would. When you didn't mention it again last night, I just assumed…"

"Yeah, I know. I just needed to process. And be honest with myself." Tania blushed, and Jacky reached across to cup her chin.

"Babe, this is me. You don't need to be embarrassed. I was totally honest with you last night. Be totally honest with me, please."

"Oh God." Tania's blush deepened. "I haven't stopped thinking about it. I was useless at work. My overriding thought was that, although I miss the taste of pussy, it will never be the same going down on someone who isn't you." She held up her hand as Jacky went to speak. "I'm not pushing you; I'm just stating a fact. I want you to be able to tell me why this is an issue for you, but I accept that it may never happen. So, I've set that aside. And now I'm focusing on the other reactions I had. I kept asking myself why I was so disgusted by it, and I finally realised that I was deflecting." She took a deep breath. "I wasn't disgusted by it; I was *turned on* by it, and I didn't want to be. I think I thought it must mean I don't love you enough if I want to do it. And yet I didn't think you loved me any less for suggesting it. In fact, I thought it showed me just how much you *do* love me."

Jacky nodded and smiled warmly with encouragement and a huge amount of relief. "It does, and I do *not* think any less of you for admitting that you want to do this. I cannot give you what you want, and I am truly sorry about that. But why shouldn't you take advantage of a place where you can get it?"

There was a pause as Tania looked at her, and Jacky held her breath at the raw emotion displayed on Tania's features.

"I want you there with me," whispered Tania. "It can only work for me if you are there. I want... I need to imagine she's you."

Jacky swallowed and nodded and leaned across the table to plant a soft kiss on Tania's lips.

"I'd want you standing behind her." Tania's voice was so soft Jacky had to strain to hear her. Tania met her eyes. "I'd want you behind her so that as I lick her, I can imagine it's you. I want to reach around and hold you while I taste her."

Jacky's clit throbbed at the thought, and she let out a small moan. Tania seemed startled and then smiled knowingly. She crooked a finger at Jacky, and Jacky couldn't get out of her chair fast enough. She stood in front of Tania, waiting to guide her to the bedroom. Instead, Tania undid Jacky's belt, pulled down the zip of her jeans, and opened the button.

"Tania...what...?" moaned Jacky as Tania's warm fingers caressed her belly and then dipped into her boxer shorts.

"Shush," murmured Tania, and she ran her fingers down on to Jacky's clit.

Jacky gazed down at her.

"I fucking love you," she whispered as Tania's fingers pushed deep inside her.

"You okay?" asked Jacky for what was about the tenth time.

Tania turned to look at her, her expression bordering on angry. "I'm fine," she said through clenched teeth. "Will you stop fucking asking me?"

"Sorry." Jacky stared ahead out of the windscreen, hands gripping the steering wheel tightly.

They'd decided to drive to the club. That way, they could leave whenever they wanted, rather than relying on train company timetables. Jacky had done a drive-by one day on her way home from work so they wouldn't get lost on the way. The quiet street that housed the club on the northern edge of the city centre was fairly nondescript, with the club itself tucked down a ways, past a block of flats and into a row of small industrial buildings. Did the residents of the flats have any idea what went on behind the black door just a few places down from their homes?

They were about five minutes away, and Jacky, despite her own calming entreaties to Tania in the two weeks since they'd decided to make this trip, was nervous as hell. She wasn't even sure what the nerves were about. Presumably just the strangeness of this situation. She wanted to laugh out loud—she and her wife were going to a lesbian sex club to find a woman her wife could go down on. Never, in all her life's experiences, had she anticipated this one. She risked another glance across at Tania.

She was sitting up straight in the passenger seat, twisting strands of her hair around her fingers. Jacky reached across and stilled her hand. Their eyes met, and they smiled at each other.

"I'm okay," whispered Tania. She looked out of the window, then turned back to Jacky. "I'm actually quite excited. Is that okay?"

Jacky nodded and grinned. "Me too."

They laughed then, big belly laughs that totally dissipated the tension that had been building ever since they left home about fifteen minutes ago.

When Jacky pulled them up a couple of hundred yards down the road from the club, they were more relaxed than they'd been in days.

"Now," said Jacky. "Before we go in, there is one thing we haven't talked about."

"What?"

"Well, have you got a particular physical type in mind? What should I be looking out for?"

Tania giggled. "Jesus, I have no idea! Can we just play it by ear? I don't know if we're going to go through with it tonight. It might just be about being there, you know?"

Jacky nodded and held Tania's hand. Tania leaned across the handbrake and kissed Jacky, long and lovingly.

"I love you," whispered Jacky against Tania's mouth.

Tania nodded.

"Let's go," she said as they pulled apart and opened her door.

They paid and wandered through to the Green Room. According to the woman working the door, it was the "vanilla" room—no toys; no bondage. Jacky laughed to herself when her eyes grew accustomed to the dim light. There wasn't anything particularly *vanilla* about what was going on. Several couples were going at it against the wall, and there was some *serious* fucking action.

She turned to look at Tania and felt her own first stirrings of arousal from the look on her wife's face. Tania's eyes were dilated, and she had a small, lustful grin on her face—both sure signs she was turned on, and it was all Jacky could do not to immediately find them their own corner and fuck her senseless. Tania looked at Jacky and nodded, and they grinned inanely at each other.

"Beer," growled Jacky, and Tania laughed as Jacky pulled her onto a bar stool.

"It's worth it just for the floor show," said Tania a few minutes after they'd sat down. They drank their beers slowly as they watched the different couples in action.

After their first beers, Jacky got them another and then motioned with her head towards the high table in the centre of the room.

"Want to get a closer view?"

Tania stood up without hesitation, and Jacky chuckled. Tania glanced at her and blushed. Her eagerness showed, and she hoped Jacky was still okay with how keen she was. One look at Jacky's face told her everything was fine. Jacky looked as turned on as she was.

They sat next to each other and scouted out the room. Quite a few more women had arrived in the last half hour or so, and some of them were not yet engaged. The new arrivals all leaned against the wall at various points around the room, sipping their drinks. Tania, perched on her bar stool, let her gaze drift over the available women.

She hadn't so much as looked at another woman since she'd fallen in love with Jacky, yet here she was actively trying to find a woman to eat out. Did it matter what she looked like? Yes, actually, it did. Finding the woman attractive would somehow make it less…clinical.

A woman walked by, heading for the Blue Room, and caught her attention. She had a lovely toned body, cute dark hair spiked up, muscles that moved nicely across her shoulders as she lifted her beer to her lips. As the woman lifted her face in profile, Tania was hit with a jolt of recognition. No, surely not?

The woman walked on, and Tania strained to see in the darkness. She'd only had that fleeting glimpse, but she could have sworn the woman was Lou, from work. Lou, the cute but extraordinarily shy woman who no one in the office ever saw and rarely talked to. How on earth would a woman that shy be a visitor to a sex club?

Jacky nudged her gently. "You okay? You look a bit shocked— can't believe you've seen anything in here you haven't already seen. Or done." She smirked.

Tania giggled. "No, stupid! I thought I saw someone from work, that's all, but I must be mistaken."

"Jesus, I hope so! I can't imagine how I'd react if I bumped into someone from work *here*."

Tania winked. "Well, given that you work entirely with men, that really would be a worry in *this* club."

"True enough." Jacky laughed. "Anyway, back to the mission— seen anyone you like yet?"

Tania shook her head. "Not yet, but give it time. I'm sure we'll find someone eventually."

"That mean you're up for it now, not just for watching?" Jacky's voice held a slight tremor of excitement.

Tania grinned. "Babe, just relax. But yes, I think I am up for it, if the right woman comes along."

Jacky smiled and nodded, and Tania suddenly wished desperately that she could kiss her, but house rules said no touching at the bar. It wouldn't do for them to be thrown out for bad behaviour before they'd even got started.

Tania took another long pull on her beer and studied the women on the wall. That's when she saw *her*, tucked into a darker corner.

She was cute. Very cute. About Tania's height, with short curly hair and a great body. Curves in all the right places, not one of those skinny twig women. Her jeans nicely hugged her full hips, and a tight tee shirt was moulded to her full breasts. She stared after the woman who might have been Lou.

A sharp, surprising, twinge of arousal hit Tania as she let her gaze drift down and then back up the woman's body.

The woman looked a few years older, but that was irrelevant, really. Tania nudged Jacky subtly with her elbow and nodded in the woman's direction.

"Yeah," murmured Jacky. "I saw her earlier." They gazed at each other, both swallowing hard.

"Come on." Tania stood up. Now that she'd decided, she didn't want to risk anyone else grabbing "their" woman—she snorted to herself—before they got there. Tania's stomach did the high jump as she walked, and she took a few deep, calming breaths to steady herself.

The woman saw them coming and stood up a little straighter after bending to put her drink down on the floor alongside her.

"Hey," said Tania, her voice a little croaky with nerves.

"Hi." The woman's eyes flitted between Tania and Jacky, clearly not quite sure what was going on.

"Hi," said Jacky, sounding just as nervous as Tania.

"I'm Tania. This is my wife, Jacky."

The woman nodded.

"We were…er…wondering…if…um…"

The woman smiled, but somehow it didn't reach her eyes. "I'm Max. I've never had a threesome, but I've always been curious. If that's what you're after?"

Tania breathed out sharply. "Sorry, I'm being pretty useless at this, aren't I?"

Max smiled again, and her expression opened up a little.

"The thing is," continued Tania, a bit bolder now, "there's something I particularly want to do. And Jacky kind of wants to watch. Would that be okay?"

Max looked somewhat unsure. "I guess it depends on what that is?"

"Oh God," said Tania, embarrassed, suddenly realising how kinky that must have sounded. "I just want to go down on you, that's all." As she said it, a flood of juice shot out of her cunt. She felt, rather than heard, Jacky groan behind her. Max's eyes widened and then darkened, and the smile that Max flashed was so hot and sexy... Tania wanted to drop to her knees right there and then.

"Yes." Max leaned forward to breathe the word into Tania's ear and sent white hot sparks through Tania's body straight to her clit.

Tania turned to look at Jacky, and they smiled at each other, and Tania suddenly knew this was all going to be okay. Jacky moved out from behind Tania.

"I'm going to be behind you," said Jacky to Max, who nodded and moved away from the wall slightly to give Jacky room to manoeuvre. Jacky leaned back against the wall, gently wrapped her fingers around Max's upper arms, and pulled her back against her torso. Max melted into her, and Jacky let out a whimpering sound of arousal. She nervously looked across Max's shoulder to meet Tania's gaze.

"It's okay, babe." Tania gazed at Jacky, understanding. "I want you to enjoy this too." She glanced at Max. "It's okay if Jacky touches you too, yes?"

Max nodded, smiling, and then turned her head towards Jacky. "Definitely." She took hold of Jacky's right hand and placed it over her right breast. Jacky groaned and massaged the breast with her palm. It was obvious Max wasn't wearing a bra, and her nipples hardened under Jacky's firm caresses.

"Oh, babe," murmured Tania. God, that was sexy.

Max caught her eye, and Tania knew Max wanted to kiss her, and she knew without a doubt she couldn't. That would be too... personal, too intimate, and the only woman she ever wanted to kiss was her wife.

She breathed out. "I'm sorry, I can't kiss you. It's—"

Max placed a finger on Tania's lips, stopping her speech.

"It's okay, I understand. This is all about using your mouth in other ways, isn't it?" Her grin was wicked, and her words sent another spark of pure lust to Tania's clit. Max curled her fingers in Tania's thick hair, and Tania shuddered from the touch.

She pulled Max's tee shirt from her jeans. Max dropped her arm back by her side, giving Tania full access. Max moaned softly and relaxed back even more into Jacky's body. Tania met Jacky's gaze again and smiled as she lifted the tee shirt up; Jacky moved her arm, and Tania pushed the material high above Max's breasts. Both she and Jacky moaned simultaneously as Max's breasts were revealed. Jacky skimmed her fingers over a bare breast and squeezed hard. Max groaned, and Tania dipped her head forward to suck on the other breast. Max groaned even louder, and Jacky gasped. Tania flicked her head up briefly to grin salaciously at her wife, who stared intently at her mouth as it worked Max's nipple. Sharing Max was clearly doing a number on both of them.

With Max's nipple between her lips, Tania could barely wait. Any reservations she'd had disappeared the moment Jacky's hand touched Max's breast. Now all she could think about was how Max would taste, how her clit would feel on her tongue. The taste and feel of Max's nipple was lovely, but she was desperate to get between her legs.

All evening, all through the car journey, all the time they were sat at the bars, all Tania could think about was what it would be like to finally go down on a woman again. She'd told herself that it didn't matter. She knew now, with it so close, that it *really* did. Her first chance in three years to feel a woman come all over her face, and she couldn't wait.

Still sucking on that deliciously hard nipple, she moved her hands to the button of Max's jeans. She flipped it open and worked the zipper down. Max gasped and pushed against Tania's hands. She smiled against the breast beneath her mouth. No, she didn't need to wait. Max was as eager as she was.

Tania knelt on the floor and pushed the jeans all the way down to Max's ankles. She stopped then, her face close to but not touching the soft skin of Max's belly. She looked up, meeting first Jacky's eyes, which blazed with desire as her fingers rolled Max's nipples between them, and then Max's, which were half-closed, her mouth silently forming the word "yes." Tania's cunt tightened in response, and she touched the waistband of Max's delicately silky underwear. She pulled them down slowly, revealing the curly, dark hair. Max's scent ratcheted up her arousal another hundred notches or so.

She reached around Max to grab Jacky's thighs. She needed to touch her, to have some connection to her while she did this. She moaned and breathed in. Christ, she had forgotten just how wonderful a face full of damp, curly hair felt. She slowly opened her mouth and pushed her tongue against that hair, teasing softly, enjoying the texture and the hint of what Max tasted like. Max groaned, as did Jacky, and Tania fisted the material at the back of Jacky's loose-fit jeans. She dipped her tongue lower. Slowly, gently. Savouring. The tip of her tongue slipped over Max's clit, and Max shuddered with it. The taste was exquisite, and she fought the urge to dive in too hard, too fast.

Jacky threaded her fingers through Tania's against her own thigh. They gripped each other tightly as Tania let her tongue probe even lower, deeper, coating it in Max's juice, drinking in the taste of her and groaning at how fucking good it felt. She licked and stroked and delved, now inside, now on Max's clit, sometimes fast, sometimes slow. She licked not to make her come but just to taste. To feel. Max writhed, panting, gasping, spreading her legs as wide as she could to give Tania better access.

To have a woman this way—and to know Jacky was right there with her—was almost too much for Tania. Tears built, but she blinked them away. She moved her focus, to keep herself in check, and concentrated on bringing Max to a crashing orgasm. She angled her head and dipped her tongue inside Max's cunt to forcefully fuck her before she slipped back up to her clit. She sucked, nibbled, and licked firmly and steadily, and Max thrust against her as Jacky's fingers clenched against her own.

She raised her head very briefly to catch Jacky's attention and said, "Fuck her."

Jacky groaned louder than Max. She ripped her fingers away from Max's breast and pushed them between Max's legs from behind. She nudged Tania's chin out of the way slightly and forced two long fingers inside, and Max gasped. When Max pushed down, clearly needing more, Jacky begun a deep, fast fuck while Tania continued licking, her mouth and chin coated in Max's wetness, her own very swollen clit throbbing against the seam of her jeans. She was close to climaxing herself.

"She's coming," whispered Jacky, her voice as rough as sandpaper, and Tania could feel it too, feel it throbbing in the clit under her tongue, feel it in the quivering of Max's thighs, and then it slammed into Max, bucking her forwards and upwards. Tania chased her with her tongue still working on Max's clit. Jacky chased her with her fingers still buried deep in Max's cunt. Max cried out, head thrown back against Jacky's collarbone, hands clutching at Tania's shoulders for support as she shuddered in their joint embrace.

They all slumped—Jacky against the wall, Max against Jacky, Tania against Max's belly. Tania smiled and then giggled, and then Max and Jacky were laughing too. Tania looked up to meet Max's gaze first. And then Tania met Jacky's gaze, and she thought her heart would burst with love. Jacky looked at her as if she were the most beautiful woman on earth, and Tania carefully stood up, wiped her mouth, and reached across Max's shoulder to kiss her wife. Max pulled Tania into her, making it easier to reach Jacky, and after kissing her deeply, Tania turned to smile at Max.

"Thank you." She caressed Max's face. "Just...thank you."

Max smiled and wriggled out from between them, pulling up her jeans as she did so. "I think you two need to be alone now," she said. "Thanks for giving me an amazing experience—I feel quite honoured to have shared that with you, actually." Her words had a wistfulness to them that caused tears to gather at the corners of Tania's eyes again. Max also seemed to have the hint of tears in her eyes as she smiled warmly at them both before she wandered away.

Tania turned back to Jacky and pressed herself close against her, the tears quietly falling now. Partly because of what they had shared, and partly at what Max had said.

Jacky's eyes looked moist too, and Tania cupped her face.

"You okay?" she asked.

Jacky nodded, swallowing hard before saying, "I am. What about you? Was it okay?"

Tania smiled. Yes, it was totally okay, and she had no regrets at all. Well, except that it hadn't been Jacky's pussy. But what she'd done to Max had been a pretty good second-best option.

"I loved it," she said a little bashfully, still not quite sure if it was all right to be that enthusiastic about it.

"Babe," Jacky pressed her forehead into Tania's, "I love that you loved it. That was totally what tonight was about, okay?"

Tania nodded and placed a gentle kiss on Jacky's lips.

"But," continued Jacky when their mouths parted again, "at the risk of ruining this tender moment..."

"What?"

"If you don't let me fuck you right now, I might just fucking explode."

Tania giggled and turned them so that she was pressed up against the wall.

"Oh yeah," she whispered. "Do me now, babe. I am *so* fucking ready for you."

It didn't take long. Jacky slipped her fingers deep inside her, hitting that soft, exquisite spot that she unerringly found every time. Tania thrust herself against her wife's hand, her arms wrapped around her neck, grunting and panting her need into Jacky's ear. Jacky found her clit with her thumb, and a delicious heat started somewhere deep inside and spread outwards like wildfire across her skin.

Jacky held her tightly as she came, and Tania didn't care who heard her scream with pleasure in the darkened room. Jacky's fingers were so tight inside her, and she gripped them, not wanting to lose that feeling of being possessed just yet. Nuzzling her neck, Jacky trailed kisses up to her left earlobe, where she nibbled gently with her teeth. Tania sighed, contented. She opened her eyes and looked deeply into the blue ones staring back at her.

"Okay?" asked Jacky, tenderly brushing a lock of hair away from Tania's forehead where it threatened to drop into her eyes.

Tania nodded. "That was…amazing," she whispered. "Like, even more so than normal." She blushed slightly. "I'm wondering if I'm turning into an exhibitionist or something."

Jacky laughed as she carefully pulled her fingers out of Tania's cunt. She brought them up to her mouth and licked them clean.

Tania groaned—that always turned her on hugely.

"Did you enjoy being fucked so publicly, then?" asked Jacky once she'd finished licking up all of Tania's juices.

Tania shrugged. "I wasn't really aware of how public it was. I was wrapped up in you and us and what we shared and how you make me feel." She paused, analysing what had just happened. "But just as I came, I had this realisation that there were many other women in this room, and that some of them could hear me and see me. I guess I was thinking about what it was like for us to watch other women earlier on and then wondering who was watching me and possibly getting off on it. That thought gave me a bit of thrill, actually."

Tania looked at Jacky, wondering how she'd react. They'd never done anything like this before, and the whole evening seemed to be opening up huge new lines of discussion between them.

Jacky nodded slowly. "I can understand that," she said. She gave a small gasp as she was suddenly pulled round by Tania to reverse their positions. "Hm," she said, smiling as Tania's mouth aimed for hers.

Tania grinned. Her mouth claimed Jacky's in a searing, forceful kiss before she asked, "Want to look around more?"

The Blue Room definitely excited Jacky, and Tania giggled at her wife as she sat at the central bar and gaped at the action. Jacky occasionally strapped on for Tania, and she wouldn't object if it happened more often after this. Jacky looked like she was getting pointers on techniques and positions.

"Maybe we should bring a notebook and pen next time," Tania teased her. Jacky blushed.

They didn't linger long in Red. They'd wanted to see it and tentatively took seats at the bar to check out what exactly went on in a BDSM room.

A woman with long blonde hair let herself be cuffed to a free-standing cross, facing forwards against it so that her back and beautifully voluptuous ass were displayed to the room. The woman who cuffed her in wore high-heeled, knee-length boots, tight leather trousers that laced up at the front, and a bodice that laced provocatively across her ample breasts. Another pair of women watched from close by.

Tania glanced at Jacky. Her eyes widened as she took in the scene, and then she gasped as the Domme extracted a short cat o' nine tails from the bag at her feet. She flicked it a couple of times in the air by the blonde's shoulders, and Tania's breath hitched in tandem with the blonde's gasps. When the fronds of the whip lashed down across the blonde's buttocks a moment later and she cried out in pained pleasure, Tania winced. She turned to her wife again to see what reaction Jacky was having to this display. She wore a matching grimace etched on her face.

"The restraining bit I don't mind so much," confessed Tania. "But the whipping thing—no thanks!"

Jacky nodded and exhaled. "Yeah, I admit I got, um, turned on when she cuffed her in. I...I could imagine doing that bit to you."

Tania smiled warmly. "We never did play with those cuffs you got in the Secret Santa last year, did we?" She winked, and Jacky laughed, blushing even more. When Jacky had brought them home and shown Tania, indignantly annoyed at the prank played by her workmates, Tania had tucked them away in their toy drawer for "another time."

They only lasted five minutes more in Red before they made their exit. They'd looked around just to see what else went on in there. A butch with a shaved head and a large dildo fucked a woman who was bent forwards and tied down over a curved bench. The position intrigued them with its erotic possibilities. Then they quickly looked back as the cries from the blonde increased in volume. The skin on her back, buttocks, and thighs was covered in thin, red stripes.

In unspoken, intuitive agreement, Tania and Jacky drained the last of their drinks. As they stood up to leave, the dark-haired woman behind the bar grinned, and Tania caught that look and laughed sheepishly. They probably weren't the first women to take a look at the action in here and decide it wasn't for them.

As Jacky drove them out of the city, past all the drunken Friday night crowds, Tania laid her hand on Jacky's thigh and squeezed lightly. Jacky glanced at her, smiling, and then concentrated on her driving.

"What?" she asked.

"I love you," replied Tania softly. "I love you so much. I still can't quite believe you were willing to do all of that for me. Thank you."

A lump appeared in her throat again, and she swallowed hard before responding.

"Babe, I would do anything for you. Anything," she said, glancing across at her beautiful wife again. "I love you."

Tania smiled, but she also blinked back tears in the dim light of the car. The silence drew out between them, becoming more uncomfortable by the minute. Jacky was well aware of what she'd just said and how untrue it was.

Shit.

Without thinking, she put the indicator on and turned left at the next side road she saw. It led into a small industrial estate, and she pulled into one of the parking bays in front of a darkened warehouse.

"What—" began Tania as she turned in her seat, but Jacky raised a hand to cut her off. She switched off the ignition and took a deep breath as she sank back into her seat.

It was time.

They couldn't share what they had tonight and then go back to normal life with this between them. She trusted Tania implicitly. She trusted her to take what Jacky was about to say and not laugh or belittle or push her into something she didn't want to do.

"We both know what I just said is a lie, don't we?" Jacky said quietly, not looking directly at Tania but somewhere off past her left shoulder. She would only be able to do this if she didn't look directly at her. "That I would do anything for you? Or, at least, it has been until now."

Jacky glanced at Tania, who nodded slowly. She looked nervous.

"I've realised a lot of things about me and about us these past couple of weeks," continued Jacky, her voice only just above a whisper. "Ever since we came up with this plan, I've spent a lot of time thinking about who we are and what we share. And tonight, after all that, I've realised I'm more ashamed to be hiding something from you than I am about what it actually is. Make sense?"

Out of the corner of her eye, Jacky saw Tania nod again, and then she slowly reached across to link her fingers gently with Jacky's on the gear stick. Jacky welcomed the connection and held Tania's hand tightly.

She closed her eyes briefly, then swallowed. "The only person to go down on me was my first girlfriend. Her name was Sandra. We met at college. She was a couple of years ahead of me, and she'd had a few girlfriends. I think she saw me as a bit of a challenge—nineteen, virgin territory and all that. I thought I was the luckiest woman on earth to score someone like her. We dated a few times and kissed and stuff, and then she seduced me one night after drinks in the student bar. Took me back to the flat she rented with two other girls."

Jacky briefly looked at Tania again and blinked a couple of times before pushing on with her story.

"We fucked each other with fingers first. She came. I didn't. She was a bit rough, and I wasn't used to that, and it made me clam up a bit. She told me to relax, told me I wasn't making it easy for her."

Tania gave a small gasp, but Jacky ignored it and carried on.

"We had another drink, some cheap wine shit she had in the fridge. It helped, I guess—I loosened up a bit. She came at me again, a bit gentler this time, and I got into it a lot more. I was getting more and more turned on and—" She stopped talking as a blush spread heatedly across her chest and throat. "She said she wanted to lick me, and although I was nervous because it was my first time, I was feeling a bit bolder from the wine, so I pushed her head down there."

Jacky closed her eyes, trying to talk past the memories without actually feeling them. "She pushed her face into me and licked me a few times, and it felt…wonderful. She asked me if I wanted her to carry on, and I said yes, and then her face was really in there, her tongue doing fantastic things to me." Her face was flaming now as she neared the crucial part of her story.

Tania released her hand to snake an arm around her neck and played with the back of Jacky's hair. It was an action that always soothed her.

"So then she started fucking me with her tongue, and that felt unbelievably good. I could feel my orgasm coming, like it was coming from everywhere, all over me. I'd never felt anything like it. And then, um, I came. Only I…I wet myself." She hung her head in shame. "All over her face." Jacky cringed and shut her eyes. The memory was mortifying. She risked a look up at Tania, dreading what she might see.

"Oh my God," whispered Tania. "You ejaculated?"

Jacky stared at her, uncomprehending. Tania seemed…intrigued, rather than disgusted.

"You…you don't think that's gross?"

"Is that what she said? That it was gross?"

Jacky nodded. "It kind of freaked her out a bit. I mean, she sort of laughed it off, but I…I could tell she was trying hard not to say anything too nasty. She couldn't wait to get in the bathroom and clean up. And, oh God, the mess it made of the bed." Jacky paused, remembering how it felt to think there was something wrong with her. "I was so embarrassed. And I left straight away. I couldn't stay there. I thought it would be okay; I could deal with knowing what had happened if I didn't see her again, but a few nights later, I bumped into her and her two best friends in a club. It was obvious she'd told them. They all made sarcastic comments about it, and although I was really hurt, she just walked away from me."

"What a bitch," said Tania under her breath but still loud enough to make Jacky smile wanly.

"So from then on, I've never let anyone do that. I couldn't risk that happening again. It's not normal."

"Oh, babe," whispered Tania, leaning forward to softly kiss Jacky. "It's not common, but it's certainly a known reaction in some women. Didn't you try and find out about it? You could have just Googled it, you know."

Jacky shook her head. "I didn't want to know. It's disgusting, isn't it? I mean, even if it is more common than I thought, who needs that happening every time someone goes down on them? God, deep down, I would love you to go down on me, and to feel that way again like I did before I orgasmed with her, but I can't take the risk that I would do that to you too. I…I couldn't bear it."

Tania smiled and pulled Jacky closer. "Sweetheart, it's not disgusting. I mean that." Her eyes were sincere, and Jacky swallowed as Tania continued talking, her fingers tenderly stroking Jacky's face. "And I don't know a huge amount about it, but I'm pretty sure I read somewhere that, for the women who can do it, it doesn't happen every time they have sex, and it happens from all sorts of different stimulation. I don't think it's connected exclusively to oral sex or any other kind of position or action. It sounds like it could even just have been a one-time thing for you."

Jacky stared at her. "You know things about it?"

"A little." She exhaled loudly. "God, all this time, and we could have been talking about this, putting your mind at rest." She didn't sound annoyed, just frustrated. "Look, I think if I didn't know it was possible for you, then yes, if it suddenly happened, I might be a bit shocked. But now that I know, even if there is a chance that it could happen again, I'd still want to try." She smiled shyly and twisted her fingers in Jacky's hand. "I have to admit, there's a part of me that would find it amazing to see it."

Jacky's mouth dropped open; her pulse raced. "You...you would?"

Tania giggled. "Yeah, I would. Does that make me a bit weird?"

Jacky shook her head, dumbfounded. Just when she thought she loved Tania with everything she had, she did or said something that made Jacky love her even more.

"You are fucking incredible, is what you are," she said roughly, choking up a little. She reached for Tania then and pulled her into her arms across the handbrake to kiss her soundly, thoroughly. "Incredible," she whispered when they pulled apart. "I love you so much."

Tania nodded slowly. "I love you too, babe. I'm so glad you finally told me. I know it was hard to do, but thank you for doing it."

Jacky kissed her again, pulling her succulent bottom lip between her teeth. "No more secrets, I promise."

"Good," replied Tania, playfully smacking Jacky in the arm in admonishment. "Glad to hear it." Then she tilted her head slightly to one side. "So..." she said carefully. "Does that mean..."

Jacky grinned. "Give me a little time, babe, but yeah, I think it probably does."

Tania closed her eyes briefly, then opened them again to gaze at Jacky before she dropped another gentle kiss on her now-swollen lips.

"Take us home," she whispered into Jacky's mouth. "I need to show you just how much I love you."

Jacky smiled against her lips and lifted her head.

"I love you," said Jacky, voice catching with the depth of her emotions, eyes tearing up.

"And I love you," replied Tania. "One hundred per cent, baby."

Jacky started the car and pulled them back onto the main road towards home.

CHAPTER 6

Los Angeles, 2001

"Hey, I fucking love your accent!"

Mandy grinned. These American women lapped up her British accent, and Mandy had been working it ever since she got to the States. Nearing the end of week two of her celebratory tour—it wasn't every year one turned forty—and it looked as though she was about to get her fifth lay since she'd first landed on US soil. Not too bad, if she said so herself. Two in New York, two in San Francisco, and now, if all went well, her first in LA. And it was only her first night in this enormous city.

She smiled at the woman and continued their conversation.

"So, this place seems popular—you been here a lot?" The professional in Mandy couldn't help but be interested in the details of every club she visited.

The woman nodded as she sipped her mojito. "Yep, I'm in here nearly every week! It just rocks. And it has the hottest women too." She winked at Mandy.

Mandy laughed. She loved the easy flirtation thing they had going on.

"So," continued the woman, putting her drink down on the table beside them, "my name's Cheryl. Do you wanna dance?"

"I'd love to." Mandy leaned in to whisper the words in Cheryl's ear. She was blonde, curvy, and very cute, and Mandy was already responding to the thought of having her hands on that body. Cheryl grabbed her hand, led her to the small dance floor, and pushed her body into Mandy's. She started a slow grind to the beat.

Mandy sank into the embrace and the dance, letting her hands roam freely over Cheryl's hips. Occasionally, she cupped her ass to draw her nearer, only to push her away slightly in order to run her hands up Cheryl's sides and graze the outsides of Cheryl's breasts with her thumbs.

Cheryl laughed, clearly loving the attention, and after only two songs, Cheryl bent forward and kissed her. She darted her tongue seductively into Mandy's mouth and out again. The tease set off a throbbing in Mandy's clit that matched the thump of the music. She grabbed a handful of Cheryl's shoulder-length hair and deepened their kiss.

When they pulled apart, panting, Cheryl nodded towards the darker area at the back of the room.

"Wanna get a little more comfortable?" she asked, leaning forward and breathing the question into Mandy's ear.

Delighted to have someone else take the lead, Mandy simply nodded and held out her hand to Cheryl. Cheryl grinned, grasped Mandy's wrist, and tugged her on a weaving path through the other dancers towards the back.

Instead of stopping at the shadowed back of the dance floor as Mandy expected, Cheryl led them down a short corridor and into a second, much smaller room. The music was still loud in here, but there was no dance floor to speak of. Instead, in the subdued lighting, Mandy could make out various little alcoves along each of the four walls, and to her shock and total delight, nearly every one of them was occupied by female couples in various positions of sexual pleasure.

Oh, fuck, *yes*—her very first proper sex room experience. The throb of her clit increased in tempo. Every other club fuck she'd had, even here in the US, had been a surreptitious sneak at the back of a dance floor or in the toilets. Here, for the first time, she'd found what she'd been ultimately looking for; the freedom to openly fuck in relative comfort, with no questions asked and without having to leave the premises. She grinned widely as Cheryl pulled her over to an unoccupied alcove.

"This okay?" asked Cheryl, but she'd barely got the words out before Mandy pinned her to the wall and lunged in for a ferocious kiss. Cheryl arched beneath her, and then it was a mad choreography of hands and lips and fingers, clothing being pulled out from jeans, skin being touched and licked.

Mandy was *so* turned on. Being able to do this, with all the other women in the room completely unfazed, gave her the biggest sexual buzz of her life.

Within minutes, she had Cheryl's jeans undone and her fingers buried deep in her hot cunt. She fucked her slowly, wanting to make it last, to savour the freedom of the moment. However, Cheryl grabbed hold of Mandy's wrist and urged her to up the speed. Never one to disappoint a lady, Mandy responded by pumping hard until Cheryl gushed all over her hand.

"Oh yeah," murmured Cheryl, her heavy breaths tickling Mandy's ear deliciously. "That was fucking *good*."

Mandy grinned and kissed her. "Indeed," she concurred. "And when you've got your breath back, you can give back as good as you got, okay?"

Cheryl grinned and nodded, still panting heavily. She leaned her head back against the wall and eased Mandy's fingers out from inside her. Her breathing calmed as she did up her jeans, and as soon as that zip was up, she took hold of Mandy's biceps and flipped her round to face the wall.

"I know what I want to do," she whispered in Mandy's ear as she reached round to undo Mandy's jeans.

Mandy moaned and pushed back against Cheryl, letting her ass settle into Cheryl's groin. Cheryl gently thrust her hips against her as she worked her hand into the front of Mandy's knickers and then down onto Mandy's thoroughly swollen clit.

"God, you're really close, aren't you?"

Mandy nodded, unable to speak. The circles Cheryl rubbed with her fingertips over her clit made her lose all train of thought. Then Cheryl pushed Mandy's jeans down enough so that she could manoeuvre her other hand into the back of Mandy's knickers and then push two—or was it three?—fingers deep into Mandy's cunt from behind. Mandy gasped. Who cared how many fingers it was? It felt unbelievably good, and Mandy's orgasm built rapidly.

Cheryl increased the pressure of her fingers on her clit just slightly, and that was enough. The climax slammed into Mandy from every which way, and she threw her head back and let out a long, shuddering groan of pleasure.

"Oh fuck," she breathed, slumping forward against the wall, bracing herself there with her forearms. "Oh, Jesus…"

Cheryl giggled in her ear. "Was that good, baby?" she crooned.

Mandy nodded and turned her head slightly to meet Cheryl's gaze.

"Yep, that was definitely good," she replied, smiling, chest heaving. Cheryl bent forward and gave her a little peck of a kiss.

"Cool. Enjoy the rest of your trip."

And with that, she pulled her fingers out of Mandy and turned and walked away, licking her fingers as she went.

Mandy stared after her, a little stunned at the abrupt departure, and then shrugged. It wasn't as if she hadn't done that herself a number of times before. She turned, leaned back against the wall, and pulled up her jeans. As she caught her breath, she tucked in her shirt and zipped up. She let her gaze roam around the room.

This was exactly the sort of place she'd been looking for. None of the women in here looked remotely embarrassed about what they were up to. And on the other side of the wall, the main room carried on dancing and drinking.

She smiled wistfully. If only somewhere like this existed back home. Well, if she got her way, one day it would. She took a few more minutes to relax and observe, making note of everything that contributed to the atmosphere—both good and bad—and then strolled back to the main room. It was early, and she was nowhere near ready to head back to her hotel. She hit the dance floor and lost herself in the music.

CHAPTER 7

Manchester, present day

Cassie jumped off the bus and dug her gloves from her pocket. Late October, and the chill was setting in earlier each evening. The clocks would go back tomorrow, and she dreaded it. Bang would go most of her afternoon light—the light she painted best by. She glanced at her watch as she pulled on her gloves. Eight fifteen, plenty of time. The club opened at nine, but Mandy liked them all there by eight thirty to set up.

Cassie had been working there for two months now. She'd got the job by word of mouth—clearly Mandy couldn't advertise through any normal channels. Between her wages here, which were generous, and her early morning Monday-to-Thursday shifts at the supermarket, she made enough money and still had lots of time for her first love—art.

She'd sketched and painted since she was young. A teacher had picked up on her potential when she was eleven, and all subsequent art teachers had pushed her along, often giving her extra lessons at weekends. And now, after years of hard work and schooling, she was on the verge of her own show at a small gallery in Glasgow. Her abstracts had caught the eye of the owner, and he had a two-week gap between more prestigious shows at the end of the year. Rather than have bare walls, he'd offered her the space to give her a short-and-sweet boost. She'd leapt at the chance. Now she just had to make sure she had enough pieces to show.

She worked in the 'studio' tacked onto the back of her cheap flat in Stretford. Studio was too fine a word for the shabby lean-to that was cold in winter and roasting hot in summer. But it was a good-sized space, and the light spilled into it freely all day, making it ideal.

As she walked away from the bus, she ran her schedule through her head for the hundredth time that day, calculating just how many hours per day she could paint in the next few weeks before transporting the pieces up to Glasgow. Which reminded her, she needed to call her eldest brother and ask—beg, plead—to borrow his van for that trip.

But first, another Friday night shift at the club.

When she'd first got offered the job, Cassie had been unsure about working there. She wasn't necessarily comfortable with such a club, but she needed the extra work. This job paid well, and that meant she could buy bigger and better canvases.

At the all-night grocers, Cassie turned off the main road and walked past the block of flats, then down towards the railway bridge. When she reached the black door, she stretched up to press the buzzer that only the staff used. The door release clicked, and she pushed the door open. The lights were up, as usual before opening, and Mandy's office light spilled out into the hallway too. She stuck her head around the door to say hello before she continued to the tiny staff room at the end of the hall.

"Hey Cassie, how's things?" Mandy called out. She was always very pleasant—something that Cassie had misjudged. She'd assumed that to run a place like this one would have to be some kind of hard bitch, but Mandy was the complete opposite. She always asked after them all, wanted their feedback on the vibe of each evening, and sought their honest opinions on how things could be run better. She genuinely seemed to care about the clientele and their experiences.

"Can't complain," replied Cassie, walking back into the office to speak face-to-face. She nodded a greeting to Dee. "Had a good week, actually. I haven't said anything about it before, in case it all fell through, but I've got a deal with a gallery to show some of my pieces after Christmas. Just for a couple of weeks, but it would be my own show for the first time."

"Wow, that *is* good news. I'm really pleased for you." Mandy smiled widely and patted Cassie on the shoulder. "Good for you!"

"That's awesome!" said Dee, looking up briefly from the laptop screen in front of her.

"Thanks." Cassie blushed a little at the praise. "So, am I in Green still?"

"Yes, if you don't mind," said Mandy. "One more week, and then I'll put you in the rotation, if that's okay? But remember, like I've said before, if you're not comfortable in either of the other rooms, you just say. It's not a problem."

"I think I'll be fine," said Cassie, grinning. "I'm a big girl now."

Mandy chuckled. "Well, let's see how you feel about that after you've done a Saturday night in Red."

Dee snorted.

"Okay, whatever," Cassie mumbled and left the office to the sound of Dee and Mandy's gentle laughter behind her.

It was a little running gag between them all that Cassie had no experience with BDSM, either as a participant or spectator, and on her first day had openly expressed concerns about working in Red. Although, after reading that anthology of lesbian erotica her best mate had given her, she wasn't sure that was still necessarily true... She'd been a little taken aback—actually, make that a *lot* taken aback—at her body's reaction to the handful of Dom/sub stories. She'd ended up so wet after reading the first one that she'd guiltily put the book away for a few days, deeply uncomfortable with this new knowledge of herself.

But like an enticing dessert that she couldn't help taking just one more bite from, she'd gone back for more. Late into the night, she'd read and re-read, trying to understand what it was about the dynamic that turned her on so much. Despite feeling that it was wrong somehow, she couldn't shake it. And the orgasms she'd brought herself to after reading had been some of the strongest she'd ever experienced.

Nina rushed down the street. She was late—again. Well, on time for opening at nine, but it was a quarter 'til now, and Mandy always liked them there by eight thirty. She didn't know where the fucking time had gone. One minute, she had two hours to get her homework finished, and the next, she was sprinting for the tram and cursing her inability to keep an eye on a fucking clock.

While she'd never regretted giving up her full-time job at the gym to become a mature student of Business & Finance at the age of twenty-eight, sometimes she did question her sanity. Then, she would remember why she was doing it, remind herself of the money that was coming her way when her gran's estate was all sorted out, and the cafe that she would open with it. That always made her smile, take a deep breath, and bury her head in her books again.

At least she'd finished that economics paper, leaving her weekend free. College commitments and helping Mum out at the gift shop had seen her "me time" disappear these past few weeks. So, this week, she'd worked extra hard, determined to have one whole free weekend to do whatever she bloody liked with. Well, apart from working at the club Friday and Saturday nights, but that didn't really feel like work. More like a voyeur's free ride.

She rang the buzzer and apologised to Mandy when she popped her head round the door. Mandy frowned, but there was a sparkle in those amazing blue eyes.

"I know, I know—I'm sorry!" said Nina, rushing past to throw her jacket and bag into her locker.

"You're lucky you've been here the longest," called Mandy as she headed back to her office. Nina grinned sheepishly, closed her locker, and then sprinted back down the hall. She waved at Dee, who blew her a kiss.

"I'm sorry," she said again, meeting Mandy's gaze. "I was cramming an economics paper, and I don't know where the fucking time went."

"Oh God, I know," exclaimed Mandy, clutching dramatically at her chest. "Those economics papers do it for me every time too."

Dee guffawed, and Nina laughed, a big, loud snort of a laugh.

"Fuck off!" she said amiably and walked off to the sound of Mandy's laughter ringing down the hallway after her.

She reached the door at the end of the hall and took a pause. She smoothed her hair, pushing the loose strands back into her ponytail and tightening it, then checked down her clothes to make sure she was all tucked in and everything was clinging where it should.

Cassie was on the other side of that door, and Nina didn't want to look anything but her best. She had no idea if her crush was reciprocated, but she planned to do something about finding out soon. Thoughts of Cassie kept her awake at night, especially on Fridays and Saturdays after working in Red during the evening. The action here fuelled her imagination. What she wouldn't give to have Cassie to play with for the night—or many nights. That woman was so fucking gorgeous it left Nina breathless. And Cassie had no idea how lovely she was. Her innocence was so attractive to Nina; it had her in a complete spin.

Satisfied with her appearance finally, she reached for the handle and opened the door.

Mandy chuckled, as Nina preened before entering Green. It was sweet, really, watching the two of them. They'd clearly been attracted to each other from the minute they met, but so far it looked like neither one of them had done anything about it. Somehow she didn't think that would last much longer. There was no way Cassie would make the first move, and Mandy hoped Nina didn't go in too hard, too fast. Cassie needed careful handling—she wasn't fragile, but she was vanilla. Nina was definitely *not* vanilla.

She smiled to herself, hearing Rebecca's voice in her mind.

Here you go again, mother hen to your little chicks.

She sighed. Yes, she was at it again. She couldn't help it; she'd always cared about her staff—the ones that mattered anyway—as if they were her little flock. Not her children; it wasn't a maternal thing. More like a big sister.

She pictured Rebecca laughing gently at her, shaking her head. The image was so powerful it left her breathless for a moment, and her heart lurched.

The ringing of her mobile phone broke her reverie, and she turned quickly towards the office to answer it.

Cassie smiled as she flipped the lights up and did her quick check for cleanliness and order. Satisfied, she dimmed the main lights and turned up the bar lights.

The door swung open, and Nina, who ran the Red bar, walked in. Cassie's stomach did that little flutter again. She'd reacted like this since she'd met Nina. Nina wasn't the physical type that Cassie would normally go for—she was the same height as Cassie but thinner. Her face was more angular, and she wore her jet black hair in a long ponytail, whereas Cassie kept her golden-blonde main cropped short. Normally, Cassie was attracted to something softer, rounder, more curvaceous. But there was something about Nina… Cassie went a little weak at the knees every time Nina looked at her. She left her breathless and unsure of herself.

"Hi Cassie, how's it going?" Nina's face lit up when she smiled.

Cassie stopped fiddling with the bottle opener in her hands and laid it on the bar. "Good, how about you?" She blushed slightly as her voice came out a little croaky. She cleared her throat. "Just confirmed that I've got a gallery showing after Christmas."

"Oh, that's awesome! I'm so pleased for you." Nina laid her hand over Cassie's, and Cassie thought her heart was going to pound through her ribs. *Oh my God, what is it about this woman?* Nina's eyebrows arched ever so slightly, and a hint of pink crept across her cheeks.

"Yeah," she continued. Nina's hand still covered hers. "It's a great opportunity."

How long would Nina leave her hand there? Maybe she'd like to move it up Cassie's arm, over to her breast—*Jesus, stop already*! She pulled her hand out from under Nina's and took a step back. A look of disappointment flitted across Nina's face. Or did she only imagine that?

"Well, um, I'd better finish setting up. I'll see you later, maybe?" She blushed again and hated herself for it. She was reduced to a ridiculous puddle of nerves—and arousal—every single time.

Nina smiled then—a slow, utterly sexy smile—and nodded, her gaze boring into Cassie. "Yes, later." She turned and walked towards the door with the small red light above it.

Cassie laughed at herself and shook out her arms to break the tension in her body.

"Way to go to make a tit of yourself."

And at that, she went back to setting up for the evening.

Fridays were usually quieter than Saturdays, but for some reason it was buzzing tonight. By eleven, Green was as full as Cassie had ever seen it. Interestingly, she had heard some German accents tonight, from a group of three women who had arrived together just after ten.

She'd seen her first threesome in action too. A couple who'd arrived together, then paired up with another woman. One finger-fucked her from behind while the other knelt in front of her, tonguing her. When she came, she wandered away, and the couple then fucked.

She often found herself musing on the lives of the clientele outside of the club, their reasons for being here, and whether it lived up to their expectations. Like that stunning woman who came in almost every Friday—short, dark hair, nicely toned body, with a hint of sadness hanging over her that made Cassie want to wrap her up in a big hug and ask her what was wrong.

That night, her thoughts drifted almost continuously to Nina through the evening. She'd been unable to shake off the excited tension that had infused her body since their interaction earlier. Nina—and fantasies of what she'd like to do with Nina—filled her brain. That bloody book hadn't helped. Not to mention the things she saw at work each week. The thoughts that came to her shocked her in a way she still wasn't quite comfortable with.

Up until now, with her handful of female lovers, Cassie hadn't been the initiator, content to be led, to take direction. Her thoughts about Nina, however, were anything but passive. If she allowed herself to dwell on it—which she rarely did—there was something about Nina that made Cassie ache to assert control over her. She wanted to subdue Nina, take back her power. She wanted to pin her down, tie her up, and listen to her beg for mercy…

God, she was so wet.

At a quarter to two, Mandy remotely flicked all the lights in the club a couple of times. That signalled a last call of sorts. At that point, the women had about ten minutes to finish and get themselves presentable for the journey home. Cassie's last couple had left shortly after one, and she was well ahead on her closing duties. She gathered empty bottles and glasses from around the room, straightened the furniture, and wiped down *everything* with a sterilized towel to pass the time until closing.

The last few women to leave started drifting through from Blue and Red. Cassie was careful not to make eye contact. They were expected to be politely professional, and on no account were they to be anything more than that with the clientele, no matter how tempting the offer. Tracey had been aggressively propositioned only once, and that woman had been evicted. Each bar had a panic button that went through to the office, and Mandy had responded in a shot, strong-arming the woman quietly and efficiently out the front door before she knew what had even happened to her. Mandy did not have the build you might expect of a bouncer, but apparently no situation fazed her.

Eventually, Tracey and Nina wedged open the doors to their respective rooms, signaling that their parts of the club were empty. She did the same to her door through to the hallway.

Cassie finished clearing up, bagged up her takings, and went to Mandy's office to hand over the cash. Tracey joined her and said a quick goodbye to both of them before dashing out the door. The beads on her braids clicked against the doorframe as she swished through it. Dee had left at one thirty, which was normal for her. As far as Cassie could tell, Dee's main job was to be a second presence at the front door, just in case. At a little over six feet tall with close-cropped hair, she could look really intimidating.

Mandy's internal phone line rang.

"Hey, Nina, what's up?"

Cassie half listened to Mandy's side of the call while she counted out the cash.

"Well, if you're sure, I won't say no—if tonight is anything to go by, tomorrow is going to be mad." A pause. "Yes, okay, I'll ask her, but I'm sure she won't mind."

Cassie looked up and raised one eyebrow questioningly.

"Nina's offered to lock up for me. Red's been a bit hectic tonight, and she needs more time to clean. But she wondered if you'd stay and help her—many hands make light work and all that?"

Cassie swallowed before answering.

She and Nina.

Alone.

In the Red Room.

Her temperature went up a few degrees at that thought. And her knickers got just that little bit wetter.

"No problem," she answered as nonchalantly as she could, pleased that her voice didn't fail her.

"Great. Nina's going to bring her cash down now. Then you guys can lock the door behind me as I go."

Cassie nodded, and her legs took her out of the office, through Green, and on into Red. She tried very hard to remain calm and failed dismally.

Nina was just bagging up the last of her cash when Cassie entered the room. She lifted her head and smiled that same deep, sexy smile at Cassie. Her stomach did a backflip in response.

"Hey, thanks for doing this; I really appreciate it." There was a hint of a smirk around Nina's mouth.

"No worries," replied Cassie. "Where would you like me to start?"

"Can you do bottles and glasses while I take this down to Mandy? Then we can put everything back in its place and tidy up when I get back."

"Sure," said Cassie as Nina left. She turned to the room. It was only the second time she'd been in Red. The first time, the lights had been in club mode, so she'd not had to look too closely. Now, with the room fully lit, she stopped in the centre and stared. The equipment in here was actually fairly tame, if that book was anything to go by. The room was meant to hint at something darker for women who had fantasised about it but didn't necessarily want to go the whole hog. There were two large crosses, various benches, and some stocks, plus a couple of other bits of furniture Cassie had no clue about. This room contained possibilities, and she was intrigued.

She wanted to strap Nina down on one of those benches, spread her naked body out to enjoy at her leisure… She blushed and forced herself to move. She grabbed the glass holder and began collecting up the empties.

Making herself busy cleared her mind of the dirty thoughts she'd been having, and she relaxed a little. Once she'd cleared the glassware and boxed up the bottles for recycling, she donned a pair of gloves and pulled a black bin bag off its roll from behind the bar. Latex gloves, tissues, spent tubes of lube—she collected it all and shoved it into the bag. She didn't get so much of this in Green, but she'd been briefed by Mandy to expect more in both Blue and Red, and Mandy had not lied.

Nina handed the cash over to Mandy, who turned and locked it in the safe.

"Thanks again. It's a while since I got out of here on time," said Mandy, smiling.

"No worries." Nina played with the loose strands from her ponytail. She was itching for Mandy to leave so that she could lock that front door behind her and then get back to Red…and Cassie.

Mandy stopped as she pulled on her jacket. "Everything okay, Nina?"

Nina fought the blush that attempted to invade her cheeks. She nodded. "Fine," she replied. "Just…fine."

Mandy cocked her head to one side briefly, her expression thoughtful, then shrugged on her leather jacket and picked up her handbag. She walked out of the office, and Nina followed behind her ready to lock the door.

As Nina closed the door, Mandy turned to her. She stared deeply into Nina's eyes until Nina dropped her gaze. Mandy's piercing stare seemed to cut straight through her.

"Be careful with her," murmured Mandy. "She's not as…*robust* as you are."

Nina stared at Mandy in surprise, and Mandy smiled back, understanding written all over her face. She nodded once and then stepped out of the door, leaving Nina to push it closed behind her.

Cassie had finished picking up all the detritus and was washing her hands in the small sink behind the bar when Nina returned.

"Oh God, you fucking star!" she said as she walked in, gazing round at the now much cleaner room. "I didn't mean for you to do that bit as well—I know it's not normally part of your routine."

Nina walked closer. Cassie dried her hands on some paper towel and turned to face Nina, her hands shaking slightly as she dropped them to her sides.

"Thank you, that was above and beyond," continued Nina, and she placed her hand on the top of Cassie's arm, just below the sleeve of her tee shirt, and rubbed gently. Electricity shot out in all directions from Nina's touch.

"You're welcome," Cassie mumbled, unable to tear her gaze away from Nina's eyes. Green, with flecks of gold that caught the light, framed by long, long eyelashes that curled seductively with each blink. Her breathing quickened as Nina's lips parted slightly, and the tip of her tongue came out to run lightly over them. Cassie couldn't stop the small moan that escaped her at the pure eroticism of that action.

Nina's eyes widened.

"It's not just me, then," she whispered, taking one step nearer.

Cassie shook her head, unable to speak, unable to stop looking at the mouth that was edging closer to her own. She was losing control, but she couldn't fight it. Nor did she want to.

"Thank God," Nina murmured as she brought her lips into contact with Cassie's. Both of their mouths opened instantly, tongues meeting, groans rumbling in their throats. Cassie wrapped her arms around Nina's shoulders to pull her slender body closer. With Nina's body pressed against the length of hers, her need to consume became almost violent. She ran her hands up Nina's neck, grasped her ponytail, and used it to pull Nina even closer. Nina let out a small whimper as she did so, a sound that Cassie felt all the way down to her clit.

They came up for air a minute later, panting, and stared at each other.

"I have wanted you since the minute I first met you." Nina kissed her way around Cassie's neck, sending exquisite shivers down Cassie's spine and making her wetter than she'd ever been before. "It has been fucking torture, these last few weeks, knowing you were in the other room, watching all these women doing to each other what I wanted to do to you." She dropped her lips into the V of Cassie's tee shirt and licked into Cassie's cleavage, making Cassie arch up into her, craving more.

Nina lifted her head and stared direct into Cassie's eyes. "There are things I want to do. Now. Do you trust me?" Her voice was husky, dripping with desire.

Nina was in total control, and Cassie couldn't find the strength to reverse that situation, despite all her fantasies to the contrary. She panted out her answer.

"Yes."

Nina took Cassie's hand and tugged her over to the far side of the room.

Cassie saw where they were heading, and a sharp bolt of want spiked inside her cunt.

The cross was free-standing, rather than attached to the wall, but bolted into the floor for stability. Soft leather cuffs were fastened to the four points, with one pair just above her head and the other at her ankles.

Nina pulled Cassie around to stand in front of the cross. Cassie swallowed. Based on what she'd read, crosses were often used for floggings or spanking, and she knew she wasn't ready for that. Yet.

"W-what do you want to do to me?" Although Cassie was a little nervous, she met Nina's gaze without flinching.

Nina stepped closer and ran a fingertip along the line of Cassie's jaw, eyes blazing with a mix of warmth and desire.

"It's okay," she whispered. "I'm not really into pain, at least not much. I am, however, definitely into teasing." She moved her fingertip slowly down Cassie's chest into the V of her tee shirt. "And tormenting." The fingertip caressed the tops of Cassie's breasts, and Cassie shivered. "And trying things I've never tried before." The fingertip crept up again, moved slowly across Cassie's lips, and dipped just inside her mouth. Cassie sucked it in and bit gently on the fingertip. A whimper erupted from Nina, and Cassie was immensely satisfied with that reaction.

"I've never had anyone tied into one of these before." Nina pulled her finger away from Cassie's lips and nudged her backwards. "But the thought of having you there, right now, is turning me on more than anything else I've ever done. So, can I?"

Her eyes smouldered, and they were filled with urgency. Nina's breathing grew ragged, and her fingers twitched where they were splayed on Cassie's waist.

Something broke loose in Cassie, something she hadn't realised was wound tight inside her until right this minute.

"Yes," whispered Cassie, stunned at her own eagerness. "God, *yes*."

Nina sucked in a breath, and she roughly pushed Cassie back against the metal of the cross. It was solid against her back as Nina buckled in one arm and then the other. The instant Nina pulled them tight, Cassie tensed with an excitement, an anticipation, she'd never known. Her clit throbbed, standing tight and proud inside her jeans and already desperate for Nina's touch.

Nina stood back a little and, holding herself a few inches away, stared at Cassie strapped in.

Cassie felt that gaze like a searing caress, and she shuddered. Nina smiled as she reached for the bottom of Cassie's tee shirt. With one quick motion, she yanked it upwards, over Cassie's bra, and then in the next moment up over her head so that it bunched behind Cassie's neck. The bra was pushed up next, just enough to reveal Cassie's small, pale breasts to the room. Her nipples, already hard, became painful points as they hit the cool air.

Nina nodded, almost to herself, and then reached for Cassie's jeans. She unzipped them and, just as roughly, pulled them down to her ankles before stripping them off, along with her socks and sneakers, completely. Cassie's knickers rapidly followed the same path, and her mouth went dry at the wantonness of being exposed this way. Her breathing became short gasps as Nina used her hands to push Cassie's legs apart. Then, she dipped even lower to attach the cuffs to Cassie's bare ankles. She was spread-eagled now, her clit pounding and her face flushed. Breasts and wet cunt open to the air, completely pinned and unable to move. It was unlike anything she'd felt before.

She loved it.

Nina moved closer but did not touch.

"I want you to trust me. I want you to enjoy this," whispered Nina close to Cassie's left ear. "But if you get uncomfortable about anything, please, just say so. I'll understand."

"I honestly don't think there is anything you could do to me now that I wouldn't want. I am aching for you. Have been since we met." Cassie's voice was hoarse.

Nina lunged forward to take her mouth in a fierce kiss, possessing Cassie's in a way no one else had ever done. After several long moments, Nina stepped back and slowly peeled off her own clothes. She took her time, teasing Cassie with glimpses of her body, turning away to pull off her shirt and bra, and then slowly turning back so Cassie could gaze at her breasts. Nina's nipples were small and pink and made Cassie salivate with the need to lick them.

Once Nina was completely stripped, Cassie's mouth watered even more at the sight of her fully naked in front of her. Flexed biceps, flat stomach, toned thighs—she'd had no idea someone so lean could excite her so much, and she groaned at the torture of not being able to reach out and touch.

Nina smiled knowingly, clearly enjoying owning all the power in this situation.

"All in good time," she murmured with a wicked grin and then reached out a hand and pulled on Cassie's left nipple with her fingertips. Cassie strained against her cuffs, desperate for more. Her own sex education was about to be taken to an entirely new level. This was the most erotic, exquisite torture. Her juices coated the tops of her thighs; she hadn't known it was possible to be that wet. The thought of what Nina could do to her in this position brought her dangerously close to the edge already.

Nina began a long, excruciatingly slow tease. Her lips and tongue and fingertips were everywhere and nowhere all at once, and sensations shot through every nerve in Cassie's body. Her cunt throbbed almost painfully. Nina pulled and sucked on Cassie's nipples until she cried out in pleasure-pain. Then, using her nails and teeth, Nina ran scorching pathways up and down Cassie's sides, her torso, her thighs. She touched her everywhere except between her legs, and it was completely unravelling Cassie. Every time she thought Nina would finally give her what she wanted, she pulled away and concentrated somewhere else.

"Nina, please," she begged and was rewarded with a small chuckle.

"Oh, it'll be soon, I promise," whispered Nina. "You are driving me insane. You are so fucking beautiful; I can't get enough of you." She kissed Cassie, deeply, yet tenderly, then Cassie watched, breathless, as Nina ran her fingers through her own juices and brought those glistening fingers to Cassie's mouth. Cassie sucked greedily, and Nina pushed her fingers deeper into Cassie's mouth.

With Nina grinding slowly against her thigh, their engorged clits close to each other and Nina's skin pressing against her, Cassie unraveled even further. Her breathing came in huge panting gasps, and her heart thudded in time with the throbbing between her legs. Finally, Nina ran one fingertip straight down the centre of Cassie's body, over her belly, and directly in between her soaking wet pussy lips. Her cry of pleasure was matched in intensity by Nina's deep groan.

Nina started stroking then, long, slow strokes from clit to opening and back again, overwhelming Cassie and making her whimper and tremble with excitement. Her head rocked from side to side as Nina drove inside her, two fingers, deep and hard. With her arm around Cassie's waist, she pulled her closer as her fingers pushed ever deeper.

"Yes, oh *yes*," screamed Cassie, and Nina pumped harder.

Cassie had never felt so consumed by someone, never felt her entire body ablaze like this. She was filled with an intense heat that threatened to engulf her. It swept through her, liquid fire that melted every bone in her body, and her eyes slammed shut as she came. She thrust once, her arms and legs straining against the cuffs that held her tight, her breath stilling as she drowned in the orgasm flowing over her. She exhaled loudly and slumped forward in the restraints. A few tears leaked from the corners of her eyes, and her heart raged in her chest. Nina held her close, pressing her skin against every possible touch point, her fingers still enclosed deep within Cassie as she kissed across Cassie's forehead.

They stayed like that for a few minutes, until Cassie could breathe normally and lift her head. She gazed at Nina, wanting to say so much and having no idea where to start.

"I don't have words," said Nina softly, mirroring Cassie's thoughts, kissing Cassie so gently it made the tears start to fall again. "Oh Jesus, please don't cry," said Nina, her expression alarmed.

"No, no, it's okay." Cassie stretched to kiss her lingeringly. "These are just 'oh my God, that was the most incredible sex of my life' tears."

Nina breathed out a huge sigh and kissed her again. She bit at Cassie's bottom lip gently with her teeth.

"God, I'm so glad. It was *so* fucking good. I couldn't stand the thought that you didn't enjoy it."

Cassie snorted. "I think you can tell I enjoyed it." She waggled her eyebrows.

Nina laughed and hugged her close. "Yep, I guess I don't really have any serious doubts on that score." She reached up above Cassie. "Now, let's get you out of these, shall we?" She unbuckled each of the wrist cuffs and while Cassie rubbed a bit of life back in her arms, knelt and undid the ankle cuffs.

As Nina worked, Cassie breathed deeply, feeling strangely absent from the moment. Her body was still reeling from her orgasm, probably the most intense she'd ever experienced, but her mind was ablaze with images of what she wanted to do now. All she could think about was getting her hands on Nina's body. Possessing her.

Did she have the courage to ask?

But should she even ask—shouldn't she just "do"?

Her deepest fantasy of pinning Nina down, spreading her legs and fucking her hard was paramount. The need drove her temperature up and made her cunt ache. She ripped off her tee shirt and bra and gazed around the room. Her attention landed upon a leather-covered bench with a rounded top. Perfect.

As Nina stood, her expression was greedy and wanting.

"My turn," Cassie said, her voice thick with desire. Nina looked shocked, and Cassie smiled. "You said you had been imagining things you could do to me in here. You're not the only one who's been wondering," she said with a strength that she'd never before felt.

Nina's moan sent hot blood throbbing into Cassie's clit. She led Nina to the curved bench, turned her around, and pushed her over it. With a gasp, Nina tried to push herself up again.

"Don't," Cassie said with a growl, utterly consumed with white-hot desire now. Every bit of her skin crackled with it. She'd never felt so…powerful, and she couldn't switch it off, even if she wanted to.

Nina looked back and caught Cassie's attention. Her pupils were so wide it made her eyes look black. She nodded slowly, smiling, and turned back.

Cassie's heart beat hard in her chest, and she took a couple of breaths to calm things down. She wanted to dive in and yet, at the same time, not rush. This was a dream coming true, and she needed to revel in it. She pushed Nina further over the curved top of the bench and then used both hands to pull Nina's legs wider apart. The scent of Nina's cunt reached her, and she smiled. She took a good look. Nina was soaked.

"I love how wet you are," she whispered. "You look amazing."

"Please," Nina begged. "Fuck me."

Cassie chuckled. "You're not the only one who can tease," she said, smiling as Nina groaned. Nina tried to turn again, and Cassie pushed her down. She wrapped her ponytail around her hand and wrist to use as leverage and forced Nina's head back down.

"Hm, are you going to keep trying to move? Maybe I should tie you down too."

Nina let out a choked sob, and sparks flashed behind Cassie's eyes as visions of her fantasy invaded her brain. She overlaid the images with the sight before her. She definitely needed to tie Nina down to complete the scene.

A rush of power surged through her, and she pushed Nina down again by pressing the ponytail into the back of her neck.

"Stay."

Nina whimpered, and Cassie's stomach lurched. Wow, what an amazing trip. Cassie had dabbled in a bit of weed and E through her teenage years, but that didn't even come close to the high she felt in this moment.

There was an array of equipment lying around the room, and she spotted some cuffs lying loose on a bench nearby. When she walked over to get them, she noticed a metal bar on the floor that had cuffs at each end. She considered it for a moment, and then, in a flash of insight that sent another dollop of juice leaking out of her cunt, she realised what she could use it for.

She picked up the loose cuffs and the bar and strode back across the room. Instead of running from her feelings, she completely immersed herself in them.

She approached Nina, who glanced up as she came near.

"You're a fast learner." Nina smirked.

Cassie chuckled, almost embarrassed, and then straightened her shoulders. In that moment, she was the dominant. She used the loose cuffs to attach Nina's wrists to two hooks at the base of the bench. Then she walked around behind Nina and took a moment to drink in the sight of her spread out like that. Nina's heavy breathing, her body arching in anticipation, heightened Cassie's enjoyment even further. Every night of sex she'd had up to this point in her life paled into complete insignificance. What she and Nina were sharing right now was, she knew, setting her on a whole new path of sexual awakening, akin to a second coming out.

She knelt on the floor behind Nina and attached one end of the bar, and then, after forcing her legs wider apart to accommodate the width of the bar, she attached the other one. Nina grunted as she did so, and Cassie sat back on her haunches and breathed for a moment. Nina was utterly at her mercy, spread wide by the bar, arms locked down over her head, and her cunt and ass on full display. Cassie's body ached with the sight—oh God, how she wanted this fuck to last.

"Okay?" she asked Nina.

"God, yes," came the breathed response. "But please, *please* just fuck me, I need you so much."

Cassie leaned forward, placing her face just an inch away from Nina's cunt. Heat radiated off her, and she could *taste* Nina in the air. Nina squirmed in her restraints, soft whimpers escaping her lips. When Cassie finally pressed the flat of her tongue hard against her pussy, Nina let out a loud cry. Jesus, she tasted so good. Cassie lapped at her, slowly, mercilessly, ignoring all of Nina's exhortations to go faster, harder, deeper. It took all of Cassie's self-control—Nina tasted so good, felt so good, the need to dive inside her was beyond anything Cassie had ever known. And yet, she resisted, prolonging the moment.

She placed her hands on Nina's ass to pull the cheeks wider apart. She darted her tongue along the length of Nina's cunt, and then, despite having never done it before, she moved her tongue upwards and began to lick Nina's ass. Nina let out a deep sigh of pleasure, and Cassie increased the pressure.

"Oh God," exhaled Nina. "That is so fucking good."

Encouraged, Cassie worked harder. She dipped her tongue just inside, her hands clenching and unclenching the soft flesh of Nina's ass. Cassie's clit throbbed with each cry. She couldn't wait any longer. She had to get inside this woman. She lifted her head and, in one quick motion, ran two fingers from Nina's clit to her entrance and pushed inside her cunt. Nina threw her head back and gasped loudly, and nothing could have stopped Cassie from diving deep and diving hard.

She rammed into Nina, opening her own knees to brace herself and give herself more leverage to fuck Nina senseless. Their cries mingled in the cool air of the empty club, and their sweat pooled on Nina's back. As Cassie kept pumping, her own cunt responded. She was going to come herself just from doing this to Nina. She struggled to hold herself back, to not let her orgasm rip through her until Nina got there too.

Then Nina came. Her cunt tightened magnificently around Cassie's fingers, and she pushed her ass back hard. The muscles in Nina's back rippled, and Cassie pushed as deep as she could. Nina held one deep breath and then let out a strangled cry as she collapsed on the bench.

Cassie was so close; she pressed up against Nina and rubbed her clit against the heel of her hand where it was still buried in Nina's cunt. Three quick thrusts, and she was there, crying out Nina's name as she flopped forward onto Nina's damp back. She kissed Nina's neck, licked the sweat from behind her ears, and nibbled on her earlobes. And all the time, Nina undulated against her, moaning softly, whispering words too soft for Cassie to hear.

After a while, Cassie stirred and shifted back onto her haunches. She carefully extracted her fingers, laughing when Nina whimpered as she did so. She reached down to unlock the ankle cuffs and removed the bar. Nina wiggled her legs to loosen up her muscles. Cassie stood, wincing slightly at the sharpness of the pins and needles that shot through her lower legs and feet, and stumbled round to the front of the bench to release Nina's wrists.

Nina groaned as she manoeuvred her body upright, and then collapsed on the floor at the base of the bench with her back against it. Cassie sat beside her, and Nina drew Cassie in against her and wrapped those muscular arms tight around Cassie's torso. She leaned over to kiss Cassie and, with just one kiss, stirred up Cassie's passion again.

Nina broke the kiss with a grin. "Very impressed you found a spreader *and* knew what to do with it," she said, winking.

Cassie laughed. "I'm not embarrassed to admit I had no idea that's what it's called or what it's for. I just kind of guessed."

Nina laughed. "Fuck, you could have fooled me! Hm, maybe we'll make a BDSM expert of you yet."

Cassie grinned and then turned serious, unsure of herself now that their passion had cooled off for a moment. "Was it really okay, to be that…controlling?"

Nina cocked her head slightly to one side. "You've never done that before?" she asked quietly, all teasing gone from her tone.

Cassie shook her head. She wanted to tell Nina everything; given what they'd just shared, she presumed it would be safe to do so.

"I've been having fantasies about you for a while, but I was a bit unsure of them. I've never felt the need to control before, to dominate, but something about you made me really…ache…to do it. It made me uncomfortable thinking about it."

"Did it make you uncomfortable doing it?" Nina's face showed some concern, perhaps worried that what they'd done wasn't really what Cassie wanted.

Cassie pulled Nina close and kissed her. "Not at all," she whispered when they came up for air. "I loved it." She felt...liberated, freer than she could ever remember feeling. Nina smiled her sexy smile, and Cassie laughed.

"So," she began, tipping Nina's chin up so that she could meet her gaze. "Are *you* a BDSM expert? Is this what you usually do?"

Nina smiled and blushed a little. "Actually, no—I've fantasised about it often enough, and working here has certainly taught me a few things, but I've never really indulged. I've had a couple of lovers who were into a bit of tying up, some role play, and the odd spanking, but nothing hard-core."

"I never really thought about it all until I came here and met you." Cassie paused, blushing. "Well, actually that's not quite true." Thoughts of the book ran through her head.

"What?" asked Nina, looking baffled.

"Oh, well, it's, um, just that a...a mate of mine bought me a book for my birthday recently, and, well, some of the stories in it kind of got me thinking. That sort of coincided with meeting you and working here, and suddenly all sorts of...naughty...thoughts were going through my brain."

Nina giggled. "Am I a bad influence?" she asked, grinning.

Cassie laughed and traced small circles around one of Nina's nipples with her fingers. "Bad, but in a good way," she murmured, entranced by the sight of Nina's nipple hardening under her touch.

"Did you prefer being submissive or dominant?"

Cassie caught Nina's gaze again. "I liked both, for different reasons. But usually you have to be one or the other, don't you? Do I have to choose straight away?"

Nina laughed softly. "God, you can be anything you want, and it can change from day to day if you want! There's no hard rules. I've seen a couple of women in here being very submissive one week, and then the next week they're totally into a dominant role. Equally I've seen the same women being dominant here week in, week out, but for all I know, they do that here because they're submissive at home. I don't want to be trapped in one role or the other, I want to play. So if that's what you want too, that's totally cool."

Cassie blushed, embarrassed at her naivety.

"Hey." Nina kissed her softly. "I fucking love that you're so open to the possibilities."

Cassie smiled, relieved, and kissed Nina harder. She loved the hot softness of Nina's mouth, so she ran her tongue over Nina's swollen lips.

"So," she said when she came up for a gulp of air, "I have a question."

"Go ahead," murmured Nina as she nibbled Cassie's neck.

Cassie hesitated a moment. She needed to know, but at the same time, didn't want to spoil where they were right now.

Nina raised her head. "What is it?" she asked softly and stroked Cassie's face with the backs of her fingers.

"I...I was just wondering if this was just one time for you, with me, or whether you...maybe wanted to see...if we could have something more." Cassie blushed profusely as the words stumbled out in fits and starts.

Nina's face melted into a tender softness as she reached to pull Cassie even closer. "Oh, I definitely want us to see if there is something more here, you gorgeous, wonderful woman."

Cassie beamed. "Wow. Okay. God, that's so cool."

Nina laughed. "You are fucking adorable; you know that, right?"

Cassie dipped her head in embarrassment, then looked up, painting what she hoped was a cheeky smile on her lips.

"But sexy, too, right?" she asked, impishly.

Nina guffawed, then gazed all the way down Cassie's body and back up again. Cassie blushed deep to her roots.

"Oh yeah," exhaled Nina, her eyes darkening.

Cassie leaned forward and kissed Nina as hard as she could, thrusting her tongue deep into her mouth. Nina's moan reverberated through Cassie's chest. She raised her head and ran her hands up to Nina's ponytail. She wanted to run her fingers through that hair. She reached for the thin band that held it altogether and met Nina's gaze.

"Can I?" she asked quietly, lifting one loop of the band with a fingertip.

Nina nodded, and Cassie pulled carefully at the band, easing it down the dense twist of hair until it was free. She took her time running her fingers through the soft, thick strands, delighting in the feeling. She'd never been with a long-haired woman before. It felt amazingly good. She dipped her face into the softness and let the curtain wash over her eyes, her nose, her lips.

Nina shivered slightly, and Cassie pulled back to look at her, one eyebrow raised in a question.

"Feels amazing," murmured Nina, and Cassie leaned in for another deeply delicious kiss.

They kissed for a while—just kissing, no touching. Simply enjoying each other's lips and tongues, alternating who was controlling the kiss, alternating the strength of it. Nibbling on bottom lips, sucking on top lips, gently biting tongues.

"So," said Cassie as they eventually pulled apart, both smiling, both breathing heavily, her boldness from earlier returning along with her arousal. "What can we play with next?"

Nina giggled, and it was her turn to blush a little. "Well," she replied, pulling away from Cassie and pushing herself off the floor. "There is one piece of kit in here I have been dying to get you strapped into ever since I first saw it used." She pulled Cassie to her feet. "Game?"

Cassie grinned. "Oh yes," she whispered and let Nina lead her across the room.

The bench was long, about eighteen inches off the ground, with two tall uprights at one end and hooks with cuffs on the four legs. Nina gently pushed Cassie onto her back, and the padded material gave ever so slightly as she sunk back into it. She gasped as Nina grabbed her, opened her legs wide over the frame, and buckled the cuffs around her ankles.

She was completely spread open in front of Nina, her ass and cunt hanging off the edge of the leather and giving Nina full access. Just the thought had her juices flowing freely again. She waited in anticipation for Nina's tongue or fingers to find her aching clit, but Nina stood up and moved away. She strapped Cassie's wrists into the cuffs at the front of the bench, leaving Cassie completely spreadeagled with her breasts pointing jauntily at the ceiling, her nipples rock hard.

"Now for the fun part." And with that, she gripped the two tall uprights, climbed over the bench as if mounting a horse, and straddled Cassie's head. Cassie whimpered with an extraordinary need.

Nina gazed down at her, her luxuriously long hair framing her face, making Cassie's hands itch to run her fingers through it again. Nina smiled wickedly as she slowly lowered herself down, bringing her wet cunt ever closer to Cassie's face. Her smell filled Cassie's nostrils, and she nearly sobbed with the need to taste.

"Now," Nina whispered, her cunt almost within touching distance. "You are going to lick me until I come, and if you do it nicely, just the way I like it, after I've come, I am going to climb off here, walk back round to where your cunt is waiting for me, and then I am going to lick you until you scream. Understand?"

Cassie nodded, the power of speech having left her some moments ago. She gazed up into Nina's wetness and licked her lips.

"Good girl," grinned Nina, her voice tight, and she lowered herself down the last couple of inches.

Cassie licked.

Mandy was still swearing softly under her breath as she pulled the car over to the kerb in front of the black door. Leaving her mobile phone in the office had been one of the more stupid things she'd done recently, although there was quite a list building day by day. Menopause was definitely not much fun—her short-term memory issues were seriously starting to piss her off.

She locked the car and fumbled for the keys to the club in the bottom of her handbag. When she found them, she slipped the first one into the deadlock, only to find it wasn't locked. What the—? Did Nina forget that bit when she locked up earlier? Damn her; that was a serious slip-up. She unlocked the top lock and stepped inside.

When she saw the lights still on in the hallway, she hesitated. Her heartbeat quickened, and she tried to control her breathing. She listened for sound of any kind. Nothing. She stepped in and shut the door quietly behind her. She tiptoed into the office. The safe was still locked and her phone still on her desk. Not burglars, then.

She grabbed the phone and held it tight in her hand as she left the office and walked carefully along the hallway. She wasn't sure what was going on, but she wanted the phone near to hand, just in case.

She walked through the open door into Green. All the lights were on, and the room was clean and tidy. Cassie had clearly finished up her own room before helping Nina out. She crossed to the door that led to Blue. A quick glance inside showed a dark room with no sign of life. She backtracked, walked a few paces towards Red, and opened her mouth to call out Nina's name. That's when she heard it. She stopped dead at the sounds coming from the room ahead of her.

"Oh, Cassie, Jesus, that is so fucking good."

Nina's voice was deep and husky, and there was no doubt about what she was experiencing right at that moment. Mandy slapped a hand over her mouth to keep from laughing out loud. Well, well, well, Nina had got her way. And from the sound of things, it was everything she wanted it to be. Mandy smiled, delighted for the pair of them, and silently laughed at their audacity to use her club for their liaison. Well, why not—if the mood had taken them and no one else was around to witness it, who cared? Although she'd have to have a quiet word with Nina tomorrow to make sure they kept it to after-hours only. Assuming there would be more than tonight, of course.

Nina's moans grew louder, and Mandy really didn't need to be around to hear her climax. She spun on the spot and left the Green Room as fast as she could.

She checked the office one last time before leaving and then quietly let the front door click after her. Still smiling, she unlocked the car and started the engine for her repeat trip towards home.

Cassie came even harder than she had earlier in the evening. Nina's tongue had been relentless, taking her to the brink many times but never quite pushing her over until Cassie was practically sobbing for Nina to let her come. When she did, her hips pushed so far off the bench that her left thigh muscles locked into a cramp. She'd flopped back down again and urged Nina to release her ankles so she could do some stretches to ease it out.

Then they'd started laughing, hysterically. Nina helped her stretch by putting her leg over Nina's shoulder to force the muscles into submission.

"God, I hope I haven't fucking broken you," laughed Nina as Cassie groaned in agony beneath her.

"I think you might have. Ouch!" But Cassie was giggling, finally able to drop her leg off Nina's shoulder and sit up.

They sat straddled across the bench, facing each other then, arms wrapped around each other.

"That was amazing," whispered Cassie in between soft kisses to Nina's face and neck. "You make me feel incredible."

Nina pulled her a little closer. "Ditto," she murmured, taking Cassie's mouth into a deep, passionate kiss that was all about feeling and emotion rather than physicality. Cassie couldn't get enough of Nina; every kiss and every touch just made her want more.

"Come home with me," Nina said as they pulled apart. "I want to wake up with you in my bed tomorrow."

Cassie smiled—a big, broad smile of joy. "God, yes please!" she said and pulled Nina to her feet.

Cassie had finished tidying her bar on Saturday night when Nina came sprinting in from the office. Her face was flushed, and she was grinning from ear to ear. Cassie raised an eyebrow.

"What's got you looking so hot and bothered?"

Nina chuckled and reached across the bar to plant a big kiss on Cassie's lips.

"Tell you later," she said when she pulled back and dashed off to Red to clean up.

"I'm coming to help you," Cassie called after her.

"Great!" came Nina's muffled reply.

Cassie giggled and switched off the bar lights. She walked into Red and leaned on the bar, amused at the antics of her girlfriend. At least, she presumed she was her girlfriend. Maybe she should check that with Nina before too long…

Nina was cleaning at a sprint, trying to do four things at once and failing badly at all of them. After a few moments, Cassie took pity and strode across the room to grab Nina around the waist from behind and pull her to a stop midstride.

"Enough!" she said in Nina's ear, lingering to gently bite her earlobe.

Nina sighed, melting back into Cassie's arms.

"Sorry, I just want to get done, so we can get out of here. I have plans for you, and they don't involve bin bags and latex gloves." Cassie giggled in her ear. "Well, maybe the latex gloves…"

Cassie snorted softly. "I'm helping, remember?"

Nina turned in Cassie's arms and nodded. "Okay, gorgeous. If it means we get the fuck out of here faster, I'm all for it."

"It does, so tell me what you want me to do."

Nina smiled and held Cassie's gaze. "Well, there's an offer," she said, her voice sultry and her eyes darkening slightly.

"Focus, Nina, focus! Cleaning tasks. What cleaning tasks do you want me to do?"

"Spoilsport," Nina mumbled as she handed Cassie the glass holder. "You do glasses and bottles, I'll do rubbish," she said in a slightly petulant tone.

Between them, they finished in record time. Nina flipped off the bar lights, followed by the main lights, and they walked out of the darkened room arm-in-arm. They switched off the main lights in Green as they walked through there and into the staff room to grab their coats and bags.

Mandy was waiting for them in the doorway to her office, smiling. When Cassie saw her, she tried to extricate herself from Nina's hold, and Mandy's smile grew even bigger.

Mandy held up one hand. "Don't bother, I know," she said, grinning as Cassie blushed. "And as I said to the other one earlier on, I'm very pleased for you both. Now, get the hell out of here and go have some fun."

Nina giggled and pulled Cassie with her to the front door. "Come on, you heard the boss—we have official permission to go get sexy."

Cassie sighed and then grinned as she looked at Mandy.

"What have I got myself into?" she wondered aloud.

"Hey, I'm right here!" Nina's pout was very cute. Cassie leaned in and kissed her soundly.

"Yes, you are," she said against Nina's lips. She turned to Mandy, grinning even wider. "Oh, and I think I'm more than ready to go into the bar rotation for Red from next week." She glanced at Nina, smirking. "I've got a lot of learning to do to keep this one satisfied," she said, and both she and Mandy giggled as Nina's mouth dropped open in shock.

"What the…" Nina's voice, when it finally came, was strangled. She stared at Cassie, who put the tip of one finger under Nina's chin and pushed up gently to close her mouth. Then she winked at Mandy and tugged a stumbling and stuttering Nina out into the cold night air.

CHAPTER 8

Manchester, 2003

Mandy gazed across the room from the mezzanine level. It was packed tonight, and she allowed herself a small, proud smile. They'd been open less than a year, but they were already the most popular club in Manchester. This was her third job in this city as a club manager, and this was the big one. She planned to do this one for about two years total, assuming they could keep this level of success going, and then she wanted to open her own club.

Working for Robbie Chapman was all right—mostly. He paid well and let her have almost full rein, but he was still the owner. He could change tack at any time, get rid her of her at any moment. He'd done that to other managers in his chain of clubs. Besides, she really wanted to run a gay club, and Robbie wouldn't touch fag clubs, as he called them, with a barge pole.

Having been on the Manchester scene for a few years now, she'd watched it develop, noting what worked well and what didn't. She'd listened in on conversations in bars and cafes to get a feel for what the gay men and women in this city wanted from their nightlife. She'd never be able to run anything this big for gays, but she was okay with that. It was all about the quality, not the size. She wanted top decor, furnishings, and facilities. She wanted top DJs and acts. She wanted a bit of gay class.

Then, of course, there was the other kind of club she wanted to run. But it would probably take a bit more time and thought to bring that one to life.

She glanced across to the main bar, seeking out Rebecca, the bar manager. She couldn't help but stare at her, safe in the knowledge that Rebecca was unawares. God, she looked fucking gorgeous tonight—tight leather trousers, with a white shirt over a black vest top. Her hair was pinned up on one side, leaving a cascade of soft brown curls to waterfall down her left shoulder. Oh, how she longed to bury her face in that neck and her hands in that hair.

She shook herself and tore her gaze away. *Stupid*. Rebecca was off limits. She was very happily straight, engaged, and she was Mandy's best friend. *Leave it*.

But God, it was so hard not to fantasize, and Mandy wondered for the umpteenth time how she'd ended up in this predicament. She, of the no-strings, nothing's-going-to-tie-me-down lifelong attitude was madly, crazily, heartbreakingly in love for the first time in her life, at the age of forty-two and with a woman she couldn't have. Life was fucking cruel sometimes.

They'd met eighteen months ago at the previous club Mandy had managed for Robbie. Smaller than this one, but he'd wanted to test her before letting her run one of his jewels, as he called them. Rebecca had been bar manager there too, and they'd quickly become friends, sharing the same sick sense of humour and love of fashion. And when Robbie had promoted Mandy to run this new club, it had been a no-brainer to bring Rebecca along to manage the bars.

It had taken Mandy only a couple of months to fall head-over-heels in love with her new friend. At first, she had found it amusing, and then it became increasingly intolerable as she realised just how deep her feelings ran. She should have put some distance between them, but she just couldn't do it. Being with Rebecca brought so much joy into her life; she couldn't deprive herself of it. So she'd learned to suppress her yearnings and make do with the wonderfully satisfying friendship that Rebecca offered.

She needed to find an outlet for her deeper desires in other places, with other women—faceless, nameless women—as she had done for years now.

True, it had been hard when Rebecca got engaged. Her boyfriend had proposed about a month ago. Seeing Rebecca so excited about being engaged, and being asked to help plan a big wedding, was painful. As was wishing it was she who would be walking down the aisle with Rebecca.

But again, she'd set her own feelings aside and been the supportive friend Rebecca needed. They already had the plans up and running. Her fiancé was quite happy to leave all that to the "chicks," as he called them, which made both of them laugh in disgust. At forty-two, Mandy was definitely too old to be called a chick, and Rebecca felt the same, even though she was slightly younger at thirty-eight. But that was her fiancé—Mr Laid Back. Or was that Mr Lazy? Mandy wasn't quite sure, and the difference between the two titles was a very thin line. To be honest, she'd never quite taken to him, but had always assumed that was because, in her eyes, no man could ever be good enough for Rebecca.

She heaved a big sigh and pushed all thoughts of wedding plans—and Rebecca—out of her mind. She turned back to watch the main room for a few more moments before heading down to her office. She had payroll to finish, and there was a very chilled glass of Prosecco with her name on it somewhere down at the main bar.

CHAPTER 9

Manchester, present day

Lou showered slowly, standing under the hot water with her head tipped back, enjoying the sensation as it gushed over her breasts and down over her abs. It was early yet, but she liked to take her time before heading out to the club. For her, this was a subtle form of foreplay. She listened to her body tell her what mood it was in. More often than not she was the "aggressor" on club nights, but that took so much energy to pull off. It was a struggle. In order to keep the interactions *exactly* as she desired them—not very vocal and at a pace *she* controlled—required *her* to be the one in charge. And yet, that went against her basic instincts.

She had learned, though, it was generally the only way it worked for her. Occasionally, she had been the one who found a spot on the wall, waited, and let someone else come to her. Usually on nights like tonight, when she was just too tired to do anything else. But those nights were always the most uncomfortable for her. She could never be sure who or what she was going to get. Battling herself was definitely wearing her down, and thoughts of how to change that had crept to the forefront of her mind lately.

It was funny, but since that time with Max, she'd struggled to find that same level of intensity. That had been, by far, her best, most… intimate…experience at the club since she'd discovered it a year ago. In other circumstances, Max would definitely be the kind of woman she could imagine having something more with, someone who could kindle that kind of passion in her with one look, one touch.

Their first kiss had been so powerful, and the sex that had followed had stayed in her memory for days, weeks. Of course, a relationship was out of the question. To build a relationship, she would have to *relate* to someone, to converse, to share, to reveal. All things Lou was incapable of.

This was why the club had been such a godsend. It was the magical solution for her. At the club, once she'd gone through all the mental gymnastics to get herself through the front door, she was able to set aside her inherent, painful shyness. She could transform herself into anyone she wanted to be.

The club gave her the physical release she needed for her inner passionate self, the hidden Lou that was desperate to be free. She just wasn't quite strong enough to achieve it in everyday life.

Her job at the insurance company allowed her to keep her interactions to email and the occasional phone call. Face-to-face situations were rarely needed, and if they were, most people just accepted that she was quiet and perhaps a little odd, but harmless enough. She was grateful for that. She enjoyed her work, and it paid well enough for her quiet lifestyle.

Tonight, because she was so tired, she would wait by the wall and see who approached. She would let someone else make all the moves and hope that person didn't push her into an uncomfortable headspace, that she would be able to release the pressure that had built up inside of her these past couple of weeks.

The taxi dropped her a couple of streets away—she never liked to be dropped right at the door. She used her time as she approached the club to gather her bravery. The cold November rain had settled in for the weekend, so she kept her umbrella close over her head to protect her hair she'd so carefully styled.

Mandy let her in, took Lou's cash, and then left her to stow her coat, soggy umbrella, and bag in one of the lockers. Mandy had introduced herself that first night, which Lou imagined she did to all the newbies, but it had taken Lou a couple of months to feel comfortable enough to meet her eyes, smile an unspoken greeting, and tell Mandy her name.

In the locker room, Lou shook herself, trying to dispel the maudlin thoughts. She arched her back a couple of times to release some tension and then, finally ready, stepped out into the hallway.

She walked through into the Green Room and stopped for a drink. It took her a while to get into the feel of the evening. On her very first night, she hadn't watched anyone much at all, too embarrassed to be caught staring. Then she'd realised that everyone was voyeuristic, and gradually, she had allowed herself to look too.

She sat at the bar with her first beer. The barwoman was the dark-haired one with the long ponytail, and she gave Lou a small smile. Lou had seen her in the gym she used each morning. She was pretty sure the woman didn't know her as their workout sessions had only crossed paths a few times. She was fit and had a nice lean body, but she was too thin for Lou. She much preferred curves and softness.

It was pretty quiet, only two couples already fully in action and two other women along the wall, quietly sipping their drinks while they watched the couples and the door to see who came in. Lou focused her attention on a couple in the corner. With their jeans and underwear down around their knees, they were taking turns fucking each other, never quite bringing each other to orgasm. It was just one endless fuck that had them both panting. She eventually realised they might have been baiting each other, seeing who would "break" first, because suddenly one of them groaned, "Oh Christ," and dropped to her knees to bury her face in the other's pussy. She licked until her partner screamed her pleasure. Lou smiled, relishing the way this club enabled anyone to let loose with zero inhibitions.

As she sipped her beer, the room gradually filled. Not everyone stopped in Green, of course. Quite a few wandered through to Blue or Red, although they invariably took their time as they crossed the room to check things out. Lou struggled to tune in to what her body wanted tonight. All she could come up with was the vague notion that she didn't want to think about it in any detail. She wanted to feel and come, and she really didn't care how that happened.

She moved to the centre bar, wondering if a closer proximity to things would help. She watched as one woman slowly fucked another. They were down on the floor, one sitting with the other straddling her thighs. With her head thrown back, the one on top slowly plunged up and down the other woman's fingers.

The position sparked something in Lou. Was it the closeness? Or maybe it was the fact that the one being fucked was also the one in control. Whatever it was, it stirred her up, awakening her. She followed the feeling, connected with it, and let it tell her what she needed.

And then she knew. A visit to the Blue Room might help, for once.

She walked into Blue and ordered her drink from the cute woman with braids who always gave her a small wink whenever their paths crossed. It was probably against the rules, but Lou had been here enough times to know all three barwomen by sight, and they all acknowledged her in some way. She smiled back and made her way to the stools at the centre bar.

She'd only visited Blue a few times in the past, purely to watch. She had never been on the receiving end, but she had fantasised about it occasionally. Tonight, it was time to make it a reality. She had a specific physical type in mind and took her time searching the room. She didn't see her ideal woman just yet, but she'd wait. If this place had taught her one thing, it was patience.

She had just finished her second beer when the right one walked in. Not too tall, solid build, leather trousers, and a very tight white tee shirt that stretched over full breasts. Her deeply black skin and strong bone structure hinted at an African heritage, rather than Caribbean. She had cropped hair, and both ears were pierced multiple times from top to lobe. Lou's cunt tightened.

Yep, this one.

She waited a few moments to make sure the woman was staying in Blue. Hopefully she was packing; the whole effect would be ruined if she expected Lou to deliver. The woman strolled almost arrogantly around the room, checking out what was on offer. Oh yeah, she would do *very* nicely. Lou grinned in relief as she finally started to slip into the right headspace for what she needed tonight.

Taking a deep breath and mustering every bit of courage she could, Lou slipped off her stool just as the woman walked past her corner of the bar. She turned her gaze in Lou's direction and stopped to look Lou up and down, slowly, hungrily. Lou's pulse quickened, and juice leaked from her cunt. She stepped slowly up to the woman and—forcing herself to be bolder than she could usually imagine being—put her hand on the woman's crotch. She was rewarded with the hardness she'd hoped to find and a sharp intake of breath from her prospective partner.

"Cheeky little bitch," the woman murmured with a smile.

"I just know what I want, and I don't want to waste time looking in the wrong place." Lou's voice came out strong even though she was a mess of nerves and fear on the inside. If she got this bit right, she'd not have to say much more.

The woman laughed quietly, without malice, and Lou sighed in relief.

"What's your name?" Her voice was deep and husky.

"Lou."

Her new partner smiled, her gaze drifting down over Lou's breasts.

"Chris," she murmured as she took hold of the front of Lou's red, silky shirt and led her to a spare space on the wall. Lou let herself tune in to groans and gasps around her, her excitement rising. She was finally, to her huge relief, in the zone, ready to submit to whatever this woman wanted to do to her.

Chris licked her lips and kissed Lou hard. She thrust her tongue into Lou's mouth and swept her hands up Lou's body to land on her breasts. Lou pushed into her, and Chris responded, squeezing and kneading through the fabric of Lou's shirt and bra. Lou's nipples tightened, and she kissed her harder. With her hands on Chris's hips, she pulled her even closer and moved her pelvis shamelessly against the firmness of the dildo between them.

Groaning, Chris pulled back slightly and reached for the bottom of Lou's shirt. She was surprisingly gentle and careful as she pulled it out of Lou's jeans. She ran her hands up inside the shirt and roughly pulled the cups of Lou's bra down to expose her breasts to the silky fabric on the inside of her shirt. Lou moaned, and Chris gave her a lascivious grin.

Lou wondered again at her own capacity to transform herself on nights like this. It gave her a freedom that wasn't possible in her daytime life. And then, as Chris slipped her warm hands over Lou's breasts and pinched Lou's already hard nipples, Lou stopped analysing and just surrendered.

As her nipples and breasts were teased until she thought she might come just from that attention alone, she pulled Chris's tee shirt from her trousers. She roamed underneath the fabric, finding warm skin and a bra filled with abundant breasts that she cupped and squeezed. They kissed again, and there was a heat in Chris's eyes that signaled that foreplay was over.

"I want to fuck you sitting on that chair," Chris breathed in her ear, and Lou nodded.

Just the thought of it made her cunt gush, delighted that Chris had tapped into exactly what Lou needed.

"It means you getting undressed from the waist down, though—is that okay?"

Lou smiled, touched by her concern. Another thing she loved about this place—yes, it was all about sex, about fucking, often without emotion, but that didn't mean it was completely heartless.

"Yes." Lou leaned in and ran her tongue softly around Chris's mouth, loving the sound of the groan that came from somewhere deep in her chest. Lou stood back then and let Chris undo her jeans and gently tug them down to her knees. From there, Lou took over. She finished removing her shoes and socks and kicked off the jeans. Chris lifted the tails of Lou's shirt and stared at Lou's hips and ass.

"Fuck, that is seriously sexy." Chris met Lou's gaze before she ran her hands over Lou's hips and hooked her thumbs under the slender waistband of her lacy G-string. As she gently peeled it down, she took Lou in another penetrating kiss.

It felt so good to be wanted this badly, to be swept up in someone else's desire. She helped Chris push the G-string down past her hips and let it fall to the ground. She felt completely exposed, but strangely, it didn't unnerve her.

Chris ran her hands over Lou's ass, stroking gently at first, and then with firmer pressure, her fingers sinking into Lou's soft flesh. She pressed her mouth into the juncture of Lou's neck and collarbone, sucking and nibbling and sending delicious shivers down Lou's back. As Chris cupped Lou's ass strongly with one hand, she ran the fingers of the other hand through Lou's wetness from behind, dipping just one fingertip into Lou's cunt, teasing her with a hint of what was to come. Lou pushed against that finger, painfully aching for more, and Chris laughed against her skin.

"Soon, sexy. Soon." She chuckled and lifted her head. "How about we get ourselves sat down now?"

Lou nodded eagerly. She was desperate to push this along and very happy that Chris seemed just as keen. She stepped back to give Chris room to unzip her leathers, salivating as the dildo was revealed; she was even more ready for this than she'd realised.

Chris caught her gaze and grinned. "Like what you see?" she asked, huskily, stroking one hand up the full length of the dildo and back down again.

"Oh shit, yes," Lou growled, as her juices flowed even more. God, it had been a very long time since she'd wanted to be fucked this much.

"Then I think we'd better sit down, don't you?"

Lou's breath caught in her throat. She watched Chris as she sat down and adjusted her hips as she settled in the chair. Once Chris was positioned, Lou straddled the chair. Staring into Chris's eyes, Lou waited there in quiet anticipation while Chris opened a condom and rolled it on.

"Something tells me you don't need lube," whispered Chris, and Lou shook her head. She whimpered as Chris ran her hands through her wetness and then used that to moisten the dildo. It looked about seven inches long, not a scary length, but it would fill Lou completely. Her breath hitched at the thought.

And then Chris placed her hands on Lou's hips and, gripping firmly, guided Lou down. Lou closed her eyes, the exquisite eroticism of the moment overwhelming her. She was panting, loudly, and didn't care. She reached down to position the dildo at her entrance and then placed both hands on Chris's shoulders.

When the dildo entered her, slowly, she groaned with every slight thrust, pushing down for more and whispering, "Yes, oh yes," again and again. When it was fully inside her, she feared she would come in seconds and didn't want to. She wanted to make it last, and so she controlled her thoughts and her breathing. She relaxed into the rhythmic thrusting and the sheer pleasure of feeling it fill her. She opened her eyes at last and watched Chris's own ecstasy playing out on her face. Chris's breath came in heavy pants, and she pushed her face into Lou's breasts, her hands gripping tightly onto Lou's hips as she rode her harder and faster.

Lou was ready now. She wanted it—needed it. She let loose the last bit of control and came hard. The flush of it spread everywhere. She threw her head back and cried out. Chris groaned beneath her, and Lou let her push deep inside once more. Then she held Chris there, clinging tightly onto her shoulders to tell her to stay.

"So good," murmured Chris near to Lou's ear. "So fucking good. I need you to do something for me now."

Lou nodded and met her heated gaze.

"Lick me."

Without hesitating, Lou eased herself off the dildo, and Chris unbuckled the harness. She pushed it and her trousers down to her ankles and dropped the dildo to the floor. She shuffled forward on the chair, giving Lou a better angle, and opened her legs. Lou smiled and dropped to her knees. She used her thumbs to push back the thick curls from Chris's swollen clit, and Chris laid back on the chair, eyes closed, chest heaving. Lou breathed in her musky scent, and then, using just the tip of her tongue, she teased her clit. Chris gasped and fisted her hands in Lou's hair.

"Faster. Harder," came the commands, and Lou obliged, pressing her face deeper into the warm wetness that tasted so sweet, letting the whole of her tongue get to work, licking and sucking. When Chris came, she pulled Lou even closer, nearly suffocating her. A long, loud groan wrenched from her throat as she thrust with each spasm of her orgasm.

Lou took her time with her second shower of the evening. She didn't normally shower at the club, but having been so thoroughly, satisfyingly fucked, she was dripping and really didn't want to travel home in such a state. She and Chris had parted with a kiss but barely a backwards glance. Chris had headed for the bathroom, too, dildo in hand. Would she come out looking for a second round? Why not? The evening had just got going; it wasn't even eleven yet. But for Lou, for tonight, once was enough. She felt utterly sated and ready to go home.

She took a cab to her small flat in Hulme. It was early enough to get public transport if she wished, but she hated the crowds on a Friday night and felt safer getting a taxi. Thankfully, her driver was quiet; she hated the chatty ones. Her shyness normally kept conversation to a minimum anyway.

She made herself a cup of tea and sat drinking it in her darkened kitchen. She always did this, replaying the night's events back like a movie and lingering over the best bits to keep the afterglow going just that little bit longer.

Lou grew blissfully tired. Tonight, she would have a deep, uninterrupted sleep. The perfect remedy after a night at the club.

Monday morning rolled around again far too quickly for Lou's liking. Since she actually liked her job, though, she didn't have too much trouble getting out of bed when her six o'clock alarm went off. She followed her normal weekday routine—a quick slice of toast followed by a bus ride to the gym with her office outfit in her daypack.

The trip into the city centre took only fifteen minutes, followed by a five-minute walk to the fitness club. Once in the gym, she cranked up the volume on her iPod and did her usual set—a mile run followed by some free weights and abs work. She finished off with fifteen minutes on the cross-trainer. The dark-haired barwoman from the club was there again, doing a lengthy run on a treadmill, so Lou made sure to use equipment at the other end of the room. She had no desire to bring a connection to the club into her everyday life. In order for the club to remain an escape, they needed to be kept separate.

An hour later, her muscles burning and her body bathed in sweat, she showered and changed into her work clothes. She walked to the office via Pret for a second breakfast and her first coffee of the day. It was always the same pattern, all planned to keep her interactions with other humans to a level she found bearable.

By eight thirty, she was at her desk, tucked away at the back of the fourth floor, sipping her coffee while she fired up her PC. She supported the electronic purchase order system for this office plus the two offices in Birmingham and Glasgow, about two hundred staff in all. The system had been in use for over a year, so the issues she had to deal with were fairly straightforward.

Today she had ten new tickets, which was a pretty good day. That would mean she would have time to mentally prepare herself for her morning meeting. Lou didn't normally do meetings if she could possibly avoid them, but the company had hired a new business analyst called Stephanie Jackson. She needed to review and map all systems and processes in use throughout the company. Stephanie had finally, after a few persistent emails, pinned Lou down to a meeting.

Lou's nerves got the better of her at about a quarter 'til eleven, and she walked quickly to the toilets, worrying that she might actually be sick. Thankfully she wasn't. Instead, she employed the breathing techniques she had learned to help with situations such as this, where she had to meet and converse with new people. It wasn't a full panic attack. She'd had a couple of those in the past. These were more like anxiety attacks, and she'd become adept at managing them, if not preventing them.

She walked back to her desk and decided it was an Ella moment. Lou loved jazz, especially the female singers from the forties and fifties, although she'd happily listen to anyone and any era.

She sat back and closed her eyes for a moment, letting Ella's velvet voice soothe her.

"Ella. Can't beat her," a woman said in a warm voice, and Lou sat upright with a start, her eyes popping open in shock.

"Sorry! I didn't mean to scare you," the woman said, voice full of concern. Instead of panicking as she normally would, Lou turned and looked up into a face so striking…so beautiful… She nearly forgot to breathe. The woman's lightly tanned skin was framed by dark-blonde hair cut into a bob. Her face was dominated by incredible grey eyes, a strong nose, and plump lips that looked utterly kissable. Lou sat up straighter in her chair. Suddenly aware that she was staring, she stood and clumsily offered her hand, trying to remove that last thought about kissing.

"Hi. I'm Stephanie Jackson, nice to meet you." She took Lou's hand.

"Hi, likewise," mumbled Lou. "Sorry. Lou Meacham, very nice to meet you."

Stephanie smiled and looked a little strangely at Lou as she released their handshake. There was an awkward pause, and Lou had the strangest feeling that Stephanie was checking her out.

She dared to return Stephanie's searching look, and the merest hint of a blush crept across Stephanie's cheeks.

"So," said Stephanie, breaking the contact first and clearing her throat. "Shall we get started?"

Lou nodded as she motioned Stephanie into the spare chair and sat back down alongside her.

Lou got home at her usual time, a little after six, and set about making herself some pasta. Chet Baker was on the iPod, and the music made her think back to her meeting earlier that day. She smiled as she cooked. She and Stephanie had conversed so easily, a first for Lou, especially when initially meeting a person.

Obviously, they'd mostly talked about work, and Stephanie had asked good questions. She even made a couple of suggestions for improvements that Lou was going to look at over the next few days. Lou had, without thinking, left her music playing the whole time they talked and had taken a secret delight in Stephanie's obvious knowledge of the tracks. She even stopped Lou at one point to ask who a particular singer was, expressing clear joy in discovering a new vocalist.

Lou had actually interacted with someone, without stumbling—too much—and without feeling as if she wanted to crawl under the nearest desk and hide. Amazing.

She sat down at the breakfast bar with her food and took a sip from the juice she'd poured a little earlier. It had been so long since she'd tried to interact with another woman outside of the club, and she had no idea how she'd got through the casual chat with Stephanie as well as she had.

She'd been single for about five years when she'd decided to try getting out there again. She'd been lonely, and the loneliness had sunk into her soul so deeply it had fought past the fear and propelled her into action. The first time she'd finally plucked up courage and made it out the door and into a club, she hadn't done too badly. She hadn't actually talked to anyone, just drank a beer at the bar and done a lot of looking. She'd been approached by a few women who asked her to dance, but she'd declined, probably too abruptly, and they'd quickly backed off, looking hurt. She'd regretted her tone but couldn't muster the courage to call them back. She'd gone home after only a couple of hours, but even that brief time had given her a tiny bit more courage. So a few weeks later, she'd tried again. This time, she did dance with someone, but found it so difficult to make eye contact that the woman had eventually drifted away.

She'd talked herself into one more visit a month after that, and that had been the last. She'd accepted dances from a couple of different women, worked really hard at eye contact, but couldn't quite manage the conversation afterwards at the bar. The first woman had just shrugged and wandered off, but the second had taken it personally and had been fairly abusive about Lou's lack of response. Despite a small part of Lou's mind knowing that such intolerance wasn't something she needed in her life, the damage was done. Lou resigned herself to being alone.

Then she'd read about the club in a magazine she'd found at the gym. It was the anonymity that appealed. Knowing she could walk in and, with only a little bravery, find some company even just for an hour. Knowing all that woman would want from her was physical, that she wouldn't have to be witty or clever or have any conversation at all.

She'd still been incredibly nervous when she'd first ventured through the black door. God, what a release it had been that first time. And not just in the physical sense. She had missed sex, of course, but she'd been able to take care of that herself to a certain degree over the years. But what she had missed most was skin and lips and fingers and touching. Intimacy. The club gave her all of that, and she had gone home that first night and cried for about an hour afterwards. The relief had been overwhelming.

For the last year, the club had given Lou joy, comfort, and, yes, intimacy—of a fashion. Now, though, she was starting to recognise that it was a false sense of intimacy, a fleeting glimpse of what could really be. For the first time in years, she yearned for something more, something deeper. She had no idea how to go about finding it, but wanting was a start.

Two days had passed since she'd met Stephanie Jackson, and she couldn't stop thinking about her. *Ridiculous.* First of all, she knew next to nothing about her. Second, she could be straight—she certainly looked it, with her fancy skirt suits, heels, and polished nails. Third, even if she wasn't straight, she might already be involved with someone.

Stupid infatuation. Going nowhere. Get over it.

The phone on her desk rang and startled her.

"Hi Lou, it's Stephanie."

"Oh, hi," she said, her palms instantly sweating.

"I was wondering if I could pop up to see you again. I have a few more questions after going through my notes from our first meeting?"

"Sure, no problem," Lou replied. Her pulse was racing. *Shit, she's coming up here!*

"Great, be there in five."

Lou hung up and immediately started tidying her desk and straightening her clothes, all the while muttering to herself to stop being ridiculous. When Stephanie appeared, she was all business, and a surge of disappointment rose inside her. But, when Stephanie got up to leave half an hour later, she surprised Lou by turning back. Her face was slightly flushed—an adorable addition to her usually professionally masked features.

"Hey, I hope you don't mind me asking, but that singer, Ernestine Anderson, was it?"

Lou nodded.

"Well," continued Stephanie, "I was blown away by her voice, and I was wondering if you had anything I could borrow, maybe take a copy of?" Her voice carried a slight tremor.

"Yeah, I do, but how about I do the copy for you. I can bring it in on Friday if you like?" Lou heard herself say the words, knew they had left her own mouth, yet still couldn't quite believe she'd said them.

"Would you? That would be great! Thanks, I'd really appreciate it." Stephanie's flush deepened a little.

"No worries," said Lou and found herself smiling. Stephanie smiled back, a small smile, but it set off a twinge of…something, deep in Lou's gut.

"Okay, well, I'll see you Friday, then," said Stephanie, suddenly looking a little awkward, and then she was gone.

Lou was left wondering what the hell had just happened. In the space of a week, Stephanie Jackson had unwittingly crowbarred open Lou's armour shell just enough for a tiny chink of light to shine through.

The next morning, when she logged in to check her email, one in particular leapt out at her.

Hi Lou,

I've got a meeting with Tania Goodman in Finance at ten, at her desk on the 5th. I know it's short notice, but it would be really useful if you could join us. Tania's got the budget for the Southampton project, and I'd like you to help us go through the timeline and check we've got all the key areas accounted for. Let me know if you can't do ten, and I'll re-arrange.

Regards,

Stephanie

Lou puffed out a loud breath. Great, so even if she begged off this morning, they'd rearrange the thing anyway to accommodate her. She leaned forward onto her elbows and dropped her forehead into her open palms. She vaguely knew who this Tania was, having seen her present some financial stuff at an IT meeting once before. But she'd never spoken to her directly, and now she'd have to do so in front of Stephanie.

Her heart rate increased, and lines of perspiration formed down the middle of her back. She took a few deep breaths, immediately recognising the start of an anxiety attack and knowing she didn't have long to get it under control.

After about fifteen minutes of using every technique she knew, Lou felt near to normal again. She had to be able to do this.

She fired off a quick one-liner to Stephanie, saying she would see them at ten. Then she sorted through her other emails and worked out the priority of the tickets. Five minutes before the meeting, she took one deep lungful of air and exhaled slowly, stood, and made her way to the stairs.

As she entered the fifth floor, she had a quick look around for Tania—she remembered her as a nicely curvy woman with long auburn hair. Stephanie's voice came from somewhere behind her.

"Hey, Lou, her office is over in that far corner."

Lou turned, masking her features to hide the pleasure she felt at seeing Stephanie. She managed a smile, which Stephanie returned, but hers held little warmth.

"Come on, let's get over there," said Stephanie, walking on immediately and leaving Lou to take a few quick steps to catch her up. Stephanie was all business again today, no hint of the casualness from yesterday. Lou shook her head in confusion. To be blanked off so completely by Stephanie this morning was hurtful. She tightened her armour; after all these years, she was very good at that.

"Have you guys met?" asked Stephanie as they stepped into Tania's office. Lou shook her head. "Okay, Tania Goodman, this is Lou Meacham."

Tania reached out her hand, and Lou nervously shook it, hoping to God her palm wasn't still sweaty. Tania smiled encouragingly, and Lou breathed a sigh of relief, finally remembering to return the smile.

Their meeting took about twenty minutes, and Lou was pleasantly surprised to find Tania an engaging and funny woman who seemed to have twigged that Lou was very shy. She made allowances for that in the way she posed questions to Lou.

During times when Lou didn't need to contribute to the conversation, she looked around Tania's desk space. There were several photos, including one that looked to be a wedding photo. Tania wore a stunning green dress that clung to her curves in all the right places. There was a small bouquet in her hands, and standing next to her, kissing her forehead with a look of total adoration was another woman. She was taller than Tania with thick, dark, spiky hair and amazing blue eyes. She was in a dark suit with a white shirt and an undone bow tie hung on either side of her open collar. Tania was smiling up at her, and they looked so incredibly happy and in love. Lou insides did a little lurch.

"That's my wedding, earlier this year," said Tania softly.

Lou whipped her head round, embarrassed to have been caught staring. Tania was smiling though, and Lou found herself shyly smiling in return.

"You both look so happy," she said before she could censor herself. She blushed at the longing in her tone. Something about the photo, the love that was obvious between the two woman, had struck a deep, aching chord in Lou.

Tania nodded. "We are—it was a lovely day."

Stephanie shuffled her papers on the desk between them and stood up quickly. "Sorry, I need to get back," she said, her voice sounding a little strained. "I'll speak to you both later." She strode off before either Lou or Tania could say anything.

Tania smirked. "Hm, think we made her a bit uncomfortable?"

Lou blushed a little, realising that Tania had clocked that Lou was gay too.

"Actually," continued Tania, ducking her head down a bit and lowering her voice. "I have a question, if you don't mind?" She had an unreadable smile on her face.

Lou shook her head. "No, go ahead." Her heart pounded at the prospect of it being something personal.

"Well, I've just made a big assumption that you're gay too, yeah?" Lou nodded.

"Great! So I'm not the only gay in the village around here; that's a relief." She rushed on before Lou could respond. Tania, she was beginning to realise, was a bit of a force of nature. "Anyway, here's the thing. I got introduced to Stephanie last week, and my gaydar has been giving me all sorts of wonky readings from her ever since. Are you getting the same vibe or is it just me?"

Tania grinned, and Lou couldn't help but smile back. She shook her head.

"I'm afraid my gaydar is a little rusty," she said quietly, startled when Tania let out a chuckle. "I-I don't know how to read her at all, but—" She caught herself. She had been about to tell Tania that she'd thought Stephanie had checked her out on the first day they met.

"What?" Tania's voice this time was gentle and warm. Lou hadn't had a gay friend in such a long time, and although she'd only met Tania half an hour ago, she had already taken to her easily. Maybe having someone like Tania to talk to would be a really good thing. Maybe a little courage now could go a long way.

"Well," said Lou, her voice a little cracked from her nerves. "The thing is, on the first day I met her, last week, I-I could have sworn she checked me out." Lou's face flooded with heat, but all Tania did was raise her eyebrows.

"Well, well. Interesting," murmured Tania.

Lou was so grateful she hadn't teased her, or worse, accused her of being full of herself.

"She is a mystery," continued Tania, her eyes twinkling. "I think you and I should keep an eye on her and see what we can find out, yeah?"

Lou blushed again. She didn't need any encouragement to keep an eye on Stephanie.

Tania looked at her, opened her mouth to speak, and then shut it again.

"What?" asked Lou.

"I... Well, I was just going to say, um..." Tania seemed to be struggling with her words.

Lou made a rolling motion with her hands to encourage her to speak up, her curiosity overcoming her shyness. The action made Tania giggle.

"All right, I'll just say it," said Tania in a rush. "You're incredibly shy, aren't you?"

Lou glanced away and nodded, but before she could respond, Tania was speaking again.

"And you really like Stephanie, don't you?"

Lou's heart pounded in her chest. Oh shit, was it that obvious? What if Stephanie had realised? Was that why she'd been so cold with Lou today?

"Hey, don't panic, please!" Tania's voice was calm, and she tentatively laid a hand on Lou's arm. "I only just realised it as we were speaking now. There's no way she knows, okay?"

Lou dared to meet Tania's gaze and found only friendliness and warmth there. She sighed. Something she couldn't really understand told her Tania would not hurt or belittle her. In fact, her gut instinct told her that Tania could be a really good friend.

"I think she's gorgeous," whispered Lou. "But I am so shy. I have no idea how to go about even finding out if she's gay, never mind if she's single or interested in me. And no, I don't have a working gaydar, but she has given me a couple of very confusing signals, and it's doing my head in."

Tania smiled at her. "I think you and me need to have lunch together today. What do you think?"

A warm flush of pure joy spread through Lou's body. She grinned and nodded.

Lou was in a dilemma. It was Friday night, her preferred night to go to the club. As she sipped her coffee and listened to Billie Holiday, she struggled to come up with the enthusiasm to go or a plan of what she might look for when she got there. She couldn't get Stephanie out of her mind.

Her amazing interaction with Tania yesterday had put her head into a spin too. It was refreshing to sit down to lunch and talk about gay things, which, of course, included her major crush on Stephanie. And talking about Stephanie meant all she could think about for the rest of that day was Stephanie's beautiful face.

Friday was dress-down day in the office, and Stephanie had turned up in jeans and a tight tee shirt that showed off every gorgeous curve.

Lou had managed to look away just before she got caught ogling. She'd chastised herself for being so...*leery*. But God, it had been years since she'd met anyone outside the club who made her look twice, and she couldn't ever remember talking so freely with another woman. Stephanie today had been the same Stephanie she'd talked to on Wednesday—friendly, a little chatty, smiling, and doing that very cute blushing thing again. Something about Stephanie, or at least this version of Stephanie, just put her totally at ease. Something no one else had ever done.

Tania hadn't helped, texting her after lunch.

Just seen the lovely Stephanie in the coffee room. Girl, she's smokin' today, huh?!

Lou had giggled and blushed and then texted back.

Not helping!!! Trying to be Ms Professional here.

Tania's reply had been swift.

Fuck professional! I say go with the lust, much more fun! ;-)

Lou hadn't responded to that one, burying her head in her work for the rest of the day, trying to keep her mind from turning it all over again and again. There were still all those unanswered questions—straight or gay? Involved or not involved? But who was she kidding anyway? Even if she knew all the answers, did she really think she would do anything about it? Of course not. Shit, why couldn't she just be normal? She wanted to be—oh God, how she wanted to be.

She slumped back against the sofa and ran her hands through her hair and then down over her face. She rubbed at her cheeks in frustration. *Don't be ridiculous. Stick with what you know, what you can handle. Anonymous sex in the club is all you're capable of, so just get off your arse, get ready, and go and find a woman to take your mind off Stephanie Jackson.*

Out of the blue, a thought came to her—a very stupid, crazy thought, but one she couldn't push away.

Lou leapt to her feet. Time to get changed. She knew what she needed tonight, knew what the plan would be. She smiled ruefully and went to the bathroom to start the ritual. It certainly wasn't the best plan she'd ever had, but it would fulfill its purpose. She hoped.

She smiled at Mandy, paid her money, and put her things in the locker. Then she walked through to Green, ordered a beer, and found a seat at the central bar. It would take time tonight, she thought, but she'd arrived a little earlier than usual to allow for that.

She watched the action around the room, but her attention never lingered long on any one scene. She was continually observing the room to see who had come in, who was staying, and who fit the bill. She bought a second beer, chose a different seat, and focused on the door, ignoring some obvious signals sent her way by a few of the other patrons.

After about an hour, Lou was wound as tight as a drum, and then *she* walked in. The height wasn't quite right, but the build was. And the hair. The hair was absolutely fucking *perfect,* and that would be enough. It was exactly the same shade as Stephanie's dark blonde and cut in a similar short bob. Lou breathed slowly as she watched the woman—what she did, where she went. When it was obvious she was staying in Green, Lou followed her journey around the room, hoping to make eye contact. The woman never once looked her way, and Lou feared her opportunity would slip by. Taking a deep breath, she stood and walked very deliberately into the woman's path. When she looked up, Lou smiled at her. Her hardened resolve gave her much more confidence than usual, and she gestured to the wall. The woman looked Lou up and down, nodded, and walked to where Lou had indicated. Lou took a deep breath and joined her.

"Hi," said the woman as Lou reached for her hips and pushed her gently back against the wall.

Lou was surprised at her own voracity. She was normally hesitant in starting things, no matter how turned on she might be. But her fantasy was egging her on in a way nothing else had ever done.

"No speaking," Lou whispered, knowing the voice wouldn't be the same, and that would spoil the illusion. She didn't even particularly want to look at the woman, so she leaned in to kiss her and let her imagination take over. She ran her hands into the woman's hair as she deepened the kiss, letting the thick, blonde strands run through her fingers. The woman was very responsive, arching into Lou's touch, groaning when Lou pushed her hands up under her bra to stroke and pinch her small but wonderfully firm breasts. Lou wondered if this was how Stephanie would respond, how she would feel. She let images of Stephanie fill her mind as her hands and mouth roamed over this stranger's body, but as she pushed the woman back, unzipped her jeans, and slipped her fingers inside her, something literally shut off inside Lou. She hesitated as she made to push deeper inside the woman.

Imagination wasn't enough.

This wasn't Stephanie she was touching and kissing. Lou had her fingers inside yet another stranger, and she knew, for sure this time, that this really wasn't the way she wanted to live the rest of her life. She almost sighed out loud at this revelation, as all her desire for the body before her simply melted away. Everything she'd ever needed from this club was now irrevocably altered by this one moment.

It changed everything.

It was bad enough she'd used this woman as a surrogate; she couldn't leave her unsatisfied on top of that. She went through the motions of bringing the woman to a quick orgasm and held her tight as she convulsed with her aftershocks. She politely refused the woman's offer to reciprocate, knowing it wouldn't do anything for her. She didn't want a stranger. She wanted Stephanie. Lou needed to be braver, to step out from behind the safety curtain and put herself in the firing line.

"Are you okay today, Lou? You seem a little on edge—would you rather we went through this another time?" Stephanie stared at Lou in concern.

At least Lou hoped it was concern and not fear. She was acting odd, but she couldn't seem to snap out of it. All she could think about was how gorgeous Stephanie was and how she wanted to get to know her more. A lot more.

"No, it's fine. Sorry, something on my mind. Carry on."

"Okay, if you're sure. So, the figures from—"

"Would you like to go out sometime?"

Oh shit.

Oh fuck, fuck, *fuck*! Where had that come from? Lou blushed deep crimson, mortified at how her mouth had taken over with no direction from her brain. She dared to look at Stephanie and knew she had made a *huge* mistake. Her face showed shock, and to Lou's perception, even a hint of disgust.

"No," said Stephanie abruptly. "I don't think so." She looked everywhere but at Lou.

For her part, Lou just wanted the ground to open up and swallow her.

"Okay, well, um, sorry." Lou looked away, fearful she would cry if the huge lump building in her throat was anything to go by.

"Let's pick this up later, shall we?" said Stephanie, her voice sharp, and she stood and walked away before Lou could say anything else.

Lou lay her head on her desk and closed her eyes. Slowly and carefully, she pushed all her armour back into place, as tight as it would go.

On Friday night, she walked into Green and passed straight through to Blue. She walked with purpose, her head up, her new persona in place. Tonight, she'd had no trouble getting herself mentally ready for a visit to the club. Tonight, she'd disappeared into a cold, unemotional place that she found frighteningly easy to inhabit. Tonight, she'd strapped on before leaving the house, fitting the dildo snuggly into her faded blue jeans, the ones that fit over it best, and she'd slipped a couple of condoms into her left back pocket and small sachets of lube into her back right.

She rarely used a dildo, but tonight it was necessary. Tonight, she couldn't face the emotional intimacy of having her fingers buried inside a woman or her tongue on their clit. Forget about having them do the same to her.

Tonight, she was ready to fuck anyone who wanted it, any which way they wanted it. It didn't matter who as long as they helped her forget.

CHAPTER 10

Manchester, 2013

Mandy pushed open the door to the cafe and spotted Rebecca sitting at one of the small tables in the corner. She looked as beautiful as ever, but even from this distance, Mandy could see something was wrong. Rebecca's face was clouded, her eyes looking dull and red-rimmed. She ordered a latte and marched across to Rebecca. They were meeting in Rebecca's local coffee shop, just round the corner from where she lived off Cheetham Hill Road. It was uber-trendy, and Rebecca had often spoken of its chic appeal. Mandy had barely a glance for the place today as it was clear her friend needed her full attention.

"Hey," she said, tilting her head to one side. "What's up, babes?"

Rebecca sighed and smiled weakly. "Hey, you. Thanks for coming."

"Any time, you know that. So, tell me, what's going on? You sounded pretty upset on the phone, and you look it now."

Rebecca sighed and looked away for a few moments. When she looked back, her eyes were misted with tears.

"James…left me. Three days ago. It seems he and his secretary have been getting…close…for some time now. He's decided that his future is with her, not me, so we're over. Just like that."

"Oh shit," whispered Mandy, reaching across the table to take Rebecca's hand. The tears fell then, and Rebecca tried not to sob out loud but failed. Mandy released Rebecca's hand long enough to dive into her bag for tissues. Rebecca took one and blew her nose. Mandy held her hand and squeezed it tight, patiently waiting for Rebecca to speak again.

"I know we hadn't been together that long, but I thought things were going pretty good. Seems like I was always just a means for him to try and stop thinking about his secretary, only it clearly didn't work."

"Bastard," muttered Mandy and grinned as Rebecca snorted. Fuck, how stupid were these men who kept leaving Rebecca? This was the third one in about seven years now after Phil the prick had practically left her at the altar ten years ago. Didn't they realise what they were giving up? Having got so used to being in unrequited love with Rebecca all these years, Mandy found it surprisingly easy to comfort her friend through these endings, but it always stunned her how these men could walk away from someone so…wonderful.

Rebecca shook her head, her curls bouncing around her shoulders. Although streaked with grey now, they still did stupidly crazy things to Mandy's libido. She clasped her fingers around her latte to ensure she didn't do anything so silly as to reach out and run her hands through the richness of Rebecca's hair. God knew she'd been tempted to do just that more times than she could count over the years.

As Rebecca blew her nose and then wiped at her tears with a fresh tissue, Mandy waited, sensing there was nothing else she really needed to say about James at this point. "Bastard" pretty much summed it up. She watched Rebecca pull herself together while she sipped her coffee.

"So, that's me," said Rebecca quietly after a few minutes. "What's new with you—feel like I haven't seen you in ages."

Mandy nodded. "Yeah, it's been a few weeks, I think. Nothing much to tell—I'm still looking for premises for the new venture but coming up blank so far. It's definitely one of those situations where I'll know it when I see it, you know?"

Rebecca nodded, and smiled. "God, I miss our planning sessions for that place." She laughed. "And if anyone had told me that a few years ago, I'd have died!"

Mandy chuckled. "Well, we can always have another session if you like—you know, go over all the details and make sure we haven't missed anything."

Rebecca smiled. "Do you know what, that might just cheer me up—when can I come over?"

"No, I still say you need a fourth person. Your girls are going to want a break now and then, even if it's just to go to the toilet."

Rebecca's voice was firm but slightly slurred after the three—very large—glasses of red wine.

Mandy grinned. "All right, all right—point taken. Okay, I'll factor in a fourth member of staff. I guess she could also help me out at the front desk or when I need a break too."

"Exactly!" Rebecca waved her glass for emphasis, sloshing a dollop of wine onto the tiled floor beside her. She glanced down at it, then at the papers spread across Mandy's table, and then up at Mandy, her sheepish expression making Mandy's heart do that little lurch it often did when Rebecca was near. "Oops, that was a bit close."

Mandy giggled. "Don't worry, all of this is on my laptop, so if anything got damaged, it's easily replaceable."

Rebecca stood up and stumbled over to the kitchen sink to grab a cloth. Coming back to mop up the wine, she grinned at Mandy. "Have I told you lately how fucking glad I am that you are finally going through with this?"

"No, you haven't, but I'm glad too. And I'm really glad I confided in you what I wanted to do, and you didn't run a mile but have helped me instead." She met Rebecca's warm eyes and swallowed. "It really does mean a lot to me."

"I know," said Rebecca quietly.

Finding the courage to share her plans for a new type of club with Rebecca had been harder than Mandy could have imagined. In telling her what she planned to do, she'd had to tell her why, and the "why" involved revealing a lot more of herself than Rebecca had ever known. That night, six months ago, when they'd both had a bit too much red wine—again—had been scary and cathartic and wonderful, all in equal measures. Rebecca had always known Mandy was lesbian, obviously, but Mandy had been deliberately vague about her love life over the years. The fact that she'd never introduced Rebecca to a girlfriend had not gone unnoticed, but Mandy had led Rebecca to believe that she was simply too busy for a relationship. When Mandy finally confessed all that night, not only did Rebecca not judge Mandy's…proclivities, she got fully on board with Mandy's dream to open a lesbian sex club. Many planning nights later, as they liked to call them, they'd got truly excited about what this club could be.

Going over it all tonight had also helped. They hadn't looked at the whole plan together for about a month, and the distance had let them come at it with fresh eyes.

Rebecca broke the moment between them with a big yawn. "Hey, can I crash here tonight? I'm knackered, and I don't fancy heading out into that right now." She pointed out of the living room windows at the rain that was hammering down.

Mandy cleared her throat, shaking off the emotion of the moment before. "Sure, guest room is made up."

"Then I am going to crash—stick a fork in me, I'm done. See you in the morning, honey."

"You sure? It's early yet, only just past ten."

"Yeah, I know, but I've been really tired lately and hitting the hay early most nights. Must be coming down with something."

"Okay, babes—let me know if you need any painkillers or anything that would help."

"Thanks, gorgeous. Goodnight." And with a wink, Rebecca headed off to the bathroom.

"Hey, you, it's me." Rebecca's voice down the phone line was unnaturally subdued, and it stirred an instant fear in Mandy's belly that she couldn't explain.

"Hey, yourself. What's up?" Mandy tried to keep her fear out of her voice.

"Are you doing anything tonight?"

"Not at all. Want me to come over?"

"Please. Any time after seven, okay?"

"I'll be there one minute after, babes."

When Mandy hopped out of her car in front of Rebecca's flat, she swallowed hard to tamp down the nausea that was swirling in her belly. Call it sixth sense or premonition or just plain old women's intuition, but something was wrong.

She strode up to the main entrance and pressed the bell for Rebecca's flat. The door release buzzed a few moments later, and she hauled open the heavy main door. She took the stairs up to Rebecca's first floor home, and the door was already open for her when she got to it.

Rebecca stood back to let her in, not smiling and not looking Mandy in the eye.

Mandy followed her down the hallway to the living room. There was a bottle of wine and two glasses on the coffee table.

Rebecca saw where her gaze had landed. "Yeah, we might need that."

"What's going on?" Mandy's voice was quiet, but it communicated her concern loud and clear.

Rebecca sat down on one side of the two-seater sofa and patted the other beside her. Mandy sat and took Rebecca's hand in hers.

"Tell me, babes."

Rebecca took a deep breath, head down, and swallowed before speaking. "I need…would like…you to do something for me."

"Anything, you just name it."

Rebecca finally looked at her, and the fear in her eyes made Mandy's stomach heave.

"I found…a lump. At least, I think I did. Before I go to the GP, I was wondering if you…would check for me."

Oh Jesus Christ.

"Babes, this isn't something to play around with. If you think you've got a lump, you should get to the GP right now." Mandy stared at Rebecca, stunned that she would waste time on something so important.

"I can't… I don't want to. I…want there to be a chance that I'm wrong…that it isn't what I think. Please, I need…if there is something, I need to be able to share this with someone who cares about me, not just some GP I don't know from Adam or Eve."

Mandy closed her eyes briefly, her mind spinning. Oh fuck, what if there was something?

Okay, don't panic. Even if there is, there's nothing that says it's cancer, is there? It could be benign. Yes, that's exactly what it could be. Happens all the time.

She opened her eyes and met Rebecca's again. "Okay, let's check, shall we?"

The look of gratitude that swept over Rebecca's face nearly brought tears to her eyes. She could do this. She had to do this—Rebecca needed her. Pushing aside the unbidden and completely inappropriate thought that she was about to see Rebecca topless for the first time, Mandy squeezed Rebecca's hand and then stood up.

"Bedroom, yes?"

Rebecca stood and pulled Mandy into a close hug. "Thanks," she whispered.

Mandy didn't trust herself to speak. She gave Rebecca a squeeze and then stepped back.

They walked to the bedroom in silence. Rebecca switched on the two bedside lamps, casting the room in a warm glow. Then she sat on the edge of the bed, her fingers going to the hem of her jade-green sweater. Mandy noted absently how that sweater was one of her favourites on Rebecca. It brought out the colour of her hazel eyes and contrasted nicely with the colour of her hair. Rebecca pulled the sweater up and over her head and tossed it to the floor. She reached for her bra, and a tightness knotted in Mandy's throat.

All the times she had fantasised about Rebecca undressing in front of her, and now she was. It was all so horribly fucking wrong. She tried to keep her breathing steady, tried not to think of Rebecca's body as a sexual thing, but when Rebecca unhooked the bra and her—God, *perfect*—breasts tumbled out of the satin, it took every ounce of Mandy's strength not to groan out loud.

Rebecca lay back on the bed and rested her arms loosely above her head. Mandy shut her eyes briefly against the sight in front of her. Under any other circumstance, she would have been panting. Willing herself to be the friend that Rebecca needed right now and not the woman who had been in love—and lust—with her for over a decade, she knelt on the bed beside Rebecca's prone body.

Rebecca laid her hand on Mandy's forearm. "Thank you for this," she whispered, her gaze intense. "I know…I know this is asking a lot from you. I'm sorry to put you in this position."

Mandy stared at her. Did Rebecca mean what she thought she meant?

Rebecca nodded slightly, reading the question that Mandy must have inadvertently shown in her facial expression.

"I know," Rebecca whispered. "I've known for years. I'm sorry… I'm sorry I could never be what you needed me to be. But I'm so glad you're my friend."

A tear slid down Mandy's cheek before she realised it had even formed. She closed her eyes. Fuck. She'd always known Rebecca was never going to be interested in her that way. And for Rebecca to acknowledge Mandy's feelings now, of all times, to admit that she'd always known and had never shirked from being Mandy's friend, while asking Mandy to lay hands on her bare breasts—oh, the fucking irony.

She nodded, opened her eyes, and took a deep breath as she gazed at Rebecca's beautiful face. Gently, she pushed Rebecca's arm above her head again and then rubbed her own hands lightly together to warm them. She winked at Rebecca as she did so.

"Can't be touching you with cold hands now, can I?"

Rebecca smiled.

Carefully, slowly, Mandy examined Rebecca's breasts. Ignoring their fullness, the wonderful heft of them in her hands, she firmly pressed and felt her way around both of them. The nipples crinkled as she moved around them.

Oh fuck. Keeping her face neutral, as her mind went reeling, she went back around them both again to be sure.

"Well?" Rebecca's whisper trembled with fear.

Mandy swallowed hard, but her voice broke anyway. "There's more than one."

The funeral was lovely, if a funeral could be called such a thing. Masses of flowers, lots and lots of people, lots and lots of memories shared of a wonderful woman who had touched so many people in her too-short life. After they lowered her coffin into the ground, after everyone had departed for the wake, Mandy stood by the graveside and cried for the first time since that night in Rebecca's flat. She had spent the last three months being strong for Rebecca, and there had been no room for her own tears. Because Rebecca's decline had been swift, there had barely been enough time to get all her affairs in order, as the expression went, and Mandy was glad she'd been there to help Rebecca do just that.

By the time the GP had examined Rebecca, by the time the biopsies had been done, by the time they'd investigated further, the cancer had already spread beyond her lymph nodes and was out of control. They'd tried all they could—chemotherapy, radiotherapy— but all in vain. Rebecca had died early one Thursday morning in a palliative care hospice. Mandy had been with her, holding her hand, telling her how much she loved her, had always loved her, just needing to say the words out loud for once.

Rebecca had smiled weakly up at her, kissed the back of Mandy's hand, and whispered, "Thank you." And then she had drifted off to sleep.

A few minutes later, she was gone.

She wasn't going to the wake. She had made a promise to Rebecca, and she was getting started on that promise right away. Some might call it callous, but it was what she and Rebecca had agreed upon, and she didn't care what anyone else thought. The money from Rebecca's will would be sorted out in a couple months, and added to the inheritance from her dad all those years ago, it left her financially ready to open the sex club.

She'd been astounded when Rebecca had told her it was all hers. Through the years, Rebecca had built up quite a nest egg through some property investments. Once all that was cashed in and taxes paid, there was over half a million coming Mandy's way. Rebecca had insisted, quite forcefully, and had also made Mandy promise that she would use the money to finally start the club she—they—had been planning all this time.

She'd found the property at last and had shown photos to Rebecca, who'd wholeheartedly approved. Now she had some contractors to engage. The builders and decorators were easy. She called in people she'd used when she'd opened her first gay club in the Village seven years previously. She was selling that club on and clearing her debts. Now all she needed to work on was the specialist contractor for the BDSM room. She'd narrowed it down to a choice between two companies and had meetings booked with both of them next week.

It was really happening, at last. Oh, how she wished Rebecca was here to see it, to share it with her. She gazed down at the coffin below her, aware that the cemetery workers were politely waiting to complete their job. She blew one last kiss down at Rebecca, turned, and walked away.

Rebecca might not be with her physically, but she'd be with her in spirit every step she took.

CHAPTER 11

Manchester, present day

Stephanie stepped off the tram and smoothed out her jacket and skirt before doing up her thick woollen coat. The fine dogtooth fabric of the suit always clung so deliciously to her body, more so than any of her other work outfits. She kept this as her "first day" and special occasions suit. She wore it on the days when she needed just a bit more assurance and verve to pull off the Stephanie Jackson charm offensive that such situations demanded. She revelled in it, and she detested it.

Today was her one-month review with the financial director at the insurance company she contracted for. She would give an update on how she'd progressed, and he'd give her feedback on her performance, and hopefully they'd both be in agreement with her staying on for the remainder of her six-month contract. She liked the job. The money was good, and the hours were easy compared to some other contracts she'd had in the last few years. And the first month had gone pretty well work-wise.

It was the other stuff around the job that was a total nightmare.

She sighed as she walked away from the tram stop, braced herself against the bitter November wind, and turned left towards the office. God, how was she supposed deal with the whole Lou situation? It was her own stupid fault. She'd spent years denying her attraction for women, kept it well buried, and never got herself into any awkward situations over it.

She was not gay; she just hadn't met the right guy yet. When she did, the sex would be great, and she'd find those fireworks all her friends raved about.

But meeting Lou had challenged her in a way she wasn't prepared for. She was drawn to her with an…intensity she couldn't begin to explain. The first time she'd met Lou, she'd been nearly speechless. She was stunned at how attractive Lou was and alarmed at her body's response when they simply shook hands.

It was obvious Lou was gay, and yet Stephanie couldn't help herself. She invented more questions to go back and talk to Lou about, leading Lou on. After their meetings, she promised herself she wouldn't do it again. And yet the next day, she'd called Lou, arranged another meeting, and talked about their mutual love of jazz. They laughed and chatted so easily it made her feel utterly at peace inside.

At night, the fantasies crept in, thoughts of Lou's mouth on hers, Lou's fingers on her skin, inside her… She would sit bolt upright in bed, panting and aching, and trying desperately to banish the thoughts, the feelings, the desires. The fears.

And now she had to deal with the fallout.

A few days ago, Lou had asked her out, and she'd been so stunned. She had been inexcusably rude and cruel, and Lou would probably never speak to her again. As she'd walked away from Lou, she'd risked a glance back. Lou's head was on her desk, and she might have been crying. Stephanie had been overcome with shame.

Lou had responded to the signals Stephanie had given her. It had clearly taken a lot for Lou to ask, and Stephanie had treated her appallingly. She hadn't spoken to Lou since, but she would have to soon. They were in the early days of the plan to roll the purchase order system out to the Southampton office, a project Stephanie had been roped into during her first week with the company. They needed to reach a place where they could work together comfortably, and for that to happen, Stephanie needed to apologise for what had occurred last week.

And she needed to work out a way not to be attracted to Lou so that nothing like this reared its ugly head again.

Lou's music greeted her as she approached. *Dexter Gordon.* She took a deep breath and steeled herself.

When she was a few feet from Lou's chair, she said, "Knock, knock."

Lou looked at her with such pain in her eyes… Stephanie nearly cried.

"I'm so sorry," she whispered before her brain could engage to keep the emotion out of her tone. "I shouldn't have been so rude to you last week, and I'm really sorry if I gave you the wrong impression about…us." *Liar! You gave her the right impression; you're just too scared to take a chance on where it will lead you.*

Lou nodded slowly, her blush creeping across her neck and face.

"Can we just forget it—please?" she said in a small voice that ached with something Stephanie couldn't identify.

She longed to wrap Lou in her arms and hold her tight. She clenched her hands at her side. *Stop it. Fight it. You are not gay. You are* not *gay.*

Stephanie nodded briskly and pulled up the spare chair.

"So." Her business persona instantly slotted back in place. "Southampton—did you get the updated figures I sent you after our meeting with Tania?"

Matt rang her on Wednesday night. He had an uncanny ability to know when she was at her lowest.

"Hey, sweet pea, how's life?" His voice, chirpy as ever, instantly put a smile on her face.

"How do you always do this?" she asked, laughing ruefully. "Do you have a sixth sense or something?" She picked up her glass of wine and took a deeply satisfying gulp.

"Darling, of course not. I'm just a gorgeous gay man who is so in tune with his BFF that he knows instinctively when she needs a little pick-me-up."

Stephanie laughed out loud. "Oh, come on, seriously, what's the secret?"

"You were supposed to call me last night. When you miss a call, that's when I know you have something heavy on your mind that needs discussion. So," he continued before Stephanie could even begin to apologise, "Friday night, our place. You bring the wine. Jake will cook."

Matt and Jake lived in a stunning former workman's cottage in Stockport that they had lovingly restored and decorated as only two affluent gay men could do.

Matt Pearce was her best friend from uni. They'd both graduated with honours in their business studies degrees and stayed in Manchester after graduation. By then, Matt and Jake were in a serious relationship. Stephanie stayed because she couldn't face starting anywhere new again, certainly not without Matt, who had become the closest friend she'd ever had.

Despite Matt's sexuality, she'd never admitted to him her doubts about her own and her fears for what it would mean for her life. He'd asked her outright once, drunk at a party, and she'd lied. It was the only time she'd ever lied to him, and he never brought it up again.

Stephanie rang the doorbell to the cottage at just after seven. Matt ushered her in from the cold and grabbed at the wine she held out.

"Shiraz, fabulous. Jake's doing some fancy beef stew, so this will be perfect, thanks."

She leaned in for the proffered hug and allowed herself to be held tight and rocked ever so slightly. She and Matt were the same height, so she rested her chin on his shoulder as he squeezed her gently. She pulled back before the tears fell. They'd been threatening ever since she left work. Probably since about four o'clock, if she was honest.

She'd had a follow-up meeting with Lou on the new project, and it had been so hard. She'd tried to tell herself that Lou looked no more gorgeous in dress-down black skinny jeans and a long-sleeved, figure-hugging white tee shirt. It had a V-neck that dipped down just low enough to give a hint of...other things. When she reached for her highlighter pen, the muscles across her shoulders and back had moved beneath the taut fabric. Stephanie's mouth had gone dry, and she'd wondered what that muscle definition must look like naked. And then she'd nearly choked on her thoughts.

They'd talked for about an hour, and Stephanie had tried to be friendly. She'd asked if Lou had any plans for the weekend and had been met with a look of hurt and a mumbled response about "doing some stuff around the flat." It was so hard to know she was the cause of Lou's pain. Shortly after that, she had left, feeling miserable and without saying much of a goodbye. She'd returned to her office, shut the door, and sat with her head in her hands, trying—and failing dismally—to stop the crazy swirl of thoughts and emotions consuming her brain.

She stepped away from Matt without meeting his gaze and walked through the open lounge to the kitchen area beyond, where Jake pulled her into an equally close hug.

"Hey, gorgeous, long time no see," he said as she stepped back out of the hug. "How about a glass of fizz to start the evening?"

"Lovely," she murmured and leaned against the breakfast bar while Matt reached up for fluted glasses from one of the cabinets on the wall and Jake pulled the chilled bottle of champagne from the fridge.

When they all had a glass in their hands, Matt raised a toast to good friends, and they each took a first hearty swig.

"Perfect," said Stephanie after the cool bubbles slipped down her throat. "Thanks, guys. I really needed this." And then, to her horror, the tears that had been threatening all afternoon spilled out of her eyes without warning. Her boys were both there, holding her close in a hug sandwich, and she couldn't stop the sobs. She cried for what seemed like hours but was probably only a few minutes.

They made comforting little noises while one of them stroked her hair and the other stroked her back. They said nothing as they waited for her to quiet and be still. When she finished, Matt took her hand and led her to the sofa. He pulled her down, and they sat on either side of her.

Jake spoke first. "Time to tell us what's going on?" His voice, although quiet, seemed loud in the hushed circumstances.

She nodded and gratefully accepted the tissue Matt passed to her. She blew her nose and used the second tissue he immediately handed over to wipe her eyes.

She looked up at them, smiling faintly. She couldn't keep it in any longer.

"I've been fighting this so long, and I don't want it to be true. It can't be, but I am getting so tired of fighting, so tired of trying to be something I'm not. And now I've met someone, only I've fucked it up *so* badly she'll probably never want anything to do with me again, and I am so totally lost. I just don't know what to do."

Before Matt could jump in, Jake stilled him with a raised hand. "Let's be clear about this. What exactly are you fighting and why?"

She stared at him, at his kind face filled with compassion, then swallowed hard.

"I think I'm gay, and I don't want to be." She started crying again—oh God, it was just too painful. She didn't want this. She didn't need her life to be complicated by this. Didn't need to risk everything she had built with her parents.

"Why don't you want to be gay?" Jake again—gently, softly, coaxing.

"Because it would just about kill my parents, and I can't do that to them! They mean everything to me, and after what happened with my uncle, I couldn't put them, Dad especially, through it again."

Stephanie's uncle Terry had been spotted having a…liaison…with another man after dark on Clapham Common in London, back in the seventies. Word had quickly spread around their community, and Stephanie's father had soon heard about it. The family row that broke out shortly after was now infamous. Terry bravely came out to his brother, was punched in the face for his "perversion," and then packed a bag and left home. He was now in Australia, living happily in Sydney with his partner. Stephanie's dad hadn't spoken to his brother since.

"But what happened with Terry was in a different age," said Jake. "Society was much less understanding and accepting then. Yes, it was awful for your dad to lose contact with his brother, but do you really think that's what he'd do with you?"

"I don't know, I honestly don't know," she whispered, shredding the tissue in her hands.

She thought of all the bigotry her dad—and by silent acquiescence, her mum—had spouted over the years. The vitriolic outbursts about "those disgusting people," the lectures she'd suffered at age eleven after she'd brought home her best friend from school, Julie. Yes, Julie was a bit of a tomboy, but that meant nothing to Stephanie. Julie was just her best mate. But it had been a massive red flag to her parents and resulted in a ban on ever bringing "that kind of girl" home again. She'd tried to explain it to Julie, but how could she when she didn't understand it herself?

Needless to say, her parents had never met Matt and Jake.

"But what about *you* in all of this?" Matt asked. "What about what you want, what would make *you* happy?" She could tell he was trying really hard to keep his voice calm and steady when clearly his emotions were in danger of getting the better of him.

What did she want? What would make her truly happy?

Unbidden, an image of Lou's face popped into her mind's eye, smiling that gorgeous, shy little smile she wore whenever they talked about non-work stuff. They hadn't spent a huge amount of time together, and she really didn't know Lou all that well, but God, she just felt so *herself* when she let her guard down with Lou. She didn't have to play games or strive to impress. She didn't know if it could ever go anywhere, but deep down, the thought of trying was significantly more exciting than it was terrifying.

She turned to face Matt, took his hand, and squeezed lightly. "I'm sorry I lied to you," she said, then smiled at his confused expression. "That party in our last month of uni. You got drunk and practically begged me to come out. That was the only time I have ever lied to you. But I've been lying to myself for years." She gripped his hand even tighter. "Now, don't scream the place down. But there's a woman I work with called Lou, and I am absolutely crazy about her."

A squeak escaped Matt's lips, and she giggled.

"I sense there is a 'but' at the end of that sentence," prompted Jake, and she looked at him and nodded.

"She asked me out."

This time Matt let out a whoop.

"But," continued Stephanie firmly, "I panicked, said no in a really rude way, and now she will only talk business with me." She sighed. "God, I hurt her so badly—she's really shy. I mean, *painfully* shy. I heard from a few other people at work that she keeps herself shut away in her little cubicle, never speaks to anyone if she can help it, and never socialises with anyone from work. It must have taken *so* much for her to ask me out, and I just slammed it back in her face, all because I was too scared to admit what I was really feeling."

"But can't you tell her? Just say everything you've said to us? Surely if she's as nice as you think, she'll listen?"

"Maybe. But that would require me to have the courage to do it. And she's shutting me out so hard these days, I don't know if she'd let me back in anyway. She may not trust me again. Plus, there's the whole other issue of me being fresh out of the closet and not having a single clue about dating women and…well, you know…the other stuff. Even if I did get to go out with her, she's clearly been out for a while now, so she'd be so much more…experienced than I am, and, well, it would be, you know…embarrassing." *Or worse*, she thought, shuddering inwardly as visions of her worst nightmare crowded her mind.

She'd always struggled with sex and intimacy. Her parents had drummed into her from an early age that sex before marriage was a sin. Although they had tried to raise her with the same degree of Catholic fervour, she had managed to rebel somewhat over the years. She'd had sex with a handful of guys, and each time had been dreadful. And each time she'd hoped it would be better than the last. It never was.

Each time, the act had also left her crawling with shame, a residue no doubt left over from her upbringing. No matter how much she tried to rationalise it, and fight her parents' doctrine, it kept winning through. Sex left her feeling dirty, confused, and…sullied. She dreaded the same would happen if she ever plucked up the courage to be with a woman, dooming her to a life without the intimacy her friends shared with their lovers.

She stood, her stomach churning. "I-I need to use the bathroom. I won't be a minute."

Before they could answer, she walked quickly out of the room and up the stairs. In the bathroom, she splashed cold water on her face and took some deep cleansing breaths. Then she dried her skin and wiped away the small streaks of mascara under her eyes.

She made her way back to the top of the stairs but paused when she heard Matt's raised voice from the room below.

"—can't bear to watch her fuck her life up any more. She's thirty-four next month, and look at her—still fighting what's inside. And for what? So that she doesn't upset Mummy and Daddy? What a waste." The last words fairly spat out of Matt's mouth.

"Hey, it's okay." Jake's voice was quieter. "I totally understand your concerns; you know I do. I'm just not sure *that* club is necessarily the answer."

What were they talking about? What club?

"I know." Matt's voice sounded calmer now. "But I guess I thought that if she tried the physical side of it, it would make her realise what she really wanted, and then she might be more inclined to get out and actually date. God knows, we've got a long list of potential candidates lined up."

Jake laughed. "I know. God, every single lesbian you meet gets added to the bloody Stephanie list. Just don't push too hard with this club idea, though. It would be a pretty bold move for someone who's struggling to come to terms with themselves."

She was intrigued now. Not only about the apparent list of potential lesbians for her to date—the thought made her giggle with the absurdity of it—but also by this mysterious club they had both mentioned.

She made some noise coming down the stairs and re-entered the room to silence from the two men. They looked at her with wide-eyed, overly innocent expressions.

"Are you okay?" asked Jake.

She nodded, blushing a little, but she wasn't sure why. They were all silent again.

Then Matt got the giggles. He raised his eyebrows to Jake and motioned with his head to something across the room.

"No!" said Jake very firmly.

"What's going on?" she asked, looking at first Matt and then Jake.

"Nothing," replied Jake, but as he did so, Matt leapt off the sofa and launched himself at the love seat. Jake tried to grab him, but he wiggled free.

"No, Matt, honestly, that's really not appropriate right now." Jake sounded really annoyed, which shocked Stephanie.

Matt stuck his tongue out at Jake, and Jake stalked off to the kitchen, muttering to himself. When Stephanie looked back at Matt, he was holding out a magazine.

"What's this?" she asked suspiciously.

Matt thrust the magazine into her hand, open to an article, and stood up. "Just read it, darling. I'll get you a top-up for your fizz." And he rushed off to the kitchen area, leaving her staring at the magazine.

It was one of the gay ones that Matt subscribed to. She glanced at the cover, an older issue from the start of the year. She turned back to the small article he'd put in front of her.

The story was about a sex club for lesbians here in Manchester. A darkroom experience for women who wanted anonymous, safe sex with no strings. Mix of clientele—regulars and new, those who were curious about sex with a woman as well as those who had already made that life decision quite comfortably. Three rooms, offering three different experiences, depending on your needs or desires. A code of conduct that all clients agreed to, strongly enforced by the management. "No touch" zones for those who just wanted to watch or weren't quite ready to participate.

She was so engrossed, she barely registered Matt coming back in with a topped-up glass for her.

When she finished reading, she dropped the magazine on the seat beside her, sat back, and sipped her champagne. A multitude of thoughts careened around inside her head. Primarily, the idea appealed. Given that her worst nightmare was how she would react to the physical side of a relationship with a woman, it seemed ideal.

A completely anonymous introduction to sex with a woman. If she realised she really couldn't cope, she could just walk away, and no one would get hurt. Maybe she should try this first, and then if—hopefully, *when*—she could handle it, she could try to restart that fledgling relationship with Lou.

And then she got the giggles. The thought that she could just walk into a club and have sex with some woman she found in there was utterly and completely ridiculous.

She walked into the kitchen, and the boys stared at her expectantly.

"I can see why you wanted me to read it, but seriously, can you see me being brave enough to try it?"

"I told you," muttered Jake to Matt, who poked him in the ribs.

"Look, in theory it's not a bad idea," she continued, trying to mollify Matt, whose expression had now taken on a sad puppy look. "But, funnily enough, one of the things I'm most stuck on is the fact that if I was going to get…intimate…with anyone, it wouldn't be with a stranger. It would be with Lou. I just don't want anyone else, and I can't imagine being…that way…with anyone except her."

She sighed, knowing the deeper truth was more than that, but she wasn't ready to share that with the boys. Not yet. What she said about Lou wasn't a lie. She had no trouble conjuring up all sorts of images of Lou in her head that made her temperature rise.

"Tell us all about her while I dish up," said Jake, turning to grab plates from the rack above the breakfast bar. "She must be pretty special to have broken through those walls you've so carefully built up over the years."

So she told them all about Lou, and the words came gushing out. Without consciously realising it, she had stored away numerous details about Lou in her memory. The way she always sat up a little straighter in her chair whenever Stephanie approached her desk. The way she steepled her fingers when she was deep in thought about something. How slender yet strong those hands looked. The way her smile made Stephanie feel a little tingle deep in her stomach. Her quiet, dry humour—always so startling coming from someone so shy. The inexplicable wave of loneliness that hit Stephanie a few minutes after she'd left Lou's presence. Her gorgeous, beautiful face. Her hot body. She talked on and on, through their starter and on into the main course.

"You *really* like this woman, don't you?" asked Jake, smiling as Stephanie blushed.

"Yes, and I don't think I realised just how much until I sat down to confess all to you guys. I mean, she's constantly been in my thoughts since I met her, but I've been fighting it. Wow." She felt a little dazed and caught Jake sharing a secret smile with Matt.

After the meal, the rest of the evening was spent talking of other things. Stephanie was emotionally drained and needed a change of topic. But later, in the cab on the way home, she found herself thinking of Lou again. Where was she on a Friday night? Who was she with? Presumably she was single, if she'd asked Stephanie out. But did she have friends she went out with? There was so much she didn't know about her and so much more she wanted to know.

Lou got to the club at just after ten. Later than she normally would, but she'd struggled to decide what to do. She was still reeling from her disastrous attempt to get to know Stephanie, and somehow that made her even more desperate to come to the club. Now that she was here, her heart wasn't really in it. She was so torn. She didn't want to lose this place; it had been her escape and was so important to her because of that.

Without it, she really didn't know what else she would do to find…company when she desired it.

She was considering the idea of seeing a counsellor, but that was almost as terrifying as trying to meet a woman outside the boundaries of this building. Opening herself up to some…stranger, trying to explain all that she felt. It made her shudder. But it might be the only way for her to avoid being single for the rest of her life.

She sat in Green with a beer, watching the activity around her and trying to tune her body into it. It was quite busy, with about a dozen couples dotted around the room. She focused on a couple nearby; they were simply kissing, had been for some time now. That stirred something in her. Yes, kissing, for now, would be nice. Just holding someone close, exploring her mouth and lips, feeling her tongue tenderly stroking hers.

The need came from deep inside. It wasn't necessarily a sexual feeling but something far more…emotional. She wondered if any of the single women in here would be amenable to that. She'd have to ask, of course, and that would take a little bravery. But somehow, in wanting it so much, the idea of asking for it wasn't that daunting.

After her last visit here, when she'd been so angry and hurt, she had gone home in a bad way. Yes, she'd had a couple of fucks that night, but they had been even more meaningless than her previous visits. She had gone through the motions and got nothing out of it. She'd let herself be talked into the second one because she couldn't believe it could be any worse than the first. She had been wrong.

Tonight, she needed almost the complete opposite of fucking. She needed connection.

She took another sip of her beer and glanced around the room once more. Her gaze fell on a cute woman tucked into one of the corners. She looked about Lou's height with straight, dark hair that fell just past her shoulders. A nice face—nothing spectacularly beautiful, but with a gentle attractiveness that tugged at Lou. And a body that was full of lovely curves in all the right places—not slim, not perfectly proportioned, but all the sexier for it.

The woman cast furtive glances around the room. She was either new here or a little shy. Or maybe she was a first-timer for a sexual experience with a woman. Lou smiled to herself. They might just work quite nicely together.

She took a deep breath, summoning some courage, and got up off her stool. Abandoning her half-empty beer, she walked slowly over to the woman, allowing her some time to realise that Lou was approaching her and giving her a few moments to get used to the idea.

As she got closer, Lou smiled gently, and the woman smiled back. Lou stopped in front of her, not touching.

"Hey," Lou said, quietly, her voice not shaking too badly. "Mind if I join you?"

The woman, her eyes wide, shook her head slightly, and Lou stepped carefully forward to cup the woman's face in one hand.

"Can I kiss you?" Lou asked. "For now, I just want to kiss; is that okay?" Her voice shook more now, and the woman's posture softened slightly.

After a second, the woman nodded and swallowed hard. Lou carefully pulled the woman into her arms. The woman moaned and tentatively wrapped her arms around Lou's waist. Her whole body was trembling.

Lou studied her. Perhaps lunging in for a deep kiss shouldn't be the next step. Not just yet.

"First time here?" she asked, looking into the woman's lovely brown eyes.

The woman swallowed again. "Yes," she said, her voice a nervous croak. "I mean, I've never... I've always liked women, but I-I've never actually done anything with a woman."

"God, you're really brave coming here," said Lou, gently stroking her face with her fingertips, overwhelmed with tenderness for her. "I'm impressed."

And she was. She couldn't imagine the strength it took to walk in here as a virgin. And she was so glad she'd been the one to go over to her, not one of the more aggressive women who sometimes prowled around in Green.

The woman blushed. "Thanks," she whispered, looking away in embarrassment. "I'm really nervous!"

"It's okay," replied Lou. She gently cupped her chin to pull her face back to meet Lou's gaze again. "We'll only go as far as you want. I'm totally okay with that. I came here tonight not knowing what I wanted, really, so even if all we do is talk, that will be enough for me. Honestly," she finished.

The woman gave her a look of utter disbelief.

"So, what's your name?"

"It's Vero, short for Veronique."

"Hi Vero. I'm Lou."

Vero nodded and huffed out a big breath, clearly trying to ease out some of her nerves.

Lou smiled. Being the strong one for this nervous-yet-brave woman made her feel calmer. Plus, it gave her some confidence. Her shyness and this woman's nerves were a perfect complement to each other. This might just turn out to be exactly what Lou needed to soothe her soul after Stephanie's painful rejection.

The woman squeezed Lou tighter. "God, you feel amazing," she breathed, staring into Lou's eyes. "Even just this feels really good already."

"Yes, it does," murmured Lou, and then she knew it was time, that Vero wanted it enough to overcome her nerves.

Lou dipped her head, and Vero's eyes widened as she did so. Then she brushed her lips ever so gently over the soft plumpness of Vero's small mouth. Vero twitched in her arms, and so she kissed her again, just as softly. The moan that Vero let out made the hairs stand up on the back of her neck.

"Okay?" she asked, pulling back to look at Vero, who was breathing heavily now.

"God, *yes*," said Vero with passion.

She pulled Lou back to her and pressed their lips together in a fierce kiss. Lou groaned and ran her tongue over Vero's bottom lip, asking for entrance, which Vero immediately gave. Their tongues met, and they pulled each other closer. The kiss was long and slow and tender, everything Lou needed it to be. She pulled Vero tighter against her body and lost herself in the warm wetness of Vero's mouth.

The next few days were a struggle for Stephanie. She had opened up one of her deepest secrets, and on the one hand, she felt lighter for it. On the other, she was completely torn over what to do next. A big part of her, despite everything she'd discussed with Matt and Jake, wanted to hide it all away again and save her parents the pain of having a lesbian daughter. Just as importantly, save herself the battle of truly coming to terms with it and doing something about it.

Every time she saw Lou, however, all of that doubt faded and was replaced by well, if she was honest, pure lust—and possibly more. Because of their project, she now had to meet with this gorgeous woman for two to three hour-long meetings each week. They were the three hours a week she looked forward to the most, in spite of the tension that still existed between them.

She had tried—gently, carefully—to break down Lou's resistance again but had got nowhere. Lou had clearly spent a long time protecting herself and was very good at it. And short of confessing everything, which she still wasn't ready for—and certainly not in a workplace setting—she was rapidly running out of ideas. She was secretly hoping that Lou would make it easy for her, that she would suddenly ask her out again. Lou would never do that, though, not after Stephanie had rejected her so completely that first time. And Stephanie had to be honest—even if Lou did ask her out again and they started seeing each other, her biggest fear would still be hanging over her head.

Night-time was the worst. She would laugh at herself sometimes. Her fantasies and dreams led to some frantic masturbation, her orgasms quick and shuddering, her mind full of images of Lou.

And sometimes she would cry, as those thoughts of Lou would be overshadowed by the voices of her parents, vilifying her for her disgusting desires.

"Hi, Matt, got five minutes?"

"For you, sweet pea, always."

She smiled at the term of endearment he'd given her way back when.

"Are you alone? It's kind of personal." Her nerves and fears started to well up, and she swallowed them down hard.

"Ooh, I love a mystery! Give me one sec."

She heard the sound of a door opening, followed by street sounds in the background. Matt was the general manager of a creative design company based in the city—not that he knew much about design itself. After uni, he'd started the company with a couple of friends who did, and they'd been very successful thanks in no small part to his business skills. Their office looked out over St. John's Gardens, and she pictured Matt strolling across the road to gaze into the trees and shrubs laid bare by winter while he talked to her.

She glanced around to make sure no one was within earshot.

"Okay, coast is clear, what's up?"

She hesitated, and he sighed with impatience.

"All right, all right," she said, and her heart started to rise into her throat as she blurted out, "I think I'd like to check out that club. The one in the magazine."

"Holy Mother of God! *Seriously?*" Matt's voice was at least half an octave higher than usual. "Talk about jumping in at the deep end! You could just ask me to take you to a bar one evening, you know?"

"Yes, I know. But this isn't about meeting someone per se, it's more about answering a more…fundamental question for myself."

"What do you mean?"

Stephanie sighed. It was now or never. "I keep going backwards and forwards about not being really sure about all this. One day I think I want to come out, go for it, see where my feelings will take me. The next, I'm cringing at the thought, thinking it's impossible that I could be with a woman *that* way. I didn't tell you guys this part when I saw you. It's kind of hard to explain."

"I'm listening," he said with love and support in his tone.

"I have a number of issues with…sex and intimacy. Not just about being gay, but that's one of the bigger ones. I don't know if you can understand this, but everything that I've ever had to listen to from my parents about how disgusting and vile homosexuality is has really done a bit of a number on me, despite being friends with you guys as a counterpoint to all of that. Somehow, on the rare occasions over the years that I've dared to fantasise about being… physical with a woman, all I can hear is my parents berating me. And it's only made me want to bury all this even deeper."

She paused and was grateful Matt kept his silence.

"But lately, since meeting Lou and having such a strong attraction for her, I've been thinking about it constantly. Although I think I know deep down that I have to do this, that I have to accept who I am and what I want, I really wouldn't want to hurt Lou any more than I already have. The idea of laying it all out to her, maybe going on a date with her, and then freaking out when things got… physical…fills me with complete dread. Because freaking out is a very real possibility. I just couldn't do that to her. I care about her too much already to put her through that."

She paused again, breathing deeply. "So, I'm back to wondering if that club might be a good way to find out if I can let myself be physical with another woman. To see if I can get past the…damage my parents have done and actually let myself experience what it could be like. I know I want it; that isn't the problem. And I know I want Lou, very much. But I have this big psychological hurdle to get past before I can act on that want, and it seems like that might be easier to do in somewhere like that club rather than in the beginnings of a relationship with someone so fragile."

She exhaled a sharp breath. "So, tell me what you think. I've… I've never told another soul about any of this."

Matt's voice was quiet and full of love. "Honey, if you can't tell me, who can you tell?" He sighed. "I had no idea just how bad it was with your parents—"

"I know," she interrupted. "There was no way I wanted to tell you guys all of that."

"I can see why," he murmured. "Okay, look, I know I pushed you about that club recently, but obviously I didn't know any of this when I did. Jake was furious with me, actually. He thought it was completely the wrong tack to take. But like you say, maybe it isn't. I don't need to set you up on a date with anyone, do I? You know who you want to be with already."

Stephanie gazed up at the grey sky above her. "Yes, I do. I'm crazy about Lou, and I would love to be able to tell her that. But not until I've got this…shit out of my system."

"Hey, for what it's worth, I think the fact that you are so wound up by this means you've already won half the battle. The fact that you want to fight this speaks volumes. And yes, I think you are right, honey. There's no way you should lay this on Lou. An anonymous encounter might very well be the answer. Only you can truly know that, but I, and Jake, will support you in whatever you decide to do."

Stephanie felt the tears drop. "Thanks." She wiped roughly at her eyes.

"Hey, sweet pea, don't cry." Matt's whisper in her ear was so tender she thanked God and whoever else for the umpteenth time for bringing him into her life.

They talked some more, about their lives over the last two weeks, and she felt so much better for having called him and telling him everything. Until he put her on the spot.

"So, if you're serious about going to that club, when do you want to go? Presumably you would like a chauffeur as moral support, which is partly why you've called me?"

She laughed, nervously. "Yes, okay, so it's a 'yes, please' to the chauffeur with added moral support! But as to when, I don't know."

"Got any plans on Friday?"

"What, *this* Friday? As in, two days' time?" Her voice sounded strangled even to her own ears.

Matt howled with laughter on the other end of the line.

"Sooner better than later," he said. "Before you have time to change your mind."

All day Friday, Stephanie couldn't concentrate on any of her work. Three times she picked up her mobile to call Matt and cancel, and each time she hung up before he answered. He never called her back either, so she knew *he* knew she was thinking of chickening out and he wasn't going to let her.

She had to do this, and it was now or never. But God, she was terrified. What if she started…something with someone and then unraveled as her parents' words slashed though her brain? How would she get out of it? Was it okay to say no partway through? What if she never even got started and left there with her questions unanswered?

She supposed she could always watch. Then maybe she could gauge how she was coping and take it from there. She calmed down at that thought. That actually sounded like a safe plan, to test the waters without committing too much, too soon.

By the time Matt came to collect her, she was in full panic mode. She had spent over an hour deciding what to wear. What *was* in vogue for a night at a lesbian sex club? Finally, she'd settled on faded, ripped jeans that clung to her legs and ass in all the right ways, a push-up bra, and a tight top with a V-neck that showed off just a hint of her cleavage.

She opened the door to find Matt bouncing on his toes like a kid about to meet Santa Claus. She burst out laughing, and that steadied her nerves a little.

"This is *so* exciting!" he exclaimed as he followed her into the living room of her small apartment.

She sat down on the arm of the sofa and sighed. Her panic returned in nauseating waves.

"I'm so glad you're finding it entertaining," she said snidely. "I am in total fucking meltdown over here, thank you!"

He laughed, sat down next to her, and slipped his arm around her waist.

"You will be absolutely fine. You look red-hot in that outfit, by the way." He paused as Stephanie took a moment to check herself out again. "Look," he continued, his voice serious. "You are smart enough not to put yourself in a situation you can't handle, yes?"

She nodded.

"And you are trying to get some answers to something very important for you and your future tonight? No matter what happens, you need to know, one way or another, right?"

She nodded again, and he reached for her hand. His touch helped calm her nerves.

"There are certain 'rules' that all the clients there follow, so if you just want to start off with maybe watching some girlie stuff, without actually any of the doing, you can, right?"

"Yeah, that's actually the plan I came up with—watch for starters and see how I feel after that."

"Exactly!" he said, a sly grin starting to form on his face. "If you find yourself horny as hell afterwards, you just grab the nearest cute chick you see and let her have her wicked way with you. Easy!"

She thumped his arm. "Not helping!" she said, exasperated.

Matt laughed, hugged her close, and kissed her gently on her forehead.

"Come on, it's going to be fine. Let's go, sweet pea. Time is ticking by."

They drove in mostly silence for the twelve minutes it took to get there. Matt parked near a railway bridge. They were near enough to see the door, but far enough away that it didn't look as though they were checking the place out.

Five minutes after parking, a cab pulled up some hundred yards from the door, and a woman in a long leather coat and leather trousers got out. She smoked a cigarette before she knocked on the black door. A small window in the door slid open. After a few words, she was admitted, and the door closed behind her.

"Do you think there's a secret password or something to get you in?" asked Matt, an impish grin on his face.

"Muppet," she hissed, shoving him in the arm.

"So, how long are you proposing to sit here, ma'am," he said in his best chauffeur's voice.

"Oh God, I don't think I can do this!" she groaned, hanging her head in her hands. What was she thinking? This was crazy. Completely insane. Her heart thumped so loudly in her chest she was surprised she could hear above it.

"Hey, you've come this far," he said softly, all joking set aside. "You've been in agony over this for years. In there, through that door, could be the answers to some fairly fucking chunky questions that could change your life. It's been so upsetting watching you struggle all these years. And hey, I know I'm biased, but I would love for my BFF to be a hot lesbian."

Stephanie snorted.

"But the bottom line is," Matt continued, "I just want you to be happy. From everything you've told us these past couple of weeks, there is a way for you to be much, much happier than you've ever been, if only you can get the answers to those questions. And one of the ways to do that is to step through that door tonight. I know it's hard. Of course it is—all the big shit in life is. But honey, the rewards are so worth it… If you're brave enough."

She looked up at him, truly moved by what he had just said. She reached out to him, and they shared a hug over the handbrake.

"Okay," she said. "Just give me a few minutes to compose myself after that little emotional outburst."

She sat back in her seat again and looked out the window towards the door of the club while silently repeating the words "you can do this, you can."

That's when she saw Lou walking down the street with her head tucked down into her collar against the icy December breeze. In that moment, it felt as though her thundering heart would stop. She sat bolt upright and gasped. Matt stared at her.

"What the fuck?" he said, alarmed, gaze swivelling everywhere to see the source of Stephanie's shock. And then he saw her.

He turned to face Stephanie.

"That's her, isn't it? That's Lou?" he whispered, and Stephanie exhaled, finally, and nodded.

Stephanie's mind was in turmoil. What the hell was *this*? Lou went to this club? Lou, who wouldn't say boo to a goose, was happy to visit a *sex* club? Unless this was her first time, of course. But something in the way she moved made Stephanie think Lou had done this before. She just looked so at ease.

She couldn't work out how that made her feel. Confused, yes. Angry, a little. Jealous—a *lot*. Stupid, she knew, but suddenly she was very jealous of all the women who must have had Lou's attention in there. How close did she get to them? Did she have regulars? Did she walk in there and laugh and…fuck…the night away with her own little harem of willing partners?

And then she stopped as pure, sudden clarity emptied her mind of all that nonsense. Lou came here because she needed to. How else would she interact with anyone? How else would her shyness allow her to meet another woman, to be intimate with another woman? In the club, she could presumably melt into the background, find an anonymous partner and—for what, half an hour, an hour?—completely forget the outside world that scared her so much. In that brief amount of time, she could be whoever she wanted. The wave of compassion that washed over Stephanie at that moment was interrupted by Matt's worried voice.

"Sweetheart, are you okay?"

She tore her gaze away from the door of the club and turned to face him. "I have to find her," she said simply.

She opened the car door and was halfway across the street when he called out to her.

"Are you sure?"

"Yes," she replied without turning back to him.

She strode up to the door of the club and knocked. She was still nervous, but it was low-level now, almost completely overridden by her need to find Lou, to talk to her. To—finally—tell her *everything* and see if they could offer each other what they both really needed. She needed to tell Lou how she felt. And somehow she knew Lou would accept her, and then all of her fears about the physical wouldn't matter any more. Together, they'd be able to work through each of their fears.

The small window in the door opened, and a pair of crisp blue eyes met hers.

"Do you know where you are?" The voice was kind.

"Yes, but I haven't been before. I read about the club in—"

"Ah, yes, the article," interrupted Blue Eyes.

The door release clicked, and the heavy black door opened to admit her. She stepped into a dim hallway, and walked through to let the woman close the door behind her.

"Welcome, I'm Mandy. As you've read the article, do you need me to give you the welcome speech, so to speak?" Mandy smiled, and her expression was reassuring.

"I think I remember most of it. I guess the only thing I'm not sure about is the, er, Red Room. I'm not sure I'd be comfortable in there."

"Easy enough to avoid. The first room you enter is the Green Room. Blue and Red are located through doors off that room. You can't stumble into them by accident." The woman's warm smile matched her soft tone.

Stephanie grinned, amazed at how at ease she already felt. Mandy was very good at her job. She reached into her pocket for her cash.

"It's twenty; is that right?" she asked, pulling out notes.

"Yes, and then you'll just pay for your drinks at the bar. Remember, sitting on a bar stool, either at the bar itself or at the central island is a no-touch zone, okay?"

Mandy's eyes were piercing, and Stephanie had the sudden thought that Mandy could see right through her.

"Yes, thanks," she replied, her voice husky with nerves.

"There are lockers here for your coat." Mandy motioned to a small room behind her.

Stephanie thanked her again, stowed her coat and bag, and pocketed the locker key. Mandy stepped to one side and pointed down the hallway.

"Through that door there, that takes you straight into Green. Enjoy your evening."

Stephanie swallowed a sudden surge of nerves and walked down the hall to the door. Now that she was here, she wanted to find Lou as quickly as she could, before anyone else did. God, what would she do if she got in there and saw Lou…involved with someone? She pushed that thought aside before complete panic could set in.

Mandy smiled as she watched the blonde step through the door into Green. A "virgin," if she was not mistaken, questioning her sexuality and hoping the club would answer that question for her. They'd had plenty of them through the door since they opened last year. Somehow she doubted this one would be active tonight. That was why she'd emphasised the no-touch zones. Mind you, with that face and that figure, she wouldn't be short of offers.

She turned back and stepped into the office. Dee looked at her.

"Wow," said Dee, wiggling her eyebrows in leery jest.

Mandy giggled. "I know. It was almost like sending a lamb to the slaughter. Do you think I should go in after her and make sure she's okay?"

They both chuckled.

"Nah," said Dee. "If she's come this far…"

Stephanie entered the Green Room, breathing deeply to calm her racing heartbeat. The room was dimly lit, similar to the hallway she'd just left. She found herself facing the bar, so she ordered a beer and scanned the room while she waited for her change. She didn't see Lou yet.

Then her focus shifted, and she realised *what* she was seeing. There were three couples against the wall, and they were all…fucking. As far as she could tell, none of the pairings involved Lou. She sat down at the end of the bar and blushed deep to her roots. As she stared at the action in front of her, she took a long gulp of her beer and tried to steady her breathing.

With a jolt, she realised her breathing was uneven not because she was nervous. She was completely turned on.

She watched for a while, gaze flitting from one couple to the next as she tuned in to her body's—and her mind's—response to it all. She watched them kissing, followed their hands as they roamed over and into each other's bodies, and listened to the sounds they made. Her mouth went completely dry. Woman-on-woman sex was hugely arousing to her, and quite possibly—God, who was she kidding? *Definitely*—this was something she wanted to experience for herself. She smiled as she realised thoughts of her parents had not entered her mind once since she'd stepped into the club. Maybe tonight she would be able to banish her demons.

That thought broke her out of her reverie and focused her back on the real reason she was there. She searched the room carefully, especially the single women leaning against the wall, waiting to be approached. None of them was Lou. Then she turned her attention to the four women sat at the central bar. She could only partially see the woman furthest to the right.

From somewhere deep inside, she drew on all her bravery and walked toward the woman. Her heart nearly stopped for the second time that evening when she realised it was Lou. She was suddenly flooded with a range of emotions—fear, desire, and compassion—and had to take a couple of deep breaths before making her wobbly legs carry her the last few steps to the vacant stool next to Lou.

Lou glanced at her, and then, in an action that would have been comical if not for the circumstances, did a double take. Her eyes widened as she stared at Stephanie.

"Hi," said Stephanie nervously, meeting Lou's gaze.

Lou still stared, and Stephanie didn't know what to say. There was such a mix of emotions playing across Lou's face—shock had quickly been replaced by confusion, and now anger was creeping across her features. Lou shook her head slightly.

"What the fuck are you doing here? What is this, some kind of sick game?" Her voice wasn't loud, but the fury in her words sent Stephanie rocking back in her seat. When Lou stood and made as if to walk off, on instinct Stephanie shot out a hand and grabbed Lou's arm.

"Please, let me explain," she said. She let go of Lou's arm and clasped her hands together to stop them from shaking. "Please? I promise I haven't come here to hurt you, or play games. I really need to talk to you."

There was an awful pause. In the end, to Stephanie's huge relief, Lou motioned with her head to the main bar behind them. She turned abruptly, and Stephanie followed her. Lou's shoulders were tense in the tight tee shirt she wore. Once at the bar, they sat back down alongside each other, politely waving off the cute blonde barwoman as she approached. Stephanie opened her mouth to speak, but Lou spoke first.

"Why are you here?" she whispered. Her voice ached with such pain that tears welled up in the back of Stephanie's throat.

The words came tumbling out. "I...I've been fighting who I really am, fighting for such a long time, and I can't do it anymore. Since I met you, I've realised what I really want, and I was terrified I'd hurt you too much by rejecting you that time you asked me out. You got caught in the crossfire of my struggle, and I never meant for that to happen." She paused and took a sip of beer. Lou waited, but her face had softened a little, which encouraged Stephanie to plough on. "The thing is, I'm... Oh God," she whispered. "I'm hugely attracted to you, can't stop thinking about you, actually, and..." She needed to plunge on, needed to lay it all on the line. "And I was wondering if you could forgive me and maybe we could start again, go out sometime, see where we can take this."

Lou's expression returned to one of shock, and she took a few swallows of her beer before speaking. "I think I was so wrapped up in my own insecurities, I didn't stop to think that you might have demons of your own. I'm sorry if—"

Her words stunned Stephanie. "No! Please, don't apologise to me, you have done *nothing* wrong in this. Nothing. I knew how shy you were. I *knew* how much it took for you to ask me out, but I was so... God, so rude to you! I'm so ashamed of how I spoke to you, and I never meant to cause you so much confusion."

Lou reached out then and gently laid her hand on Stephanie's bare arm. The heat of her fingers on Stephanie's skin made her breath catch. A ripple of desire snaked its way down her body to land somewhere deep inside her. She met Lou's gaze and found, for the first time tonight, warmth there, along with the hint of a smile around her eyes.

"I think you and I can stop apologising to each other now, don't you?" said Lou.

Stephanie nodded and smiled.

"But, I have to ask," continued Lou. "What are you here for? You say you're attracted to me, but you came to a sex club on your own. Your words don't fit your actions, and...I don't know which to believe." Lou looked confused and pained.

Stephanie knew the next words out of her mouth were fundamentally important if she was ever going to convince Lou to take a chance on there being something between them. She took a deep breath. "Okay, first, I couldn't ever imagine telling you how I felt about you. Or even a situation where that might be possible. You had shut me out, quite rightly, and I couldn't find a way back in. Second, I was still coming to terms with my sexuality, and a friend suggested this would be a good way to find out if I could really...be physical with a woman. I...I didn't want to date someone, get to the intimate stage, and run out on her. That would be awful. I-I have some issues with the physical side of things. Or at least until tonight I thought I did." She smiled ruefully as heat crept over her face. "I'm really not sure that's true now. But when I first decided to come here, I figured if I changed my mind or couldn't cope with it, it wouldn't matter so much if I was with a stranger."

Lou nodded slowly and dropped her gaze to the beer bottle in her hands. Stephanie waited, giving her time to process what she had heard. Lou finally lifted her haunted eyes and said, "Are you disgusted by me being here?"

"God, no!" replied Stephanie forcefully. "I think I understand why you come here, and I'm glad you've been able to find this."

Lou inhaled sharply, her relief palpable, and then she finally smiled her full, glorious smile, the one that utterly melted Stephanie's insides.

"Thank you," said Lou, obviously relieved, and then she snorted out a laugh, tipped her head back, and gazed at the ceiling. "God, this is just crazy. I can't believe I'm sitting here with you having *this* conversation in *this* club." She brought her head back down and turned to look directly into Stephanie's eyes. "I-I've...liked you since I first met you, but you know what my problem is. This isn't going to be easy for me."

Stephanie shivered from the intensity in Lou's eyes. She reached out a hand to touch Lou's arm. "I know," said Stephanie. "But actually, don't you think that suits me? I really...like you too, but I need to take this...us...slowly. I've got a lot to discover about myself, so maybe you are just perfect. If you were all full of yourself and jumped my bones, I'd probably run a mile."

Lou laughed and gazed into Stephanie's eyes, and Stephanie laughed with her. The craziness of the evening was catching up with her. Then, somehow, they were holding hands, and an extraordinary jolt of desire struck Stephanie again, just from that simple touch. She stopped laughing. Lou looked at her, looked down at their hands, and sighed. She looked back up into Stephanie's eyes.

"So what now?" Lou swallowed. "You came here for a purpose—do you still need to go through with that?" Her tone was neutral, if a little forced.

"No," whispered Stephanie, her throat suddenly tight. She gazed at the stunning woman in front of her, shaking her head slightly as all her fear faded to nothing and was replaced by pure desire, hot and all-consuming, coursing through her body with a strength that left her aching. For all her talk about needing things to go slow, the feel of Lou's warm hand in hers sent all ideas of slow out the window.

"I don't. I don't need sex with a stranger to figure out what I can cope with...to figure out what I want. I know what I want. I want... you."

Lou gave a small groan, and a thrill shot through Stephanie at the sound. Her breath caught as Lou slowly, cautiously, reached out a hand and, with shaking fingertips, stroked Stephanie's face in a lazy, languorous line from her eyebrow, down her cheek to her lips. There was a discreet cough behind them. They both turned in a daze to find the barwoman leaning on her elbows next to them.

"Sorry, guys, I can tell you two know each other, but rules are rules—no touchy stuff at the bar, okay?"

Lou laughed, blushing, and dropped her hand. "Sorry... completely forgot where we were."

The barwoman winked and moved away.

Stephanie waited for Lou to meet her gaze again. She trembled from that merest of touches along her face, and all sorts of crazy thoughts rampaged through her brain. All sorts of good thoughts and nothing negative or scary or damaging. It was as if that brief touch of Lou's fingertips had somehow opened a floodgate, and she was having a *very* hard time fighting the urge to grab Lou and...do things to her.

And then, as if in slow motion, Lou stood, took hold of Stephanie's hand, and pulled her to her feet. She led her away from the bar and into the main room. Stephanie didn't resist. She didn't see anyone else, didn't hear any sounds; all her senses were targeted only at Lou leading her to a space on the wall. Lou turned, placed a hand gently on Stephanie's hip and eased her back against the cool brick, never taking her gaze off her. Stephanie pressed back as Lou moved closer. Her heart hammered under her ribs, and her body thrummed with an anticipation she'd never known before.

"I know we said slow," said Lou. "But all I want to do right now is kiss you, and I think you want that too, but if—"

Stephanie stopped her words with a gentle finger on Lou's lips. Even just that simple touch sent exquisite pulses of want shimmering through her body. The heat of Lou's hand searing through her jeans and the soft whisper of her words were a heady mix of nerves that made Stephanie tingle. Lou was pushing her own boundaries here, and although it was taking a lot, Stephanie loved that Lou was willing to try so hard for her.

"Kiss me," she whispered, shocked at how much she wanted it, needed it.

Lou bent her head. Her breath was hot on Stephanie's mouth in the moment before their lips touched. It was feather light, but oh *God*, it set off a firestorm of feeling through every cell in her body. Lou kissed her again, lingering longer this time, yet still so soft, so careful.

And then Stephanie didn't need careful anymore. Just these brief kisses had banished any last doubts or fears she'd ever had about being physical with another woman. The want running through her veins, scorching her body, suffocating all the mental damage her parents' vitriol had ever done to her, was testament to that.

When Lou's lips touched hers a third time, she moaned, opened her mouth, and Lou's tongue slipped in between her lips, met hers, and began to dance. Stephanie felt as if she might explode. Lou moaned and grabbed two handfuls of Stephanie's top, pulling her tighter as she deepened the kiss. Stephanie went willingly, throwing her arms around Lou's shoulders and pressing her body up against Lou's.

Stephanie ran her fingers into Lou's short hair, gripping tight where she could to bring them even closer together. She pushed her tongue deep into Lou's mouth, finding the passion in herself that had been dormant all these years. Lou kissed her with a ferocity that sent sparks shooting down to her toes. She felt herself getting wet, soaked in fact, and nearly laughed at the joy that discovery gave her. All her adult life, she had waited for the fireworks, and now here they were. And they were beyond anything she had ever dared to imagine.

Lou eased away slightly, slowly backing out of the kiss. She panted heavily. Stephanie's own breathing was haphazard, frantic. Her hands were in Lou's hair, urging her to come back for more.

"Wait," whispered Lou. "I'm… God, I'm in real trouble here. We said slow, but I am one kiss away from tearing your clothes off. We have to stop, cool off for a while."

Stephanie smiled shyly and shook her head. "Slow went out the window the minute you kissed me," she said quietly. "I want you so much right now, I am not going to stop you if you do start tearing my clothes off." The thought filled her with thrilling anticipation.

Lou groaned, and her hands clenched in the fabric of Stephanie's top again. She bent her head and crushed Stephanie's mouth with a fierce kiss, her tongue probing and teasing, triggering another flood of juice from Stephanie's throbbing cunt. And then Lou stopped, took a breath, and her mouth moved to Stephanie's ear.

"Not here," she whispered. "It isn't right. I…I want you to be more than this to me, to be…different from everything I've ever done here."

She raised her head then and looked tentatively at Stephanie, who smiled and nodded in understanding. She kissed Lou briefly. God, she loved the feel of Lou's mouth on hers. She found Lou's ear and whispered, "Take me to your place?"

Lou raised her head and swallowed nervously. "I've…I've never… at my place," she confessed, her cheeks tinged pink in the low light.

"Hey, it's okay. I just assumed you'd be more comfortable there," said Stephanie, softly. "We can go to my place if you like?" Deep inside Stephanie's mind, she wondered just who the heck she was to be so bold; she was loving this new version of herself.

Lou shut her eyes for a moment, then exhaled. As she opened her eyes again, she smiled widely. With that, Stephanie knew they'd just crossed a big hurdle. They were going to be all right.

"I'd love it if you came back to mine," said Lou, kissing her softly. "Please?"

Stephanie kissed her deeply in response and then pulled away and reached for Lou's hand. "Lead on," she whispered, her body trembling with a delicious mix of nerves and excitement.

Mandy watched in quiet amusement as the nervous blonde virgin who'd only arrived about thirty minutes ago walked out of Green with that gorgeous dark-haired regular, Lou. It had taken her months to get Lou to respond to her friendly overtures, to find out her name, to share more than a quick smile when Lou appeared each Friday.

They retrieved their coats from the locker room, and there was something a little different in the way they looked at each other and interacted with each other. They had a familiarity about them that they wouldn't get from less than thirty minutes of acquaintance, and Mandy suddenly twigged they must know each other from elsewhere. Oh, how cute—had they stumbled across each other here and realised they wanted to explore something more than a quickie in the club? She smiled, laughing at her repressed romantic self. Looking at the adoring looks these two were giving each other, she sincerely hoped that was exactly what was going on here.

Rebecca would laugh, dig her in the ribs, and call her a big softie. Mandy chuckled as Lou shyly took the blonde's hand and then, in true chivalrous fashion, opened the door for her. She chuckled some more when the blonde blushed slightly but looked at Lou with nothing short of reverence as they stepped out onto the dark street together.

Damn, those two were seriously cute. And something told Mandy she'd just lost a regular punter.

She turned back to the office as the front door shut. Dee was grinning.

"Did our gorgeous virgin just pull in record time?"

Mandy nodded, matching Dee's grin. "But there's more going on there, I think. Anyway, just going for a stroll," she said.

Dee smiled and waved her off.

Mandy entered Green and walked over to the bar. Cassie was serving a curvy little redhead in a short skirt, pouring her a glass of white wine. Mandy waited, taking in the atmosphere in the room. It was reasonably busy, and it looked as though nearly everyone was paired up. Good. She hated seeing too many women unoccupied whenever she did her strolls, as she called them.

"Hey, boss," said Cassie, next to her. The redhead wandered off into the main room. Mandy turned to face Cassie, smiling.

"How's things? Seems a good crowd."

"Yeah, it's been good. Lots of coming and going between here and Blue, I think."

Mandy nodded, turning her gaze back to the room.

"Good," she murmured and then wandered off, through Green and into Blue.

Still holding hands, Lou and Stephanie left the club and wandered up to the main road to flag a cab. They rode in silence with their hands tightly locked together as they shot shy glances at each other. The longer the journey went on, the more nervous Stephanie became, regardless of how their kisses back in the club had made her feel. She was about to get naked with another woman, and she was fearful she wouldn't know what to do, that she would fumble around like a teenager. Just as she started to go into a little panic, Lou squeezed her hand, and Stephanie looked across at her. Lou's smile was so warm, her expression so understanding, Stephanie wondered just how she had known. She was grateful that she had.

Lou paid the cabbie and led Stephanie up to the second floor, not once letting go of her hand. Inside the flat, they both kicked off their boots in silence, and then Lou reached out a hand. Stephanie exhaled and stepped forward.

Without speaking, Lou unzipped Stephanie's coat, turned her to pull the coat off from behind, and threw it casually onto the sofa nearby. Lou's breath tickled on her neck, and Stephanie shivered with desire and then moaned softly when Lou's lips started a sensuous journey across the back of her neck and up into her hairline. Her body hummed with a physical yearning she'd never, ever experienced.

"You are so beautiful," murmured Lou in between kisses.

Tears pricked at Stephanie's eyes, and she blinked them back. The emotion of being here, now, threatened to engulf her. She swallowed, pushed her thoughts away, and concentrated on what was happening to her body right now.

Lou shrugged out of her own coat and dropped it to the floor, and then Lou wrapped her arms around her waist, pulled her back, and kissed her neck more insistently. Hot waves of need washed through Stephanie. She turned in Lou's arms, needing her mouth on hers, and they both whimpered softly.

As the kiss deepened, Lou pulled gently at her top, tugging it out of her jeans, and then, oh God, Lou's hands were on her skin, roaming over her abdomen, around to her back, and then returning to move upwards gently. When Lou's fingers ran over the lace of her bra, she gasped and arched into Lou, needing, *craving*, more. Her nipples tightened underneath the lace, underneath Lou's hands, and she wondered how she was still standing.

Lou lifted her head, removed her hands from under Stephanie's top, and pulled her towards the bedroom.

"Okay?" asked Lou.

"Yes," Stephanie replied, smiling as she squeezed Lou's hand in reassurance, although not sure if for herself or for Lou. Lou switched on the bedside lamp, and they lay on the bed. Stephanie took Lou's hand and boldly placed it under her top. "Where were we?" she asked.

"Here, I think." Lou smiled shyly but with a deliciously naughty sparkle in her eyes as she cupped Stephanie's breasts.

"I want to touch you," Stephanie murmured.

She watched, entranced, as Lou stood to peel off her shirt and then, more shyly, her bra. Stephanie groaned and reached out, cradling Lou just below her breasts. She stared at the perfect shape of them, the dark nipples hardening under her gaze, crinkling in a way that made her cunt ache. She moved her thumbs against Lou's nipples, rubbing them slowly, enjoying the feel of them and the way they responded to her touch. Lou gasped as she lowered her mouth and tasted her breast. Stephanie licked and sucked and pulled the hardened tip with her teeth and lips, and she knew, with absolute certainty, this was what she truly wanted, where she absolutely needed to be.

Lou grabbed her shoulders, and Stephanie looked up at her.

"I want you naked, now."

Stephanie didn't hesitate; the desire in Lou's voice sent sparks shooting through her belly to her cunt. Stephanie yanked off her top and let Lou reach behind her to undo her bra. She pressed herself into Lou's hands as she cupped her naked breasts, and they kissed, slowly and deeply. Stephanie went to unzip her jeans, but as her fingers brushed down her belly, they rubbed over the zip of Lou's jeans. Lou let out a soft moan, and Stephanie lingered and caressed and dipped her hand down deeper, feeling Lou's moist heat even through the denim.

She felt no shame, no embarrassment, and no coyness. She knew exactly what she desired, and she couldn't believe she'd denied herself this for so long.

She pulled Lou's zip down to slide the jeans over her hips and off her entirely. Lou stood in front of her in nothing but a black lacy G-string. Her toned body looked amazing in the soft light, and Stephanie didn't think she'd ever seen anything sexier. She ran her gaze over the full length of Lou's body. She reached out a finger to trace the tattoo on Lou's right thigh—a serpent twining its way up her leg from just above the knee to her hip. Lou twitched beneath her touch.

"God, you're gorgeous," Stephanie whispered, and she let her hands wander all over Lou's skin and muscles, revelling in Lou's small gasps of pleasure. She undid her own jeans and stepped out of them, and then Lou was pulling at the waistband of her underwear. Stephanie trembled as Lou peeled her underwear down and off. Stephanie stepped away, lay down on the bed, and watched breathlessly as Lou removed her own G-string. Then Lou fit her body on top of Stephanie's, and Stephanie sighed, marvelling at the feel of Lou's soft, hot skin on her own.

"Jesus," she murmured as Lou moved gently up and down over the full length of Stephanie's naked form. "You feel incredible."

Lou moaned, muttering something indecipherable, and then her mouth was on Stephanie's, her hands clutched tightly in Stephanie's hair.

They kissed and kissed, and Lou caressed and stroked Stephanie's body until she was so turned on she almost couldn't take any more. Lou used her lips to travel down Stephanie's body from her neck to her ankles, licking and sucking and making Stephanie arch and moan and beg. Stephanie stifled a cry and arched her back when Lou ran her tongue up her thigh to her pussy.

She began with long, slow licks, going from entrance to clit and back again, slow and firm. Then she pushed inside Stephanie with her tongue, and Stephanie cried out, unable to believe the intensity of the pleasure now swimming through her body. She came, embarrassingly quickly, and clutched at Lou as spasm after spasm ripped through her limbs.

"Oh God," she whispered. "Sorry, that was ridiculously fast." She blushed, but Lou pushed herself up Stephanie's body and lay over her again, and she was smiling.

"I don't care." Lou grinned and kissed her. "I loved it, loved knowing I could make you feel like that." She kissed Stephanie again. Tasting herself on Lou's lips kick-started Stephanie's desire, and all she could think about was what Lou might taste like. She rolled Lou onto her back, reversing their positions.

Hesitantly at first, but gaining in confidence the more she did and the more Lou responded, Stephanie taught herself Lou's body. She licked and kissed and touched and stroked, working her way downwards, enjoying those pliant breasts centred with hard nipples, the wonderfully firm abs, and that deliciously flat stomach, until she reached her goal. Lou groaned as Stephanie nibbled the inside of her thighs. She breathed in Lou's scent, her own wetness increasing again as she did so. And then she shyly dipped her tongue into Lou's juices and licked and tasted. She moaned at the sweetness of it, the rightness of how it felt, and she sunk her tongue deep into Lou and began slowly fucking her.

Lou called out her name over and over and writhed underneath Stephanie's tongue. When she came, her thighs gripped the sides of Stephanie's head and powerful spikes of want throbbed between Stephanie's legs. She slid her body up over Lou's until she was facing her again.

"Please," she moaned. "Inside me?"

And Lou, despite her lungs heaving deeply in the aftermath of her own orgasm, moved her hand between Stephanie's legs and plunged inside her, first with one finger, and then adding another. Stephanie rocked on Lou's fingers, riding her body up and down Lou's. Sweat pooled between them as they both gasped for breath. Her orgasm built slowly this time, like liquid honey oozing all over her body, and when it came, it wrenched a long, guttural moan from deep in her throat. Lou's free arm tightened around her waist and held her close. She collapsed across Lou, chest pounding.

When she could eventually move her head, she lifted it just enough to meet Lou's gaze.

"Incredible," she murmured against Lou's lips. "Just beyond everything I ever imagined."

And Lou squeezed her close again, her mouth opening against Stephanie's as their soft kiss became frantic and their desire flared hot again. Stephanie pushed Lou's arms up above her head, pinned her to the bed, and kissed her hard. Lou groaned and squirmed beneath her, gasping out her need, which Stephanie obliged by slipping a finger slowly into Lou's cunt. The wet heat that enveloped her left her breathless. She slowly fucked Lou, watching her face intently. Lou's eyes were barely open, her cheeks flushed, beads of sweat on her brow. Stephanie leaned over to kiss her as she pushed a second finger deep inside.

"Oh God, *yes*." Lou threw her head back. "Don't stop…please… don't stop."

Stephanie fucked her harder and deeper and held her tight as she came. Lou slumped back on the bed beneath her, and Stephanie rested her head on Lou's breasts.

They lay quietly, limbs askew, as Lou softly kissed her hair. Stephanie felt torn open, as if she were somehow starting life all over again with a whole new set of instructions. It was wonderful.

"I can't believe how that felt," she whispered eventually, and Lou smiled against her forehead. "You... God, just looking at you, I want to do all of that over and over again." She reached for Lou's nipple and stroked gently, almost involuntarily. She smiled as Lou moaned softly.

"So," began Lou, hesitantly, "you might...um, might be interested in doing this again? I mean...not just a one-night stand?"

"Are you crazy? I could have a hundred nights of you, a thousand..." responded Stephanie without thinking, pressing closer to Lou to emphasise her feelings. And then she wondered if her words might be a bit too much too soon for her shy lover—*lover*— and raised her head to see if she needed to apologise, only to be met by a stunned but grinning Lou.

"Wow. I never... I couldn't have imagined this would be possible after that time you shot me down."

"Well, believe it now, please." She raised her head a little more to look directly at Lou. "And before you ask, it's not just about the incredible sex—I'm not just experimenting here, in case that's what you're worried about." She saw the look of relief that quickly flashed across Lou's face and reached up to kiss her. "Yes, I've been struggling with my sexuality for years, but this is all about you. I've felt really connected to you since the minute we met. It was part of the problem of coming to terms with this—realising that I could imagine something more with you. Maybe a...relationship. When we talk about music or cooking or any of the other non-work stuff, I just feel...I don't know, just calm and relaxed and myself. You make me feel like me. The real me."

Lou smiled and kissed her tenderly.

"You are amazing, so confident in saying stuff like that," whispered Lou. "I...I have been feeling the same way, but it would have taken me months to tell you."

Stephanie snorted. "Trust me, this confidence is surprising me as much as you. I didn't know I had it in me."

Lou smiled at her, and Stephanie reached up for another kiss just because she could.

"Lou, why are you so shy?" Stephanie wrapped her arms tighter around Lou's slender form.

"God, I don't really know. I just always have been. Never been able to say two words to anyone without blushing or having my throat close up in fear." She paused. "Family stuff didn't help. But let's save that for another time."

Stephanie cupped Lou's face and stroked the line of her jaw. She wondered what family drama had played such a big part in Lou's history. Clearly, it had shaped Lou as much as her own had. A shiver ran through her body. Suddenly, memories of her uncle Terry, and all the anger and bigotry, tumbled through Stephanie's mind. She forced those thoughts away—nothing like that needed to intrude on what she was sharing with Lou now.

"You okay? Cold?" Lou reached for the duvet and pulled it higher up their entwined bodies.

Stephanie shook her head but snuggled closer to Lou anyway.

"Just…my own stuff." She kissed Lou's chest. "Let's tell each other, one day. I really want to know you, Lou. All of you."

"I'd like that too," replied Lou, her smile wide. "I want you to know me, to know all about me. Just the same as I want to know you. In all the talking we've done at the office, I've found it so easy to be with you."

She suddenly laughed, and Stephanie looked up at her.

"What?"

Lou blushed. "I was just thinking about work. About being with you there, you know, now that we've done this. How am I supposed to keep my hands off you in the office?"

Stephanie grinned. "Oh dear, I hadn't thought of that. Hm." She ran a hand down the length of Lou's warm torso. "Maybe we'll have to find secret places we could meet. I think the back stairway is hardly ever used." An image of them flashed into her mind—wrapped up in each other on the stairway, pushed against a wall, knowing someone could interrupt them at any minute but unable to stop, fingers seeking wet heat... She swallowed against the arousal that steamrolled across her body.

Lou shuddered, and goose bumps broke out on her skin underneath Stephanie's touch.

"You like?" Stephanie's voice took on a seductive huskiness she didn't know she possessed.

"Mm, very much."

Lou placed a hand on Stephanie's ass and began rubbing slow circles across it. She teased Stephanie, her fingers occasionally dipping down to where her thighs met.

"You're like magic," murmured Lou after a few moments. "I don't know how you did it, but somehow something about you made me forget all my other crap, made me almost forget how shy I was." She chuckled. "Well, until you knocked me back, of course..."

Stephanie poked her in the ribs. "Something tells me I am going to have to make that up to you for a while, huh?"

Lou smiled slyly. "Maybe..."

Stephanie grinned, raised herself up on her elbows, and leaned in for a kiss that started softly but quickly became anything but.

"I think I'll start now, then," she murmured and let her tongue drift down Lou's neck, across her collarbone, and onto her breasts.

"Oh...good start..."

Stephanie woke at daybreak, desperate for a pee. Lou was fast asleep beside her, and she eased herself gently out from the bed and carefully left the room to go in search of a bathroom. Once she'd taken care of that, she stretched a few times in front of the bathroom mirror, grinning inanely at her own reflection. *Oh, my God, what a night.* She chuckled—she'd had no idea it was possible to feel that good, that extraordinary, with another human being. Why, oh why, had she waited so long to find this? Well, no point torturing herself about that now—she just needed to be thankful she *had* found it and with someone as wonderful as Lou.

She left the bathroom and headed for the kitchen. She smiled to herself. She wanted to make breakfast in bed for Lou, surprise her, look after her. She had such feelings of…tenderness towards her. It made her feel all quivery inside. She never knew she could be such a romantic fool.

The kitchen was a small open-plan space off the living room, with a narrow breakfast bar separating the two areas. She glanced around at her surroundings, noting the cool, minimalist furniture, which didn't surprise her. Some gorgeous pieces of artwork were sprinkled around the room as well. They were full of warmth and passion, which did surprise her a little. She thought a bit more closely about it, and about the gorgeous woman she had just spent an incredibly passionate night with, and then it made sense.

She turned back to the kitchen area and quietly set about opening cupboards. She found teabags and mugs and filled the kettle. She'd just discovered a nice crusty loaf in a bread bin and was hunting for a bread knife when the bedroom door crashed open. She yelped with fright and dropped the loaf on the countertop. She whipped round to find a stunned and slightly bedraggled-looking Lou framed in the living room doorway.

Her mind registered the panicked look on Lou's face, but the rest of her couldn't help but notice the magnificent sight of that toned, lean body braced by two outstretched arms gripping the door frame. Muscles flexed, breasts perfectly pert, and legs slightly parted. Wetness pooled between her legs before her brain took charge and told her to deal with the panic Lou was expressing.

"God, you scared me! Are you okay?" asked Stephanie, gently.

Lou's eyes were a little wild as her gaze flitted from Stephanie to the tea things out on the counter and the bread nearby.

Oh no, I've made a massive assumption that it's okay for me to still be here in the morning, making myself at home. It's too much…

"I'm sorry," she whispered, "I shouldn't have—"

"No, no, it's okay. It's me, I thought…" Lou looked embarrassed.

Suddenly the penny dropped. "Oh God." Stephanie's voice was still a whisper. "You thought I'd gone?"

Lou nodded slowly, and Stephanie's stomach did an excited little lurch. She walked over to Lou, her smile widening as she got closer and Lou started to relax. She leaned in and kissed her, letting her tongue slip teasingly over her bottom lip before murmuring, "You're not getting rid of me that easily."

She gasped as Lou's mouth suddenly devoured hers, pulling Stephanie close, pressing their breasts together, their bellies, their thighs. Lou lifted her head and placed her hands on Stephanie's hips.

"I need you." Her voice was low and strained, and her breathing was laboured.

Stephanie's cunt pulsed. She nodded and gasped again as Lou turned her around and pushed her towards the breakfast bar. Stephanie placed her hands on the granite top and shuddered as Lou pushed her legs apart with her thigh. Lou draped her body over Stephanie, pressing her hard nipples into her back, running her hands between Stephanie's legs from behind to skim lightly through her wetness, teasing her clit with her fingertips. When she pulled those fingertips back to circle the entrance to her cunt, Stephanie groaned and pushed back for more.

"Yes…oh *yes*…"

And Lou didn't hesitate. She pushed one finger deep inside, as far as she could go, and then pulled back out slowly, driving Stephanie crazy with desire, want, need.

"Oh God, fuck me," she pleaded, her voice a rough whisper, startling herself at her use of such coarse language but loving it at the same time.

Lou groaned and pushed inside her again, two fingers this time, and their groans melded together as Lou fucked her. As Stephanie wantonly bucked her hips, groaning loudly, Lou reached around with her other hand and brought the tip of one finger to rest on Stephanie's clit. She let Stephanie's own hip movements dictate the pressure, the speed, and Stephanie worked it, rubbing herself against that single point of contact harder and faster. Lou's fingers filled her, and she came, crying out, head thrown back and calling out Lou's name.

Stephanie sat on the sofa, naked, gazing down at the equally naked woman sleeping half under a blanket across her lap. The winter sun glinted brightly through the gaps in the blinds, sending soft shafts of light over Lou's body.

It was Sunday morning. Stephanie hadn't gone home since they'd arrived here Friday night. Saturday had been spent in bed—making love, talking, eating, making love again.

On Saturday evening, while Stephanie cooked for them, enjoying pottering around Lou's kitchen, Lou had texted Tania. She had shown the text to Stephanie before sending, and she'd smirked as she read Lou's words.

Not sure u'll believe this & it's a long story, but Stephanie Jackson is half-naked in my kitchen right now.

They'd both laughed out loud at Tania's reply, which arrived moments later.

WTF ???!!!!!

Lou had arranged to meet Tania before they started work on Monday, and Stephanie was so pleased—her girlfriend needed a friend like Tania. Her girlfriend. She smiled as the phrase repeated in her brain.

She stroked Lou's hair now, gently so as not to wake her, but still needing to touch, even if she was asleep.

Her phone buzzed on the table beside her. She looked at the caller display and rolled her eyes. Matt. Of course. She hadn't contacted him since she last saw him Friday night, other than a quick text on Saturday morning to say she was okay and would call him later. Of course, that was before Saturday melted into a haze of delicious lovemaking and time ceased to have any meaning.

"Well, it's about time!" snapped Matt when Stephanie swiped to answer.

She giggled.

"Did I wake you?" he asked, his tone still strident.

"No, not at all," she replied, in her quietest voice, mindful of the gorgeous woman dozing below her.

"Hey, why so quiet, sweet pea? Are you sick or something?"

Stephanie chuckled softly. "No, not sick." She paused. "I'm just keeping quiet so I don't wake my girlfriend."

There was a silence. And then Matt screamed, "Your *what*?"

Stephanie smiled from ear to ear.

EPILOGUE

Manchester, present day

Laura took a deep breath as the cab pulled away behind her. Was this the craziest thing she'd done in her life? She looked up at the dark sky above her, blowing out a breath. She brought her head back down slowly and stared at the black door across the street. It had been such a long time since she'd actively done this, and she still couldn't shake off the thought that surely she was too old for this game now? Back in the day, when she'd had her flat stomach, her fitness, her cocky confidence, all of this would have been so easy. Too easy, really. She'd regularly gone out and pulled some gorgeous chick for a quick fuck in the dark somewhere.

But now, at fifty-one years old, it seemed ridiculous to think of doing the same thing with this older, slightly flabbier, certainly stiffer body. And yet… There was a hunger still deep within her; it was what had brought her here. A hunger that had gone unanswered for four years now. Four years she'd been a widow, working her way through her grief, slowly but surely. Having only done the settling down thing at the age of forty, then to have lost her wife to a heart attack a mere seven years later. They'd barely started on their life together; so many plans that never came to fruition. She shook thoughts of Kelly out of her head. She definitely didn't need to be thinking of her tonight.

She glanced at her watch; nearly ten. She had no idea what time things warmed up in there, but they'd been open for about an hour now. She doubted she'd be the first through the door on this cool

Saturday night. It had been a pleasant enough April day, but the nights were still chilly, and she presumed enough women would seek some…warmth…somewhere like this on such an evening. She hoped, anyway.

She also hoped the club was as dark as she'd heard; she didn't want to highlight the fact that she'd probably be one of the oldest women in there. She knew she still didn't look bad for her years—her face had aged pretty well, and her cropped hair, still bleached blonde, always made her look younger than she was. Still, she figured most of the clientele behind that door would have a good fifteen or twenty years on her.

She wished a club like this had existed back in her twenties, when all she was interested in was nothing complicated, just physical. And now, years later, she'd discovered it was out there, and she couldn't help but want to experience it, just to see what it might feel like again after all this time. God knows, after Kelly, she had no mind to get serious with anyone again. They'd have to be someone pretty amazing to get her to give up her heart again. No, once around that ride was enough, but there was life left in Laura, and she wanted to live it. Or relive it.

A tremor of excitement rumbled quietly through her belly. And lower. Fuck, she hoped this was all it was cracked up to be. Her days of fucking a stranger in smelly toilets and dark alleys were definitely over. The excitement had never quite outweighed the risks in the long run—yes, the naughty thrill of possibly getting caught had always added a certain something to the occasion, but after that night in Brixton, things had never quite been the same for Laura.

God, she hadn't thought about that night in a long time, but she'd never forgotten it either. She couldn't remember the woman's name. Just those eyes. Jesus, eyes so crystal blue they were etched on her memory forever. She'd never quite forgiven herself for legging it that night either. Yeah, of course the chick said she was okay, but how gutless was it of Laura to just leave her bleeding on a bench in the street at nearly midnight? She could at least have walked her to the Tube.

Yeah, not her proudest moment. She'd looked out for her at every club and pub she'd visited for the next few weeks, thinking if she saw her, she should at least apologise for walking away. But she'd never seen her again, not once.

She shook off the memories, pulling her focus back to the black door across the street. "Come on, tiger," she muttered to herself. "Get yourself in there and see what you can find."

She strode across the street and pressed the bell next to a small covered window in the centre of the door. After a few moments, the window shutter slid open, and a woman's eyes stared out at her from within the small opening.

Crystal-blue eyes that had been etched into her memory.

About A.L. Brooks

A.L. Brooks currently resides in London, although over the years she has lived in places as far afield as Aberdeen and Australia. She works 9-5 in corporate financial systems and spends many a lunchtime in the gym attempting to achieve some semblance of those firm abs she likes to write about so much. And then promptly negates all that with a couple of glasses of red wine and half a slab of dark chocolate in the evenings. When not writing she likes doing a bit of Latin dancing, cooking, travelling both at home and abroad, reading lots of other writers' les-fic, and listening to mellow jazz.

CONNECT WITH A.L. BROOKS:

Website: www.albrookswriter.com
Facebook: www.facebook.com/albrookswriter
E-Mail: albrookswriter@gmail.com

Other Books from Ylva Publishing

www.ylva-publishing.com

Nights of Silk and Sapphire

(Nights of Silk and Sapphire – Book #1)

Amber Jacobs

ISBN: 978-3-95533-511-3
Length: 309 pages (113,000 words)

Dae is rescued from desert slavers by the mysterious Zafirah Al'Intisar and placed as a prize in the Scion's harem. At first, Dae struggles with desires she has never before experienced, but as love and lust collide these two women slowly forge a bond.

Heart's Surrender

Emma Weimann

ISBN: 978-3-95533-183-2
Length: 305 pages (63,000 words)

Neither Samantha Freedman nor Gillian Jennings are looking for a relationship when they begin a no-strings-attached affair. But soon simple attraction turns into something more. What happens when the worlds of a handywoman and a pampered housewife collide? Can nights of hot, erotic fun lead to love, or will these two very different women go their separate ways?

Don't Be Shy

A Collection of Erotic Lesbian Stories

Astrid Ohletz & Jae [Ed.]

ISBN: 978-3-95533-383-6
Length: 350 pages (139,000 words)

From kinky phone sex to unexpected, steamy encounters with the new neighbor. Fun with a love swing and unexpected relaxation techniques. This anthology has it all.

Twenty-five authors of lesbian fiction bring you short stories that focus on the sensual, red-hot delights of sex between women and the celebration of the female form in all its diverse hedonism.

Are you in the mood for something spicy?

Hot Line

Alison Grey

ISBN: 978-3-95533-048-4
Length: 114 pages (27,000 words)

Two women from different worlds. Linda, a successful psychologist, uses her work to distance herself from her loneliness. Christina works for a sex hotline to make ends meet. Their worlds collide when Linda calls Christina's sex line. Instead of wanting phone sex, Linda makes an unexpected proposition. Does Christina dare accept the offer that will change both their lives?

Coming from Ylva Publishing

www.ylva-publishing.com

Just My Luck

Andrea Bramhall

Genna Collins works a dead end job, loves her family, her girlfriend, and her friends. When she wins the biggest Euromillions jackpot on record everything changes…and not always for the best. What if money really can't buy you happiness?

Grounded

(The Flight Series – Book #2)

Amanda Radley

Olivia Lewis is coming to terms with her romantic failure by throwing herself into work. But when clients leave in their droves, Olivia realises that she is losing everything. Meanwhile the world of flight attendant Emily White comes crashing down when she loses her job. With no income, large debts and a five-year-old son things can't get any worse. A twist of fate brings them together again.

The Club
© 2016 by A.L. Brooks

ISBN: 978-3-95533-654-7

Also available as e-book.

Published by Ylva Publishing, legal entity of Ylva Verlag, e.Kfr.

Ylva Verlag, e.Kfr.
Owner: Astrid Ohletz
Am Kirschgarten 2
65830 Kriftel
Germany

www.ylva-publishing.com

First edition: 2016

Credits
Edited by Gill McKnight & Jove Belle
Cover Design by Streetlight Graphics
Vector Designed by Freepik.com

Made in the USA
Lexington, KY
12 February 2019